IF YOU CAN GET IT

BRENDAN HODGE

IF YOU CAN GET IT

IGNATIUS PRESS   SAN FRANCISCO

Cover photo and illustrations:
Unsplash.com & iStockPhoto.com

Cover design by John Herreid

© 2020 by Ignatius Press, San Francisco
All rights reserved
ISBN 978-1-62164-345-6 (PB)
ISBN 978-1-64229-127-8 (eBook)
Library of Congress Control Number 2020931927
Printed in the United States of America ∞

Contents

I

The cell phone buzzing in her hand was a reproach. Jen had promised herself she would avoid screens and spend her Sunday morning relaxing. Instead she had been checking her work e-mail, and now Katie was calling.

Jen set the phone on the table to let it vibrate its way through the six rings that would send the call to voice mail. She smoothed out the newspaper to read the front-page article, knowing even as she did so that she was going to pick up the phone and answer it at the last moment, because Katie always got what she wanted.

"Hi, Katie. What's up?"

"Um. Hi."

Katie's phone skills had clearly not improved during the last few months. The seconds dragged on as Jen declined to probe why her ten-years-younger sister had called.

"So. What are you doing at the moment?" Katie finally asked, as if it were Jen who had called out of the blue.

"You know how it is here. Busy at work," said Jen, turning over the page of the newspaper and scanning the inside headlines. "I'm heading into the last month before a product launch I'm in charge of, so I don't know when I'll next have a quiet morning to call my own. What are you up to since college? Sorry I couldn't fly back for graduation."

"I've been looking for a job and stuff. Well. Mostly I

guess I've been fighting with Mom and Dad. Being home really sucks now that they're in this holy-roller phase."

"Mmm hmm? I bet."

"Actually . . ." A hesitation was followed by a rush of words. "After having been on my own for five years, I just can't stand being back home. Mom's always asking me why I've been out late. Last week she freaked out because she said I had too much alcohol in the house."

"That hardly sounds like her. She never noticed my stash, and that was in high school."

"Yeah, well she notices now. So I had to get out. I'm moving."

"Where are you going?"

"Well . . ." The pause was just long enough for Jen to realize what was coming. "I was hoping to move in with you. Just for a while. Until I can get a job and get my own place."

Jen loved her family—even liked them on most days—but it was a love that had been nurtured by having the Rocky Mountains as a privacy screen for the last eleven years. "Look, I dunno, Katie. It's really expensive here in the Bay if you don't have a good job. And I'm barely going to be home over the next month. Maybe you should think about it a bit. Do you have any college friends you could move in with? Maybe closer to home or in a more affordable city?"

"How often have I asked you for anything?"

Jen silently tallied the "Mom and Dad said they didn't have money for . . ." calls over the past few years: textbooks, study abroad, car down payment.

"Look, I'm sorry. I know you're busy," Katie pleaded. "I just need a few weeks. I'm not going to cause any trouble.

I'll stay out of the way." The words were coming faster, and she sounded close to tears. "Please?"

What kind of sister am I? Jen sighed. "Yeah. Okay." Compulsively she got up and began neatening: coffee cup and breakfast plate to the sink, newspaper folded. "When are you thinking of coming? The next couple weeks are really crazy, but—"

"I'm parked out front now."

"Now?" A few steps and a look out the condo's front window showed Katie's red Focus parked on the street, with boxes and bags visibly piled in the back seat. "Katie. What were you thinking?"

"I'm sorry! Mom was just so—" Words apparently failed, and she began again. "Thursday night she just totally reamed me out for literally no reason."

"Literally?"

"And I decided I had to get out, so I started throwing things in the car. I was going to call you, but I kept worrying you'd say no."

"So, you just showed up? Katie, that's . . . . Oh, it's stupid talking on the phone when I can see you. Come up here."

Jen hung up the phone, opened the front door, and went out onto the balcony she shared with the condo next door. She watched Katie get out of the car, stretch, and come up the stairs.

"You look like you overslept an 8 A.M. class," Jen said, surveying Katie's battered flip-flops, plaid pants, tank top, and bedraggled hair.

"You look like Sporty Mum escaped from some *Stepford Wives* compound," Katie shot back. "Ugh, I feel terrible. Can I use your bathroom?"

Jen pointed, and Katie dived for it, leaving the door slightly ajar. From inside, Jen could hear the sound of retching. After a moment, it ceased and water ran. Katie emerged, wiping her face with the hand towel. "That's better."

"Are you sick?" Jen demanded.

"I spent the last two days living off Red Bull and Doritos and taking naps in rest areas. I feel disgusting."

"Why didn't you get some decent food and sleep in a motel?"

"Do you have any idea what they put in that fast food? There's this stuff called pink slime in the meat, and I bet the potatoes they make into fries are genetically modified and crap. Besides, I barely had enough money just for gas. Can I take a nap before I bring my stuff in?"

Jen went to open the door to the spare bedroom, but Katie threw herself down on the couch, pulled one of the cushions over her head, and was still.

For a moment, Jen stood, contemplating the motionless form before her and the fading prospect of a quiet Sunday. Still, the interruption was quieted for now. She went back into the kitchen for another cup of coffee. Maybe there would even be time for a run before Katie woke up.

When Jen emerged after her shower, feeling damp but virtuous, she ventured back into the living room and saw that Katie remained motionless on the sofa: one leg hanging off, plaid bottom in the air, her head under the cushion, as if the couch were some monster that had paused halfway through consuming its victim.

Nonetheless, her sister's presence somehow constituted an obstacle to the planned lazy day. The couch and its occupant continually drew her eye, and Jen found herself cleaning the condo, moving the filing cabinet out of the spare bedroom, shifting books off its shelf and onto the one in her own room, and generally reorganizing to accommodate two rather than one.

Memories of the first weeks after Kevin had finally moved out came back to her. The sense of "no one else here" had been overpowering. However increasingly unwelcome that presence had been in the final months, the lack of it, after three years, had been palpable, and she had cleaned, replaced furniture, reorganized, and redecorated until she no longer expected to see him sprawled in the recliner or crouched over a cup of coffee in the kitchen. Now "someone else here" seemed to radiate through the condo, and she felt the need to deconstruct the order that had been hers and hers alone, rather than allow the presence of a new resident to violate it.

Six o'clock found Katie still asleep and Jen sitting in one of the armchairs opposite the couch, staring at her phone. She called Mandarin Garden and ordered dinner. Their "Should be there in twenty-five minutes" promised a clear end point to the conversation if it became difficult. Then, with that protection, she called her parents.

"Hey, Dad. It's Jen," she said when the familiar voice answered. Instinctively she drew her legs up and wrapped an arm around them, as if she were a child again, creeping into his easy chair to tell him about the unfairness of some teacher or the betrayal of some friend. Dad had always been the sympathetic one to talk to, even if she had drawn no more than an "mmm hmm" from him while the game played in the background.

"Hi there, sweetie. It's been a while. How are things at work?"

It was always his first question and one that she could not resist answering, so she did.

"Good. Good." She launched into a narrative of the project, but he cut in at her first pause. "I'll get your mother for you."

"Dad, wait."

"I know your mother wants to talk to you about Katie."

"And the Cubbies are playing?"

"Sixth inning and down three against the Phillies."

"All right, Dad."

For a moment Jen could hear a mixture of TV sports and her parents' conversation in the background, then her mother's voice.

"Jen, I'm so glad you called. So Katie's with you?"

"Yeah, she got here this morning."

"Oh, praise God!"

"You could have called and told me she was coming if you were so worried, Mom."

"Oh, well . . ." She could picture her mother's dismissive gesture. "Katie gets upset so easily. I half thought she'd come back after a day or two. I didn't think she'd really drive all the way to California. You know Katie. She doesn't stick to things."

"What happened between you two? She's been asleep since she got here."

Her mother gave one of the earth-shattering sighs that Jen remembered well from her teenage years. "I don't know what it is. She's been so difficult since she moved back in. I just ask what any good parent would ask: tell me where she's going, be home by midnight, come to Mass with the family, don't drink all the time in her room. You'd think I was trying to keep her under lock and key! She came in at one thirty on Thursday night, smelling like alcohol, and when I asked her if she had any respect at all for our family rules, she just exploded. Cursing. Digging up all sorts of old family laundry. I don't know what got into her. You were never like that."

"Mom, what are you talking about? There were never any kind of family rules when I was a teenager, much less home from college."

There was a pause.

"Well," said her mother, in a tone that warned against contradiction. "I think we always had respect for ourselves as a family."

"We may have respected ourselves, but we did it pretty separately. Things were a little different with you then, remember?"

She let the last word hang for a moment, but her mother refused to rise to the bait.

"Besides, you can hardly expect Katie to want to follow rules now that she didn't have when she was sixteen."

"All I can do is my best as a mother," her mother replied with dignity. "I'm sorry if I failed you girls at times back then, but I'm trying to do the best I can now."

It was Jen's turn to sigh. "Yeah. I know, Mom. I'm glad you're better."

Mother and daughter were silent for a moment.

"So, you two had a big fight about house rules, and she left. She's not pregnant or on drugs or wanted by the police or anything crazy like that?"

"Oh . . . Do you think she is? I hadn't thought about that."

"No. No, Mom, I was kidding. I just mean, there's nothing really *big* wrong, is there?"

"I worry a lot that she struggles in her spiritual life."

"Her what?"

"She never wants to come to Mass with us. I don't think she prays. But I think it bothers her. Even that degree of hers, studying all those Eastern religions—I think she was just trying to run away from what she knows is true."

"Sheesh, Mom, we only used to ever go to church on Christmas and Easter." As soon as she said it, Jen knew this would elicit some kind of guilt-ridden response, and she elected to take the easy way out. "Shoot, I'm sorry. The Chinese food is here. I'm sure it's going to be okay. I'll talk with you in a few days and let you know how she's doing. Tell Dad I love him."

Jen sat staring at the darkened phone for a moment, then crossed the room and shook her recumbent sister's shoulder. "Katie. Time to get up. Dinner will be here in a few minutes. Let's get your stuff in from the car."

The sisters sat across the dinner table from each other with well-heaped cartons of Chinese food between them.

"I called Mom and Dad and told them you'd got in safe," Jen said.

Katie rolled her eyes and hunched her shoulders forward. "Mom tell you I'm some kind of a drunk or slut or something?"

"No. She was pretty calm compared with the old Mom outbursts."

"Gotta love the meds."

"Is it a lot better?"

"Yeah. Remember the way she used to just refuse to talk to people all day when things were going wrong? There's never any of that now. She talks, she asks how you're doing, she wants to be around you. It's nice actually. The last couple years, it's like getting to know her for the first time." Katie paused, staring out the darkening back windows for a moment. "That's the good part. The bad thing is that once she got herself together with the meds, she had this religious conversion—reversion, I guess. I think it's helped her in a lot of ways, but the moralizing is a total buzzkill."

"I heard a bit of that on the phone. I can see how it would be frustrating to move back into that."

Katie nodded but didn't respond.

"Isn't that kind of your field, though? With the religious studies degree?"

"Yeah, well, I picked religious studies because I wanted to learn about other world religious traditions, not because I wanted to live with the local branch of Nags for Jesus."

"I suppose you could have done that without the student loans. What do you do with a religious studies degree anyway?"

Katie put down her chopsticks with decision. "Don't even start on the 'what do you do with that degree' crap, Miss Business Degree! Do you seriously think I haven't heard that one before?"

The vehemence of Katie's response brought Jen up short. "I'm sorry."

"Don't think I haven't asked myself why I studied something like that in such a terrible economy. It's not like I can just go down to the local religion shop and get a job. But I couldn't imagine wasting college on something I wasn't interested in. I mean, seriously, what do you guys learn in four years of studying business? How to balance a really big checkbook? Watch the last century's greatest television commercials?"

"There's a lot that goes into running a business that's worth studying," Jen began.

"Yeah, fine. I know. Maybe I'm just talking smack. But I'm probably going to have to spend the rest of my life dealing with business stuff. College seemed like the time to deal with the important stuff in life. And there's so much there. I mean, sure, a lot of Christians are self-satisfied, but when you look across the world at all the different religions, it's like you're seeing lots of bits of one big picture. Religion tells us something important, about humanity at the very least, and maybe something more."

Katie poked at her food for a moment.

"But if you want the religious studies answer, I think the issue with Mom right now is that with her recent reconversion she's adopted a strongly law-code-based notion of morality along with a sort of prosperity theology, meaning that she sees virtue primarily as following specific rules and believes that if she could just get me to follow those rules, I'd be happy and do well in life. Whereas, if she'd put aside *Scripture Soup for the Soul* and read the book of Job out of her own Bible, she'd see that real Judaism and Christianity have never said that God's will for your life is some kind of virtue-operated vending machine that pops out good fortune."

"Oh."

Katie shrugged. "See, I learned stuff in college. But you don't care about all this stuff, do you? How's work? You got some kind of a promotion a year ago, didn't you?"

"I got the job almost a year ago. I'm a product-line manager for AppLogix."

Katie looked blank.

"You've probably seen their iPhone apps. PocketDJ?"

"Oh, yeah, I know PocketDJ. Everyone had that at college last semester. There was even a guy who hooked it up to the student-union stereo system and DJed a whole party off it. You work on that?"

"A product-line manager is a cross-functional position. I'm in charge of talking to all the teams working on the project and making sure that they're meeting objectives, getting the product to stores on time, advertising them correctly, the whole thing. And the product line I'm working on is the PocketDJ Player that will be in stores this Fourth of July."

"What do you mean 'Player'? Is it a new version of the app?"

"No, it's a dedicated device for PocketDJ. It's got a touch turntable and sliders and everything. Really slick industrial design."

"But . . . what's the point? People don't want to carry around another thing in their pockets. They want to use PocketDJ on their iPhones. That's the whole point: that it's a turntable on your phone."

Jen shrugged, stacked the dishes, and carried the leftovers into the kitchen. This was the frustrating thing about working on such a visible project. Everyone thought they could just go with their instincts and predict what consumers would want. No one realized how much research went into product planning.

"Of course a lot of people will still be happy with the iPhone app, but the dedicated device has a better sound chip, a 6.3-millimeter audio jack, and other features that hard-core fans will care about. It focus-grouped really well. And it lets us do an end-run around Apple, which insists on treating us like any other app developer and won't give us some of the access we want."

"Oh. Well, I guess you guys must know what you're doing."

Jen arrived early at the AppLogix campus the next morning, as was her wont. This promptness earned her BMW coupe a parking spot that would be shaded by the nearest building by the time she came out in the evening, and it gave her time to prepare before her weekly project call with members of the PocketDJ Player team from all over the world. Designed more with the intention of being a "walking campus" than for convenience, AppLogix consisted of eight small, single-story buildings, each named after one of the world's tallest mountains. Jen was in Kangchenjunga, a name so uniquely intimidating in its spelling that its residents habitually referred to it as "Kanga" instead and had procured for the lobby a huge stuffed representation of the Winnie-the-Pooh character of the same name, at whose feet wags would leave assorted votive offerings.

At eight o'clock, having fortified herself with coffee and updated spreadsheets, Jen dialed into the conference call and began cataloguing her team's achievements and failures. The

Singapore design center retained certain doubts as they tested specimens of the finished product. Shanghai assured her that the shipments for Amazon and Best Buy would arrive in the United States on time yet became evasive when asked when they would ship and how long the shipment would take. The documentation team bombarded her with questions as they prepared the training materials that would allow telephone service representatives to confuse themselves and others in response to customer queries. These and dozens of other details were gathered, debated, scheduled, assigned as action items, and crossed off lists. As she lapped the first hour, Jen was in her element and was mildly gratified that there was less to fault than she had expected. The launch of the PocketDJ Player was exactly the sort of project to showcase her mastery of detail. Take that hand from the tiller, and any number of needs would be forgotten, deadlines missed. And if all went well, it would be the faultlessness of this launch that would bring her the promotion to director, acknowledging the level at which she had already been performing for the last six months.

In the midst of this well-managed whirlwind, her cell phone buzzed to proclaim the arrival of a text.

Katie: "do you have spare hdmi cable?"

Jen shoved the phone angrily away, but the knowledge of the unanswered question disrupted her concentration until, while the lead of the programming team in Slovakia explained an obstacle to meeting the delivery date for the second-generation Player software, she seized the phone and replied: "Bottom left computer desk drawer in my room. What are you doing?"

"setting up xbox"
"I'm at work! BUSY!"
"ok chill"

The Xbox proved to be the nexus of conflict over the following days. When Jen arrived home at eight o'clock that night, with the sense of glowing self-worth that being absolutely needed in the office for twelve hours at a time provided, she found Katie crouched on the floor in front of the TV, controller in hand, a half-empty "family-size" bag of Doritos and several crumpled Coke cans spread out around her on the cream-colored carpet.

"Have you seriously spent the whole day playing a video game on the Xbox?" Jen demanded. "Did you even get dinner?"

Katie made a dodging motion and pressed frantically on the controller. Jen scooped up the bag of Doritos, dropped into one of the armchairs, and consumed several chips.

"I went to the store and got stuff," Katie said, indicating the Doritos. "I wasn't really that hungry, and I didn't know if you would pick up dinner."

Jen popped another chip into her mouth, licked the livid orange dust off her fingers, and disappeared into the kitchen. The fridge door sounded.

"Two fridge packs of Coke and no Diet?"

"Diet is disgusting. If you're going to drink soda, drink it for real."

A popping sound confirmed that Jen had followed this admonition.

"Oh man, you got Nutella?"

Katie was immersed in her game and did not respond. After a few moments Jen entered, bearing a can of Coke and a Nutella sandwich. "I haven't had Nutella in ages."

"It's right there in the store."

"I don't buy it. All this stuff is horrendous, Katie. It's going to make me fat."

Katie shrugged. "So don't eat it. But you're not fat."

"That's because I don't stock the house with carb cocaine. If this junk is here, I'll eat it."

"Some willpower you've got there."

The theme played out with variations the following days.

"What the hell is with you sitting around all day playing some video game?" Jen demanded Wednesday night, dumping her laptop bag on the couch, kicking off her shoes, and tucking her feet under her.

"It's not 'some video game'; it's *Skyrim*. This is epic stuff."

"Still on your Doritos and Coke diet?"

"I found some money of yours and ordered in. There's a container for you in the fridge. I got you something vegetarian because I saw you'd eaten two of my Pop-Tarts this morning, and I figured you'd still be feeling guilty."

Jen pulled herself out of the chair and padded into the kitchen. "Yes, I ate your Pop-Tarts for breakfast. Why didn't I just invite a drug pusher to move in with me?"

"Oh, come on," Katie called after her. "It's just Doritos and stuff; it's not like I'm snorting coke or something. Loosen up!"

"At least cocaine shouldn't show on my carpet like the Doritos crumbs."

Thursday night, Jen came up the stairs from the garage, then stood rooted just inside the kitchen door, staring at the table. Her hand mirror lay in the center of the table with two little lines of white powder on it. A razor blade and a short length of soda straw lay handy nearby.

"Katie!"

"Mmm? What?" a muffled voice called from the living room.

Jen picked up the mirror with a hand that she suddenly realized was trembling and strode purposefully into the living room. "What is this, Katie?"

"I ran out of Doritos," Katie said without turning around. "And since you were so upset about all the junk food . . . As habits go, I've heard it's slimming. Models do it."

"Katie! Put that damn controller down and look at me! Where did you get this?"

Katie turned around with an impish smile. "From your cupboard. It's baking powder."

Jen stood motionless and openmouthed.

"The look on your face!" Katie chortled uncontrollably, kicking her feet against the floor. "Doritos! The gateway drug!"

Jen stalked icily back to the kitchen and dusted the baking powder off into the trash. Reentering the living room, she planted herself between Katie and the TV. "All right. Very funny. You know what? It's been a week. You need to decide whether you're going to move in here or drag your sorry ass back to Mom and Dad's house. If you want to live with me, I'm going to tell you just once: *Get . . . a . . . job.*"

It was on Friday that the Shanghai team finally admitted that the Players had not shipped on time. They were aboard ship now, Jen was assured, but they would not arrive in the United States until two weeks after the planned launch date. Frustrations ran high, and when appealing to authority, Jen found her boss, Josh, the vice president of product marketing, curiously impassive.

"Do we need to push back the launch date a couple weeks?" he asked.

"No. I'll get units here," she assured him. "We'll have to air them in. It just adds three dollars a unit to the cost. With all the advertising lined up, it would cost a lot more to delay than to fly supply in."

"All right. Sounds like you're dealing with it."

Back in her office, she opened her mind briefly to fear. Had the Player become a "troubled project"? Was the all-important entrance into hardware, with the unaccustomed difficulties that it entailed, being overshadowed by whatever the app launch of the week might be? For a moment, she envisioned herself in the same office, with the same title, three or four years hence—the oft-seen but never regarded manager of a product line that no one cared about, her hopes that this would prove the avenue to promotion replaced with the dull resignation that this was all she was fit for. End of the line.

She quickly shook off these feelings of self-pity. This was simply an example of why it was essential to have someone like her in charge of the launch. Josh and the rest of the leadership team trusted her to surmount obstacles and get the product out in a creditable fashion.

Working late at the office can serve two purposes: to get more work done than can be accomplished in the traditional eight or nine hours of the workday, or to emphasize to others, and perhaps most of all to oneself, that one is an important person weighed down with essential duties.

At 6:00 P.M. on Friday, Jen was forced to admit that she was engaging in the latter. For the last fifteen minutes, she had been staring at her big presentation, the product launch deck, without seeing it. In two weeks, just five days before the PocketDJ Player arrived in stores, she would get up and deliver this to the entire executive team: why the product was essential; how she had brought it to market; the sales strategy; and how she had overcome all obstacles to assure a smooth launch. This was the career maker.

All she had done since opening the deck, however, was consider the placement of a comma and adjust the font size on a few text boxes.

She snapped her computer shut and headed out.

In the lobby, Kanga cradled a plastic light saber in her paws: a sentinel standing guard until the new week brought the building's inmates back to work and plot and plan and play foosball.

Walking back to the car, she pulled out her phone.

"Hey, Katie. How was your day?"

"You'd be pleased. I went out and filled out a bunch of applications this morning. Starbucks called and asked if I'd come in for an interview Monday."

Jen held back the inquiry: Starbucks? Could you get any more stereotypical? At least she had applied somewhere.

"It's been a long week, Katie. Want to get some clothes on and we'll go out to dinner?"

"Yeah, I'd like that."

"I'll be home in twenty minutes."

2

The last time the Nilsson sisters had lived under the same roof for any extended time had been thirteen years before, when Katie was ten years old and Jen, lacking an internship, came home for the summer after her sophomore year of college.

Compared to living with a roommate or a boyfriend, the current situation was unsettling. It seemed clear that she and her sister ought to have some sort of relationship, but the passing days make it clear that they did not share similar habits, preferences, or aspirations. Rather than a younger version of herself, with slight variations to add interest, Jen found herself living with someone who *looked* very much like her younger self, right down to her painfully familiar college cafeteria pudge, but who was in every other respect a stranger.

Roommates and boyfriends were chosen, however poorly. That she should find herself in a close, inseverable relationship with someone not chosen seemed simultaneously unfair and intriguing. Was this how Uma at work had felt when she flew back to India last year to marry a man from her village of whom she had known only that he had fit the two criteria she had given her mother: he must have a college degree and he must not smoke? The idea of moving in with, much less marrying, someone about whom one knew so little and expecting happiness had seemed, to Jen, utterly mad. And yet what, really, did she know of Katie, other than that they shared genetic code?

Jen was not sure whether to conclude that Starbucks was hard up for workers, or that a Midwestern religious studies major was exactly what they had been searching for, but Katie's Monday morning interview had ended with the question "When can you start?" This had not decreased the likelihood of Jen's returning home to find Katie recumbent on the couch, because answering the application question "When are you available?" with "Any time" had landed Katie with the opening shift on Mondays, Wednesdays, Fridays, and Saturdays.

"Five A.M.!" Katie wailed from the couch on Friday evening. "This is worse than eight A.M. classes. I'll never get to sleep in again."

"Welcome to adulthood," Jen responded without sympathy. "They've only scheduled you for twenty-eight hours a week. Do you know how many hours I worked last week?"

"But you make lots of money. I make ten bucks an hour."

"That is an excellent reason to find your way out of the service sector."

As the launch meeting loomed, it came to take up an ever larger share of Jen's mind. The weekend before, she spent half of each day in the office, the other half at the kitchen table with her laptop, endlessly fiddling, rearranging, and considering.

In the shower, she recited, "Our market study has suggested a domestic first-year market for this product of over three million units and a significant secondary revenue stream through monetizing the online user community experience." At night, she awoke with a start from a dream in which she recited those words to the leadership team while still dripping and wrapped in a towel.

On Wednesday night, she called Katie into her room to inspect the potential outfits she had laid out on the bed for the presentation.

"Your presentation isn't till Friday," objected Katie.

"That," explained Jen, "is why I'm making this decision tonight. Tomorrow night I'm going to be all prepared and go to bed early so I'll be fresh. You're an objective set of eyes: Dress, skirt, or pants? What do you think?"

"I think it's pathetic that the only choices I have for my evening are planning your business wardrobe or watching *The Expendables* on FX. What's a girl have to do to get a date around here?"

"Write your phone number on some guy's latte."

"I did, but he never called me!"

"Wait, you wrote your phone number on a guy's latte? Really?"

"No. Sheesh, where's the sense of humor?"

Jen had a momentary flash of annoyance with herself; after three weeks, she should at least be able to tell when her sister was scamming. But Katie had disappeared into the closet, and Jen returned to contemplating her clothing options. The skirt and blouse were her favorite, but the COO was a leg watcher, and although she didn't mind holding his attention, she wanted him to hear what she was saying as well. The dress was slightly longer and would perhaps look less out of place on a Friday, which would see even most of the executives in jeans. The dress and her good-luck pumps.

Katie emerged from the closet. "How about if you wear these shoes?" she asked, holding up a pair of five-inch platform heels that Jen recalled, with sudden irritation toward her younger self, wearing to a Halloween party with Kevin.

"Don't be ridiculous. I'd never wear something like that in the office."

"What do you have them for?"

"I don't know. It's been years since I've worn those."

"Can I borrow them?"

"Sure, sure. You can have them. I don't want them."

On Thursday, Jen's diligence caught up with her. Everything was ready for the launch, so there was nothing left to do but worry. She stalked the halls and dropped by other people's cubes, but there was no update to be had on her project and no room in her mind for anything else.

She considered going home early, but she pictured Katie sprawled on the couch, eating snacks, and felt no desire to expose her raw nerves to her sister's jibes. Instead, she called the hair salon and wheedled a last-minute appointment. Next door to the salon was an auto detailing place, and impulsively she pulled in and ordered the BMW a full round of pampering while she went for her own. Freshly highlighted, trimmed, and blown out, looking at her reflection in the glistening black hood of the car, she told herself that she looked like a director already—a director who launched products effortlessly.

Coming up the back stairs into the kitchen, she found the condo in a state of tumult. Katie had been cooking. Onion skins, bell pepper ends, and food wrappers were scattered across the counter, and the scents of pizza and microwaved popcorn filled the air.

"What is all this?" Jen asked, setting her laptop bag in a corner and kicking off her shoes.

"Watch out for the tomato sauce on the floor," Katie cautioned, a moment too late. "Sorry! Here's a paper towel."

Some sort of occasion was clearly in the offing. Katie had exchanged her usual flannel pants and flip-flops for a skirt and ballet flats.

Jen gritted her teeth as she scrubbed at her foot with the paper towel, then put her shoes back on to forestall further accidents, reflecting bitterly that she couldn't even count on the floor of her own condo to stay clean anymore.

Katie pulled a package of popcorn out of the microwave and shook it into a bowl. "I thought you'd need to unwind before your big presentation," she said, "so I made pizza and popcorn and checked out the original *Die Hard*. And I got wine coolers. Girls' night in. Just what you need."

"Gosh, Katie," Jen said, surveying the kitchen. "My stomach's already tied in knots thinking about tomorrow. If I start gorging on all those carbs, I'm going to be sick. I was just going to have something light and get to bed early so I'll be rested."

Katie was pulling the pizza out of oven. "Oh, come on!" She clattered the pizza pan onto the stove and kicked the oven door closed. "If you can't drop the uptight-business-chick act for a night, you're never going to be relaxed

31

for your meeting tomorrow. What you need is pizza and popcorn and movie violence. I even bought cookies 'n' cream ice cream. That used to be your favorite, didn't it?"

"Look, Katie, this is nice of you," Jen said, trying to mask her irritation over the dirty kitchen, the greasy smells, and the very presence of anyone else in her home when, of all nights, she wanted nothing out of place. "But this is not some college cram session. I have to get up tomorrow morning in front of my boss and the senior vice presidents and the whole leadership team and give a presentation that's the culmination of everything I've worked on over the last year. I need calm, and . . . and . . . not action movies and junk food."

Katie was shaking her head. "I thought I'd try to do something nice for you. Something . . . I didn't have to be sitting around your place getting yelled at. Abby and Myra from work asked if I wanted to go out with them tonight, but I told them I couldn't go, because I thought you'd need some girl time before your big meeting. And instead you're just . . ." Katie reached for words, then pounded the stove with a satisfying clang instead.

"Sheesh," said Jen, the kitchen mess grating on her as much as her sister's anger. "If you wanted pizza, we could have just ordered some. This place is a wreck."

"Fine! You know what? Have your calm," Katie announced. "I'll call up Abby and get out of your way for the night." She stormed into her room and slammed the door. Jen contemplated going after her but couldn't decide if she felt the need to apologize. A few moments later, Katie issued from her room, phone to her ear, evidently talking to her friends from work. She had traded in her top for a tighter one of shiny material and put on the heels that Jen had given her the night before.

She paused by the front door. "Just a second," she told the phone, and then, turning to Jen, she delivered the parting shot she had evidently been saving up since the first confrontation: "Nice hair. I hope the business-bitch look sells your iPhone wannabe."

The door slammed, and she was gone.

Jen surveyed the wreckage of the kitchen coolly. Then she changed out of her work clothes, cleared the counters —dumping the popcorn in the trash—and mopped the floor. She left the pizza out in case Katie was hungry when she got in. With the kitchen clean, she opened the freezer and found the pint of cookies 'n' cream Katie had bought. With this she retreated to the couch.

Jen had set both her alarm clock and her cell phone, determined that no accident would result in her oversleeping, but she found herself wide awake at five, staring up at the ceiling in the dim first light of a summer morning. She tried to think whether it was nerves that had wakened her, or some sound made by Katie getting ready for work, or just the knowledge that she *must* be up on time.

Getting ready took less time than she had allowed, and she considered going in early, but the memories of sitting in her office with nothing to do but think about the presentation warned her off. She made eggs and coffee instead and perused the newspaper. Katie's pizza remained untouched on the stove. She felt a sudden craving for the iniquity of morning pizza, but if Katie had not yet touched it, she was reluctant to capitulate so visibly by taking the first piece. She let it be.

When she pulled into the parking lot at work, it was already much fuller than at her accustomed hour. Since it was too late to get a spot that would be shaded, she parked well out, where no one would park next to the newly detailed coupe and ding it. She strode along the sidewalk toward her building, her good-luck pumps giving a commanding *tic, tic* on the sidewalk. Kanga, on guard in the lobby, was wearing a Shriner fez and cradling a Hindu god in her paws. Jen glanced at the lobby clock: 8 A.M. One hour to go. She pulled out her phone and checked her e-mail as she walked to her office. Candice in Accounting, with whom she had spent many hours calculating how different types of packaging affected the number of Players that fit on a pallet, and thus per-unit shipping costs by air and sea, had sent a note: "Big day. Good luck!!!" Josh, her boss, had sent one as well, "Stop by my office when you get in."

She set her laptop on the desk and headed down the hall to Josh's office. The glass door was shut. She could see Josh cradling a paper cup of coffee and talking on the speakerphone. He waved in response to her knock, then held up a finger, signaling, "Wait a moment." After a moment, he stabbed the phone off and came to open the door.

"Sorry to keep you waiting. Come on in."

Jen took the seat opposite the desk. Josh sat, tapped a few stray papers into a more precise stack, and set his coffee to one side.

"All of us appreciate the work that you've done on the

PocketDJ Player project," he announced. "I know that all of the leadership team have been impressed with your hard work and ownership of the process. So I know that you will understand this is in no way a reflection on you personally or your performance. As part of a major new partnership and restructuring, the leadership team has decided that a hardware device is not the right direction for the company."

The meaning of the flood of cushioning corporate-ese in which the essential message was wrapped suddenly struck home, and Jen found herself watching Josh speak as if from a distance, hearing only the key phrases.

". . . is one of the positions no longer required under our new plan . . . given your length of service at AppLogix that severance will be four weeks' pay . . . this additional severance is contingent on your signing of the noncompetition agreement . . . any unexercised options . . ."

It was not yet 8:30 when Jen found herself passing through the lobby again, feeling unnaturally light with no laptop bag, only the folder of HR paperwork in her arms. ("You can make an appointment next week to go through your office and collect personal possessions.") Two programmers in shorts and comic tees were playing noisily at the foosball table. Kanga leered derisively from under her fez.

Outside, the light seemed unnaturally bright—it was a time of day when she was usually indoors. She realized that she was shaking. Feeling a sob welling up within her, she bit her lip and redoubled her speed in order to reach the shelter of her car. As her pace neared a run, she placed a foot wrong and twisted her ankle hard, biting back a cry of pain. She kicked off the shoes and carried them the rest of the way, feeling the rough warmth of the pavement under her bare feet. Her reflection in the glistening black hood looked tauntingly similar to the day before, but with red-rimmed eyes looking out from beneath the hair that had inspired such confidence in her then.

Once she was muffled in the warm, leathery interior, she leaned her forehead against the steering wheel and allowed herself, for a long moment, to cry. Then she wiped her eyes, forced herself to breathe slowly, and started the engine. Katie was scheduled to work until two. At least she would have some hours of solitude to gather her thoughts before facing anyone.

Back in the condo, she sat at the kitchen table, a cooling cup of coffee in front of her, numbly staring at her personal laptop and willing herself to update her résumé. Perhaps it would have been satisfying to break down and drain all the emotions away through tears until she could go to sleep. After the last few weeks, she must need rest. But since that first flood in the car, tears would not come, nor would rest, only overpowering numbness.

The sound of the front door opening only half registered with her, and it was a moment before she looked up to see Katie coming in, still wearing the clothes she had left in the night before and carrying her heels in her hands. Their eyes met, and Katie froze.

"You're supposed to be at work," Jen stated.

"I didn't make it home last night." Katie responded with the equally obvious fact. "I met a guy while I was out at the bar." She shifted uneasily from one foot to the other as

Jen continued to fix her stare on her younger sister. "His name is Brian," she supplied, as if this clarified matters.

"You met some guy. Named Brian. At a bar," Jen summarized in slow sentence fragments, her voice still shaky with the last hour's emotion, her pain and frustration converting to anger as she spoke. "And you went home with him and blew off your shift at work. Threw away your new job."

"It's a stupid job. You said so yourself."

"Threw away your job," Jen repeated, rising to her feet. "What kind of a stupid, irresponsible *slut*—"

With an inarticulate shout, Katie hurled one of the shoes at Jen. The throw was so unplanned, so poorly executed, that the shoe flew high and wide, bounced off the kitchen counter and clattered onto the stove, where it came to rest on the still untouched pizza.

"What the hell?" Jen yelped.

"Shut up!" Katie demanded, brandishing the other shoe, her own voice sounding dangerously close to tears.

For a moment they stared each other down. Then Katie dropped the shoe and rushed for the bathroom, wailing, "Oh man, I'm going to be sick!"

Jen stood listening to her younger sister's misery for a moment; then, after a glance at the shoe lying in the ruins of the pizza, went after her into the bathroom.

Katie was crouched in front of the toilet, leaning her arms on the rim. It was impossible to remain angry with this image of suffering. Jen knelt behind her and smoothed her hair back out of her face.

"You look terrible. Can you get anything out?"

"No," moaned Katie.

"Have you taken any Advil?"

Katie nodded.

"Can we get you to your bed?"

"Okay."

Jen helped Katie up and guided her gently into the spare bedroom, where she crawled into bed and lay, huddled and miserable, in the middle of it. Jen put the trash can where Katie could reach it easily if she needed it and pulled the blanket up over her.

"Are you ready for anything to eat or drink yet?"

Katie shook her head.

"All right. Get some rest. I'll see you in a bit."

Shutting the door of Katie's room quietly behind her, Jen finally felt exhaustion settle upon her and knew that she could rest. She went into her room, collapsed onto the bed, and—conscious even in her numbed and battered state of the luxury of being able to sleep in the middle of the day— fell immediately asleep.

3

The daylight filtering into Jen's room through the blinds tracked slowly across the walls. Drained as she was by her weeks of preparation for the launch, the shock of the layoff, and the fight with Katie, she might easily have slept all day, had the presence of someone next to her not wakened her. She half sat up with a start and then saw that it was Katie, clad in her accustomed tank top and plaid flannel pants, her hair looking recently washed, who had nuzzled into bed next to her like an oversize teddy bear.

Katie opened her eyes and regarded her. "Did I wake you up?"

Jen flopped back on the pillow and stared at the ceiling. "It doesn't matter. I've been asleep a long time."

"What happened?" Katie asked. "Did something go wrong? Are you sick?"

"I got fired," Jen said flatly.

"What do you mean you got fired?" Katie asked, incredulous.

"Fired. Laid off. No job."

"But . . . Even I didn't get fired. I called Mandy, my boss, and told her I was really sick. She said next time I better call and tell her that before my shift started. But that's it. She didn't fire me. How could *you* get fired?"

"It's not personal." Jen shrugged. "There was some kind

of strategy change, and they cut the whole Player program, and a lot of us who were working on it got laid off. They don't need me. That's it."

"I'm sorry." For a moment there was silence. "What will you do?" Katie asked.

Jen sighed. "Well, I'll have to find a new job. I guess there wasn't much I could do today anyway. I'm so tired. I'll clean up my résumé over the weekend and start searching on Monday."

"I can help pay the rent till you get a new job," Katie offered.

"Kiddo, do you have any idea what the mortgage on this place is?"

Katie shook her head.

"Thirty-eight hundred dollars a month."

Katie made a strangled noise. "Will we have to move?"

"Only if my new job is somewhere else. I've got six months' expenses saved up. We can get by for a good while. Maybe order out less, but we'll have plenty of time to cook."

Katie burrowed into the sheets and pillows. "I'm nowhere near to making it on my own out here, am I?" she said in an unusually small voice. "Are you going to send me back to Mom and Dad?"

Jen raised herself on one elbow and regarded her sister's half-buried head. "No, I guess not." She saw Katie's shoulders relax.

Jen reached out and stroked her back, like a parent comforting a small child. It was some small sop to her sense of self that, despite the layoff, she was so obviously more able to provide for herself than Katie was. "I'm sorry. This must be hard for you. You're used to having someone take care of you. And I haven't been paying any attention. I've been so busy."

She felt Katie's shoulder shaking gently under her hand. It was a moment before she realized that her younger sister was sobbing silently into the pillow.

"What? What's wrong, Katie?" she asked, leaning close.

Katie's shoulder gave a last shake or two, and her hand pounded the pillow. "No! It's not like that at all! No one keeps an eye on me except to tell me when I'm screwing up. You're the one who's all grown up and Mom and Dad are proud of. And I'm just . . . No one even remembers me."

"What are you talking about?" Jen asked, surprised by this seemingly self-indulgent outburst. "You were always the baby. Mom was always worrying about you."

"Only because she wasn't proud of me, like she was proud of you. Remember that time I got locked in a trunk for hours at Grandma's house? Nobody noticed. That's what it's always like with me."

"What?" Jen sat upright. "What do you mean locked in a trunk? You were never locked in a trunk."

"I was!" Katie contradicted, in a half sob. "Don't you even remember? I'd just turned five. All the cousins were over. I got locked in a trunk up in the attic. For hours."

Jen wondered for a moment if this was another of Katie's scams, but her voice remained at the edge of sobs. "I'm sure I'd remember something like that. Locked in a trunk?"

Katie sat upright and kneaded the pillow in her lap.

"We were over at Grandma's for . . . I don't know. It must have been in the spring, because I had just turned five. I was playing hide and seek with the cousins—Jamie and Ann, and Tim and Bobby—and they helped me hide in one of those old trunks up in the attic. And then . . . when the grown-ups asked them afterward, they said they'd gone to play another game and forgot I was still hiding. The latch must have closed. I couldn't get out, and no one could hear me. No one thought to look for me till dinnertime. It was hours, and I'd screamed until I'd given up. I had nightmares after that for years about being trapped in the dark. Mom and Dad yelled at you afterward and said you should have been keeping an eye on me."

This detail finally jogged a memory in Jen—her agitated parents holding the sobbing Katie and grounding her on the theory that she should have known where her younger sister was. As if she would have been playing with the little kids.

"Okay, I think I do remember something about that. You can't have been in there for hours, though. Maybe ten or fifteen minutes."

"It was hours. I'd cried myself hoarse."

"It can't have been hours. You kids ran off while we were all finishing dinner, and we realized you were missing when dessert was served, and you were the only kid who didn't show up. Twenty minutes tops."

"How do you know?" Katie demanded fiercely. "You didn't even remember five minutes ago. It was hours."

"I remember. I just didn't connect it with what you were saying because it wasn't that big a deal. You cried for a few minutes, and Mom and Dad yelled at me, and then you fell asleep and were fine."

Katie cast herself, facedown, on the pillow. "It was a big deal!" she wailed in muffled tones. "You just don't remember because you didn't care."

Jen watched her shoulders shake, then gradually settle into rhythmic breathing. Though still tired, she no longer felt like going to sleep. Instead, she looked at her sister, trying to reconcile her own memories with Katie's deeply felt ones. That she had nearly forgotten something so essential to her sister's memories of their childhood was unsettling to her view of herself and her family. They had never been the closest family, but she had never thought of them as being the sort of family in which dark memories bubbled up. Nor, she was sure, could Katie's memory of this event be correct. There was no way she could have been missing for hours without anyone noticing. And yet the very fact that the incident had barely impinged upon her memory except as a case of her parents' blaming her unjustly seemed to underscore the possibility that Katie's memory of it was more accurate.

After turning the issue over for several minutes, while Katie continued to sleep in apparent peace, she lay back down next to her and drifted off into uneasy sleep, but with a protective arm around her younger sister.

The light was beginning to fade outside when they both stirred again. Katie swung her feet to the floor and sat up.

"How's the hangover?" Jen asked.

"Better."

"Feel like you could eat?"

"Definitely."

"Let's go see what we can find."

In the kitchen, the pizza confronted them, one shoe still embedded in the clammy cheese and toppings.

"I think the pizza is a goner," Jen ruled. "Do you still want the shoe?"

Katie accepted it and wiped it off with paper towels while Jen slid the pizza into the trash.

"What do you feel like eating?" Jen asked.

Katie opened the freezer and peered inside. "Where's that pint of ice cream I got for us?"

"I ate it after you left," Jen confessed.

"After all that grief you gave me about carbs, you ate my ice cream?" Katie demanded. "You *bitch*!" But the imprecation was delivered fondly.

When Jen sat down in front of her laptop, the news from PocketDJ had apparently hit the wires. E-mails flooded in.

"I saw the news release about Apple investing in App-Logix—is that good or bad for your PocketDJ project?" "Heard that thirty people got walked from AppLogix today. Are you okay?" "All of us in the hardware development group got laid off this morning. Are you in the same boat?" "My boyfriend is getting a recruiting company going. Let me know if you want a referral."

Jen found herself curiously distant from the flurry of news and requests. By Monday, if not sooner, she knew these would be urgent to her. But after the last few hours, they seemed a distant concern. Instead, the sisters made dinner, then baked cookies and watched *Die Hard*.

Jen had thought it would be Saturday—when Katie went off to work her shift at Starbucks—that her state of joblessness would suddenly become painful again. Instead, she cheer-fully went for a run and stopped by Starbucks for coffee near the end of Katie's shift.

Sunday evening, she found herself thinking about how long the inventory being aired in would last, and when the sea-shipped Players would arrive, and suddenly the real-ity that had seemed distant smote her with its fullest force since her long walk across the parking lot: I don't have a job.

She had seldom stopped looking for the next job over the last ten years. There had always been a certain exhil-aration to thinking, "I've been at this job long enough. I could be looking for my next opportunity." But now, for the first time, she was one of the great unwashed horde of outsiders: those who were looking for jobs but did not have one. Tomorrow morning would roll around, and it would not matter to anyone but her whether she got up or not.

"Your profile has been viewed by 19 people in the last 15 days," LinkedIn assured her. But when she consulted this list, she found that half of these were among her fellow sufferers, other people late of AppLogix who were "now looking for my next great opportunity". In the past, her LinkedIn profile had been like an employment lottery—that slim chance hovering on the horizon of probability that someone would contact her and offer her a better job than her present one. Several times this had, in fact, worked. She had made no effort to find AppLogix; they had found her. But now it seemed a capricious friend. I, too, can summon career prospects from the vasty deep, but will they listen when I call?

"What am I going to do?" she asked Katie.

"They're still hiring at Starbucks. Do you want to take a temporary job there while you're looking?"

For a moment, she imagined herself as the ideal boot-strapper, taking a service job rather than sitting idle. There she'd be, mixing lattes and cheerfully greeting people at the drive-thru—until, after just a week or two, she'd overhear two patrons discussing a business plan and provide some staggeringly good piece of advice. Or, as she handed an iced coffee to a harried executive, something about Jen would stand out from the usual tattooed and pierced people behind the counter, and the customer would ask her, "What are you doing working here?" "Oh, I'm just doing this to fill a few weeks while I look for a new job."

The fantasy shattered as she considered exactly how she would have reacted to the story of a Starbucks barista "between jobs" in the tech industry. Heartlessly or not, her world was even less inclined to take seriously the holder of a "between jobs" job than the "actor" waiting tables. That, at least, fit a certain stereotype.

"There's nothing more permanent than a temporary solution," she said, clearing her mind of these fantasies. "Besides, if I take a job, I'll have to give up unemployment benefits."

"That's dumb," Katie observed curtly but had no further advice.

In defense of sanity, Jen quickly developed a routine: Get up at 6:30. Take a three-mile run. Clean up. Put on business clothes. Make breakfast and coffee. Sit down at the laptop to consult job listings, check e-mail, search for new professional connections.

By the end of the first week, she had had several inquiries via e-mail, filled out multiple applications, and even had one interview scheduled for the following week. She had let all the recruiters she was connected with know that she was "looking" and forced herself to exert a conscious effort not to check back each day to ask, "Anything yet?"

Although she assured herself that it would be normal to take up to three months to find a job, the difference between her accustomed level of activity and her current one was so sharp that it made her panicky. Her world closed in, and before she talked to anyone outside her enclosed, jobless existence, she had to remind herself, "It's been nine days now. Two days since I scheduled that interview. One day since I talked to that recruiter. Three hours since I sent that e-mail."

The clock of her anxiety ran far faster than that of the world outside, and she feared that in a moment of unawareness, she would reveal her isolation from the outside world by saying something that would constitute an admission that an hour was long to her, a day an eternity, a week unthinkable.

"I need to get out," Jen announced on Friday evening. "I need to see people."

Katie, who had taken to heart Jen's decree that they would eat out less, was creating chaos in the kitchen under the guidance of a book titled *The Raja's Garden: Exploring the Delights of Indian Home Cookery.* "Where are you going to go?"

"I don't know," Jen admitted. "Out."

"Are you going out for dinner, or will you eat here and go out afterward?" Katie asked, with an edge of annoyance in her voice.

"I'll definitely eat here," Jen reassured. "That smells really great. What is it?"

"Dal palak. And rice."

"I wouldn't miss it. I'm going to go check around. Someone must be doing something tonight."

"A wine bar?" Katie asked, when Jen pitched her plans over dinner. "Who's going to be there?"

"I dunno. Dan said maybe a couple dozen people. I know a few of them from when I was at Stanford for my MBA. There'll be wines to try. Snacks. Nothing crazy. We'll probably be done by midnight."

Katie shrugged. "Everyone will be ten years older than me, and I have to be at work at five tomorrow."

"Are you sure?"

Katie nodded. "Yeah. You go ahead. It'll do you good to get out for a bit."

"Thanks." Jen reached across the table and touched her sister's hand. "This food is really good. Thank you."

Katie smiled. "I'm glad you like it."

"Hey, don't worry about the dishes. I'll take care of them when I get home, or in the morning. Go ahead and relax for a while before you have to go to bed, okay?"

"Okay."

The tasting room of the Budding Grove was moderately crowded when Jen arrived. Besides Dan Fischer, she knew none of them well, but there were several she had met before. A glass of wine found its way into her hand, and she mingled. The scene seemed so much a part of her world before the layoff that, somewhere during her third glass of wine, she found herself answering the question "So how are things at AppLogix?" with an extended and enthusiastic description of the PocketDJ Player project. The plans that she had described so many times over the last year rolled off her tongue in well-practiced phrases, until she realized what she was doing and ended the story abruptly with "But then Apple bought a stake in AppLogix, and the leadership team decided hardware wasn't in our future. So that was that, and we're all looking for work."

She felt a hand on her shoulder and turned to see Dan.

"How are you doing?" he asked.

"I'm doing great! This evening is just what I needed. I'm glad I called you up."

"I'm glad it's helping, but you're getting just a little loud," Dan advised.

"Am I?"

"Just a tiny bit. Let's go find a booth and talk. It's been a while."

Dan guided her away into a quiet niche. Jen had turned apologetic.

"Was I loud? I'm sorry. It's been a really rough week. Very loud?"

He shrugged. "No more than some others. It's a wine bar on a Friday night. But we haven't had a chance to talk in a while."

"Thanks." She stared down at her glass and felt the gloom trying to take hold. She shook it off. "What have you been up to?"

"Oh, the usual. Everyone hates a lawyer, but everyone needs one sooner or later. How about you. How's the job hunt?"

"It's okay. I've got an interview on Tuesday."

"Where?"

"Aspire Brands. They're starting up a line of computer bags, and they're hiring a product-line director."

"Director is what you've been wanting for the last year, isn't it?"

"Yeah . . . I dunno. Like you say, this sounds like just what I've been wanting. And it's moving fast. They want someone to start by August. It just sounds a lot like the App-Logix job did: trendy company getting into a product category they haven't done before. That, and . . ." She shrugged and looked away, feeling uncomfortable meeting Dan's gaze. "I've had so much time to think about these things over the last week. I keep having this fear I've topped out. Everyone has their level of potential. What if I've hit mine, and this is as good as it gets?"

Dan cracked a half smile. "That's just tiredness talking. I don't think you're washed up at thirty-three."

"That's why it scares me. Just the sound of it is so pathetic. Promoted to the level of my incompetence."

"Hey, cheer up." He reached across the table and lifted her chin. "Loud was okay. Let's not start on morose."

Jen smiled wanly. "Okay. There's nothing more pathetic than being the fragile girl at the wine bar anyway."

"That's the spirit. Now, it's getting late. Are you okay to drive home?"

"Yeah."

"All right then. Good luck on that interview."

"Thanks."

The evening air was cool and cleared her head. She stood by her car, taking deep breaths and feeling, already, that she had made a fool of herself.

One week out of work—she reflected with disgust—and I'm practically sobbing on Dan's shoulder over a glass of wine. Way to go, girl.

She took a last, deep breath, concluded that she was ready to drive home, and got into the car. The streets were empty and quiet. The garage door opened its maw obediently and swallowed her and the coupe. She ascended the stairs and let herself in quietly, knowing that Katie would be leaving for work in less than six hours. Going into the kitchen, she found the counters clean, the dishes done. A note from Katie sat beside the sink: "I thought you really did need a break, so I took care of the cleanup. Hope you had a great time out with your friends. See you tomorrow."

The kitchen's glistening cleanliness blended with the memory of Dan's hand under her chin. She was not alone. People cared.

Monday morning found Jen, as per her routine, in business clothes and sitting at the kitchen table. She was looking at the phone, a number already dialed, summoning up the confidence to hit Call, and reflecting, as she did so, that she would have made the call without a moment's hesitation if she had still had her job—if she had not needed so much to make the call. She exhaled and put the phone to her ear.

"Search Solutions. Can I help you?"

"Hi there. My name is Jen Nilsson. I'm calling for Lauren Baird. Is she available? I'm returning her call."

"Please hold while I see if she's available."

Relentlessly innocuous music blared at her for a minute until the receptionist returned abruptly to the line and stated that she would put Jen through.

"This is Lauren."

"Hi, Lauren. This is Jen Nilsson. You'd sent me a note about a product-line manager position and said to call anytime."

"Jen!" the voice on the other end of the line greeted her with the overwhelming familiarity of the professional networker. "Good to talk to you. Yes, I've got an opportunity that I'm trying to fill here, and from your profile I thought you might be a fit for it. Do you have a few minutes to talk right now?"

"Sure."

The conversation followed familiar lines. Was she willing to relocate? Yes. Can we just talk a bit about your experience? Jen described her recent work history. What are you hoping for out of your next position? She did her best to tailor her answer to the few hints that had been dropped about what this job might be like and to suggest that she had clear ideas and standards. Shouting, "Look, right now I just really need a job!" would not be the right answer. What were her salary expectations?

"I'm not in this just for the money. The biggest issue for me is finding the right opportunity. But, of course, I expect compensation to be competitive and to recognize the importance of the position."

Lauren acknowledged the cleverness of this response but firmly asked how much Jen had made at her last job, to which Jen could not but comply.

At last, Lauren performed the ritual reveal: "Based on our conversation, I think that you could be a good fit with our client. They are a manufacturer of premium power tools named Schneider and Sons, located near Chicago. Would you be interested in my forwarding your information to them so that you can be considered for this opportunity?"

The name meant nothing to Jen, but, since power tools had not heretofore been an area of great interest to her, this was not an indicator of the company's worth one way or another. She felt a momentary disappointment that it was not a company she knew or a field that she found interesting. Her goal right now, however, was simply to get offers on the table.

"Yes, I'd definitely be interested in having my information passed on and hearing more about the role there. Actually, I have ties in the Chicago area. My parents live not far from Chicago, and I have other family back there as well. So that area would be a great fit for me."

They closed the call with the usual assurances. Jen set the phone down and sighed out her tension. Talking about herself was almost addictively gratifying, but the stakes made each call an utterly draining experience.

After a few moments of slow breathing and walking around the apartment, Jen sat back down and typed up all the details of the conversation for her prospects file. This made the fourth prospect that had reached the point of her résumé's being sent to the hiring manager. Thus far, she had only the one interview scheduled, and none of the job prospects gave her enthusiasm. Still, they were jobs. And a job was what she needed.

The headquarters of Aspire Brands was up in the City. Jen drove over to where she could catch Caltrain and made sure she allowed herself plenty of time. Nothing untoward occurred, so rather than arrive forty minutes early, she found a coffee shop in which to cool her heels and calm her nerves until closer to the interview.

The building, when she reached it, was glisteningly modern, and in front of it, an utterly abstract tangle of iron beams stood twenty feet tall astride an inverse fountain. In the lobby, Jen announced herself to the receptionist, provided identification, and was rewarded with a visitor's badge.

"Here's your schedule," the receptionist said, handing over a clipboard. "It looks like you're a few minutes late for your first interview. Kim Martinez from Human Resources is waiting for you in the atrium." She waved a hand in the direction of a tall, slim, dark-haired woman who was already approaching the front desk.

Jen felt a brief wave of panic. She was ten minutes early. Wasn't she? She started to pull out the printed schedule, then thought better of it and hurried to greet the woman approaching her.

"Jen?" the woman asked, extending a hand.

She shook the hand firmly. "Yes. Kim?"

The woman nodded. "Trouble getting here?"

Jen focused on keeping any sound of nervousness from entering her voice. "You know, there must have been some kind of mix-up. The schedule I was sent had the first interview starting at ten o'clock. Luckily, the receptionist gave me a clipboard with the updated itinerary, so I'll be okay from here on out."

Kim shrugged. "They must have updated your schedule and forgot to send a copy to your recruiter. Well, that's how things are here. Fast-paced. Two things you'll have to be comfortable with if you're going to fit in at Aspire are speed and change. Change, change, change! Our corporate value for the year is 'Dealing with Ambiguity.' Come on, we'll talk as we walk to your next interview. That way, we can still get fifteen minutes in despite this scheduling mix-up. Now, my goal is to see if you'd fit in well with our culture here at Aspire. Can you tell me what you liked most and least about your last job?"

She set a rapid pace. Jen struggled both to keep up and to answer her questions thoroughly.

"Now, your next interview," Kim announced, cutting Jen off in the middle of a discourse, "is with Alexia Astov. She's the senior vice president in charge of our flagship Sylvia Lytton clothing brand. She's also been one of the executive sponsors for the Courier brand revival, so while this role would not report to her, she has a major stake in finding an outstanding candidate to see the project through."

They came to a stop outside a curving glass wall that enclosed an office of unsettling elegance. A woman of uncertain age but unquestionable pocketbook was talking animatedly to the speakerphone from behind the massive desk, whose design resembled a flattened amoeba made of highly polished mahogany. She waved to Jen and Kim, then continued to address the phone. The wall successfully obscured all sound, making Alexia's performance, complete with expansive hand gestures, a pantomime of "woman having an urgent conversation".

"I have to get to my next meeting", Kim announced. "One of the talent acquisition admins will meet you here in thirty minutes to take you to your interview. Good luck!"

She rushed off, leaving Jen to reflect that although she had often been accused of overformality in the tech industry, in the Aspire Brands headquarters her fashion ethic appeared conspicuously plain.

Alexia's phone conversation lasted long enough to allow Jen to contemplate the question of whether to attempt to look composed by standing with her hands at her side or to assume an appearance of busyness by checking her phone for e-mail, but not long enough to reach any resolution. Then the vice president stabbed her phone off with decision, rose, and pulled open the door.

"Jen Nilsson?" Her hands enclosed Jen's in something that was more of a clasp than a handshake: cool, dry, and without pressure or movement. "Come in, come in. Have a seat," she said as she indicated a chair that proved, once Jen sat in it, to be designed such that one was forced to choose between either sprawling back comfortably in it, or perching carefully on the edge, back straight and knees together. Jen perched.

Alexia resumed her place behind her desk. Until that moment, Jen had not given much credence to the claim that sitting behind a desk implied power because the person behind the desk had her legs hidden, while the person facing her had hers exposed, but this claim now seemed readily believable.

Alexia leaned forward, elbows on her desk, and entwined her hands thoughtfully as she regarded Jen. "Now, I've read your résumé, and you seem like a very capable young woman," she began, her voice betraying no clear accent, yet somehow expressing an unmistakable foreignness in tone and rhythm. "However, at Aspire we do not look merely for the capable. We require some element of the extraordinary. Not just anyone can work here. And having been, if I may say, the inspiration behind the acquisition of the Courier brand, I feel strongly that we must have *the right* person in this role. Our last line director was not quite *right*."

Jen offered tactful sympathy over the difficulties of not having *the right* person.

"Essential to my vision," Alexia continued, "is that we must insist at every turn upon the integrity of the brand. Courier is an *iconic* brand. It must again be inconceivable that a business woman not have her Courier with her. And for the modern woman, that means a *technology* bag. Do you know *technology?*"

Unaccustomed to such an open-ended, not to say unanswerable, line of questioning, Jen attempted to provide a satisfactory answer to this. Alexia fixed her with a look of complete attention that seemed to interject "not enough yet" at every pause, and Jen quickly began to feel herself both running on too long yet not having said enough.

At last, Alexia cut her off in midsentence. "Well, well. Of course, this role is not a creative role. We have the very best designers providing creative input to the line. This role is responsible for assuring that that vision is executed flawlessly. Can you explain your ability to execute flaw-lessly?"

This seemed a challenge that must be met with a challenge in return. "I don't think you'll find someone who can tell you honestly she delivers flawless execution. As a product-line manager, I've been responsible for coordinating the work of teams all over the world. Errors are inevitable. The key is developing checks and processes such that problems are identified early and addressed quickly." She attempted to illustrate this with several examples.

"Yes, yes." Alexia waved a hand somewhat dismissively. "But in so many companies, this simply means making sure that you follow the plan, that you obey authority. Organization, problem solving: these I can see you have. But are you able to work without direction? No, no. Not enough. Are you able to challenge authority, challenge conventional wisdom?"

"Surely if I simply say yes, that is itself utterly conventional?"

"Examples!" Alexia cried. "Always examples. Can you provide an example of a time you challenged authority?"

After briefly marshaling her thoughts, Jen laid out an example where she had turned her management around on an issue.

Alexia shook her head. "No, no, no. That's just a case of standing up for what you think is the right thing to do. Very good, but what I want to know about is a case of standing up to your management. Slaying sacred cows. Those times you have to fight, fight, fight."

Jen tried another example.

"Once again," Alexia replied, with a theatrical expression of despair. "This is simply a case of arguing for what you think is right. When have you fought authority? Really fought it?"

Fighting down rage, Jen decided that the time to defy authority was now. "In that case, I'm not sure how I can answer your question. Why would I fight authority if it wasn't a case of arguing for what I thought was right? Would you respect me for having confronted authority in order to argue for something I thought was *wrong*?"

Alexia threw up her hands. "You see? It's so hard. We need people who are willing to stand up against authority and conventional wisdom. But what is business? You come in, you have your list of things to do. You have your boss to please. You play by the rules. You seem like a very, very smart young woman, but just the other day I was telling someone younger than you, 'I don't know if I can hire you. It may be that other businesses have spoiled you and you can't think anymore.' Not everyone can work here. It takes someone who can really *be* an Aspire employee."

A willowy young woman with very blonde hair was standing outside the office, tapping on the glass. Alexia held up a finger: "one minute."

"What do you think," she asked, fixing Jen with an appraising gaze. "Can you be an Aspire employee?"

Jen shrugged and spread her hands. "I don't know how you can expect me to provide a useful answer to that question. If I say yes, I may just be saying it. And why would I say no when I'm here interviewing for a job?" She rose. "It looks like it's time for my next interview. Thank you so much."

She reached out, and Alexia performed the not-quite-handshake again. The two women regarded each other for a moment. "Good luck!" Alexia said and opened the door.

"Hi!" The young woman introduced herself by a name that Jen instantly forgot, and she explained that Kim had asked her to escort Jen to the next interview. Jen desperately wished she could have a moment or two to regain her calm, but that was not how the game was played. Instead, she followed the admin, meditating on the fact that, in addition to having a comparatively plain fashion sense by Aspire standards, she was also, despite her athleticism, a heavyweight.

"You're going to be meeting next with Larry Burkett. He's the vice president of Marketing Analytics. Most people really like Alexia," the admin confided. "But Larry is a tough interview. Still, you look tough."

"Thanks," Jen replied, wondering what a tough interview would be like if the last one had been easy.

Larry resided in another curve-walled glass office, which was different from Alexia's in every furnishing except for the awkward chair. Larry himself was an even greater contrast: well over six feet tall, heavy, dressed in a plaid flannel shirt, suspenders, and studiously tattered khakis, with ragged hair that was pushed back from his face without apparent styling of any sort.

"I'm responsible for marketing analytics," he explained, "which means, of course, that I'm at constant war with all those who are 'fashion' driven. You see, there are two ways to look at the world: gut and facts. Which way do you look at it?"

"Given the intro, does anyone answer 'gut'?" Jen asked.

"Is that a fact-based answer or a gut answer?" Larry countered.

"It's not based on numbers, but it's based on observation of human tendency."

Larry smiled. "All right then. Give me an example in which you've changed your beliefs about something based on data."

Jen had begun to sketch out an example from experience when the door opened and Alexia entered.

"Larry, do you mind?" she asked. He shrugged. "Jen?" she asked. "Did you think our interview went well?"

Jen's mind reeled. "I thought I did the best that I could," she answered.

Alexia fixed her with an appraising look. "I believe you thought it went rather badly. You did well, though. I'm impressed with you. You did very well. What do you think about that?"

The rapid changes in tone were taking their toll on Jen's calm, but she fought down frustration and kept control of her voice. "I'm glad you found it revealing. I tried to answer everything as well as I could."

"I just wanted to tell you that I was impressed," Alexia said and left as abruptly as she had entered.

Larry fixed her with an appraising gaze.

"How did that conversation with Alexia make you feel?" he asked.

"I'm glad to hear that it went well," Jen responded.

"How were you feeling about the interview when you finished it."

"I couldn't tell."

"Fit is incredibly important here," Larry explained. "You

wouldn't be here if you weren't incredibly smart and if you hadn't proved yourself in your previous jobs. The reason for talking to you in person is to find out if you have what it takes to work here and not only survive, but thrive. What do you think so far?"

Jen attempted to sketch out an answer that expressed her eagerness to be challenged and her excitement about the opportunity itself—anything other than the baldly stated "I really need a job", which was, in fact, the only thing keeping her sane.

Larry cut her off. "Do you always talk so much when you're nervous?"

Jen seethed. "No."

Larry cocked an eyebrow, but Jen held any further words in. Silence stretched out to the point of agony. "All right," Larry said. "Let's go back to my last question. Tell me about a time you've changed your beliefs based on data."

Two more interviews followed. If Jen had been asked to provide a detailed account of them later, she would have found it difficult to do so. Then she was shown back to the lobby and stepped out into the street. Again she confronted the tangle of modern sculpture above the inverse fountain, though now that she saw it from the vantage point of one leaving the Aspire Brands headquarters, she noticed that the metal beams aligned to form an italic *A*.

Walking to the station and riding Caltrain, she felt herself still under scrutiny, holding her expression rigidly neutral. By the time she reached her car, control had become a necessity. She drove home in tooth-gritted silence.

"How was the interview?" Katie asked as Jen entered the condo.

Jen stalked to the liquor cabinet, pulled out a bottle of Buffalo Trace, and poured herself a couple fingers' worth. With this she retreated to the armchair.

"Bad?" Katie asked.

Jen took a slow sip. "It could have been better," she responded.

Her phone rang. Jen answered it and heard the voice of Cathy Bradford, the recruiter who had contacted her about the Aspire job.

"Jen! How's it going?"

Jen segregated all her feelings about the interviews from the sound of her voice and pushed out a cheerful tone. "Oh, just resting up after the interviews. I feel like I did the best I could."

"Well, they were very impressed," Cathy replied. "They would like to extend you an offer if you are interested."

The sheer unexpectedness of it, the contrast with the way she had been treated in the interviews, seemed an offense. She crammed all her frustration to the back of her mind and responded with faux excitement.

"That's great news. I need to see the offer, of course, before I know my response, but I'd certainly be excited to consider an offer."

"Wonderful. They'll be very glad to hear that. I think you can expect to see a copy of the offer letter via e-mail tomorrow morning."

"I'll be looking out for it. Thanks." Cathy hung up.

Jen threw her phone at the couch as hard as she could and hurled a stream of profanity after it.

"What's wrong?" Katie asked.

"They offered me the job."

The offer arrived midmorning on Wednesday, and it was everything she could have wished, except that, after her interview experience, the idea of working for Aspire gave her almost the same stomach-churning feeling as thinking about her current unemployment.

She printed out the offer letter so that she could stare at it more easily. The salary written on it was deeply gratifying. And surely working there couldn't be as much like psychological warfare as the interviews had been. She wouldn't be reporting to Larry or Alexia, perhaps would not even see them often. The interview with her potential boss, a blandly managerial woman named Bryn Masters, had not gone badly, although, as the final interview of the four, Jen could remember few details from it. Why let a couple of bad interviews turn her away from an opportunity this good?

But even as she tried to convince herself that she should take the job, she knew that she did not want to.

Shortly after noon, an e-mail from Cathy Bradford came through. "Just wanted to see if you'd received the offer from Aspire and get your thoughts."

Jen wrote back, "I got the offer, and it does look like a good one. I need a day or two to think about it, as I may be on the verge of receiving an offer for another position as well."

Then she e-mailed the recruiters for the three other jobs she had heard back about, warning them that she had just received an offer for another job, but telling each one that she was, in fact, very enthusiastic about that opportunity instead. This ploy, however, did not produce the results she had hoped for, as, over the next several hours, each one wrote back cautiously expressing congratulations and saying that, although she would pass along the word that time was of the essence, she could not make any promises.

Katie came home in the afternoon to find Jen watching daytime TV.

"So, did you get the offer from that job?"

"Yes," Jen confessed. "I got it. It's a good offer, too."

"So . . . is that good? Are you happy?"

Jen flipped channels listlessly. "I don't know. That was the most psychotic set of interviews I've ever had. And I don't know why they offered me the job so quickly. I'm worried they're crazy to work for, or they're in some really bad situation that I'll be blamed for, or just that I'll really hate working there."

"So . . . are you going to turn them down?"

"I don't *know*." They both stared at the TV. A dubbed Japanese game show was playing in which contestants had to pick which of three doorways to try to crash through: two covered over with white paper, the third with drywall.

"Should I make dinner, or are you planning to sit here and zone all night?"

"I don't know."

Katie retrieved a Coke from the refrigerator and sat down next to her sister. "Look, Jen, this isn't good. If the job makes you this unhappy, don't take it. You said you've got enough money to keep going for six months. You're smart. You'll get another job."

"What if I don't?"

"You always have before."

"But I haven't gone turning down good jobs before. This is a good job. It pays more than my last one. A lot more. It's a promotion. It's being product-line director for the Courier bag relaunch. It's a great opportunity. I wouldn't *deserve* another job if I turned this down."

"Was that a Courier bag that Grandma always used to carry?"

"See? Iconic. Even you know what it is. I can't turn that down, can I?"

Katie shrugged. "I don't see why not. If it makes you unhappy, don't do it."

Jen sighed. "Why are we watching this?" She flipped channels until she settled on a cooking competition in which men and women in chef outfits seemed to be competing to see who could cut vegetables most violently.

"If you don't like what I have to say, maybe you should call someone else about it and ask their advice. Call Dad."

"Dad's had the same job for the last fifteen years. What would he know?"

"Well, I don't know then," Katie said in an exasperated tone, getting up from the couch and heading into the kitchen. "I'm making enchiladas and Spanish rice for dinner. It'll be ready in thirty minutes, so if you want to call Dad before dinner's ready, turn off the TV soon."

"Hey, Dad," said Jen, in an unusually meek tone. "Do you have a little time? I really need your advice."

"Sure, honey. What's up?" Even over the phone her father's voice carried the tone of bedtime stories and checks for monsters in the closet. Jen found herself instinctively curling up and hugging a couch cushion.

She described the job at Aspire and her fears in relation to it.

"Look," her father said when she had finished. "I don't have your experience with trading jobs and all that. You've had an amazing career, and you know your mother and I are both really proud of what you've done. But I can tell you this based on my experience: You spend more hours each day working than you do at home. You'd better make sure that it's something you can be happy doing. It's normal to feel a little nervous when you're starting something new, but if you really think you'll be unhappy at this place, don't take the job. It's not worth it."

Next, she tried Dan, but the advice was similar.

"You know me, Jen. I tried one year of corporate law and decided it didn't matter how much it paid: I'd rather be stuck writing wills and divorce decrees than combing through merger documents sixteen hours a day. If you think you'll enjoy it, go for it. If you think you'll be miserable, it's just not worth it."

Jen slept badly, and the next morning, rather than going for her run or getting dressed, she sat at the kitchen table in her pajamas, coffee cradled in her hands, and stared at the acceptance e-mail. Each time she questioned it, it responded with the same bland phrases and compelling figure. Finally, she hit Reply and typed out, "I would be happy to accept this offer. Please let me know what the next steps are."

Within the hour, e-mails from Aspire's HR Department started to make their way back: Background check. Drug test. Tax information. Tentative start date in ten days, assuming no problems showed up on the above.

Later in the day she received an e-mail from Bryn. "So excited to have you joining the Aspire team, Jen. Just wanted to check: Do you have a passport? I'm going to need to have you go to China the week after next."

4

It was still fully dark when the alarm began to bleat at 4:00 A.M. With the familiarity of routine, Jen got out of bed and trudged across the room to turn it off, then headed into the bathroom without giving herself time to stop moving. Four A.M. in Guangzhou meant 1:00 P.M. in San Francisco, and she had to be on the phone with Bryn at 2:00 P.M.

Forty-five minutes later found her in front of her laptop, a steaming pot of room-service coffee at her elbow to help her face the day. The laptop had become her lifeline during her stay in China. Alone in a sea of 1.3 billion people, e-mail, Skype, and Facebook provided the only connections to all that was familiar. And this, more than anything, kept her, whenever possible, at her downtown hotel, with its privileged tourist access through the Great Firewall, by which modern China kept out the barbarian hordes of the outside world.

She skimmed the work e-mail that had accumulated while she was asleep, then snuck a glance at Facebook. The site had become a peculiar form of torture to her as her trip dragged on. At first, she had posted frequently: places she had visited, pictures, new foods tried. This, however, seemed to give others the idea that she was on an extended vacation, or at least wrapped up in some experience beyond their ken. Now she simply pored over everything posted by her friends.

She hoped to see some evidence that she was missed, that there remained an empty slot in others' lives that only her presence could fill. What she found instead was that their lives continued just as before, despite her absence. It was like the sort of dream in which the sleeper finds herself dead and watches with increasing anxiety as everyone moves on and forgets her life had ever occurred.

It was thus with near delight that Jen saw an update from Katie: "Got hate mail from the city. Sister forgot to put the trash bill on auto-pay before she left. PANIC!!!" At least in some prosaic fashion she was missed. She left a comment reminding Katie that she'd put her name on the checking account and reassuring her that nothing dire would happen until the bill was more than forty-five days late.

Then she pulled up Skype and called Bryn at work.

Bryn's rounded features and close-cropped blonde hair appeared on the laptop screen. "Rise and shine, campers! How's the Far East this morning?"

The ritual greeting was starting to grate in the way that anything heard repeatedly at five in the morning would, but it was at least familiar and spoken in unaccented American English. "Doing all right. What's yesterday's news?"

"Those cases finally came in with the first-production-run samples for the line. I guess the Trade Winds people were telling the truth the last time they told you they'd shipped."

Jen felt significant relief. The often-promised, always-delayed first production run had been one of the prime things keeping her in China longer than planned. "So, that's good, right? I really will be coming home on Saturday?"

Bryn shook her head fractionally. "Nope. Started a total

shitstorm. You should be glad you were on the other side of the Pacific."

"Oh no."

"Oh yes, I'm afraid. The three o'clock call is going to be a fun one. I don't know what they're thinking, but we're going to have to go all the way down their throats: make them take you to each factory and find out why they're not producing product that looks like the prototypes. Some of these aren't even close. I had Travel go ahead and cancel your flights. And they're having your visa extended through the end of the year."

"End of the year? Bryn, I've got a condo and bills and —I was supposed to be here five days, and it's already been almost three weeks."

"I know. I know. Calm down. You're not staying through the end of the year. This just saves time and money on extensions. China hands out six-month visas like candy, so why make paperwork? Two to three weeks, and you should have this all squared away and be sipping gin and tonics in business class on the way back."

The three o'clock was, as Bryn had predicted, quite a scene. The Courier line had been planned to include six initial designs, each of these available in several leathers and also a "cruelty free" material. The manufacturing was being sourced and coordinated by a Chinese company, Trade Winds, and the initial prototypes had been everything that one could wish.

As initially envisioned, Jen's visit was to have included meetings with the Trade Winds executives, a tour of one of the factories, inspection of the initial production run of product, and then handshakes and paper signing. With the product of this initial short run, the Aspire Brands sales force would have proceeded to win the hearts and minds of buyers for department and specialty stores everywhere, making them eager to participate in the triumphant return of the Courier brand—resplendent in memory even if recently sold at bankruptcy auction by the holding company, which had bought but failed to turn around the struggling company.

That was the vision. But, as with so many apparitions, this vision was suffering difficulties in realization. Trade Winds had been curiously reluctant to show the products to Jen upon her arrival, taking her to dinners and tours aplenty, but providing no wares for her inspection. Then they had announced that the products had been aired directly to Aspire Brands. And now, as Bryn had revealed, in the latest episode of this melodrama, it proved that Trade Winds had exercised an unacceptable degree of creative license in the products they had sent: Nine designs had been sent rather than six, and yet some of the original six were not even among this superfluity. Moreover, on the four designs that corresponded, to varying degrees, to their legitimate forbears, the materials and designs were subtly (or even distinctly) different from those in the prototypes, invariably in ways far more beneficial to Trade Winds' costs than to the potential acclaim of the brand.

"It is at times like these," Alexia intoned, for the benefit of all those on the conference call, "that we are allowed to prove our enduring passion for the Brand."

It was with feelings of endurance, but little passion, that Jen, after business hours in California, went down to confront the hotel's breakfast buffet and meditate on her fate.

At first, the manager of their account at Trade Winds, a middle-aged man who insisted on being called Eddy, made himself unable to understand the problem.

They had wanted to see the first product samples, yes? The samples had been sent. More samples had been sent than had been asked for. Very good samples. When could he expect an order? The production samples did not match the prototypes? Of course they didn't! These were off the production line. The prototypes were merely prototypes. Scale up to production always involved changes. Surely it was the job of Trade Winds to execute these changes. It was their expertise.

Finally, Jen pulled rank: either he could take her to visit the factories where these production samples were made and help her sort out why the production samples did not match the prototypes, or else the president of Aspire Brands would call the owner of Trade Winds and say that Eddy was not meeting their needs. Which did he prefer?

This, at last, focused Eddy's attention on the problem, and he promised that he and a driver would pick Jen up at her hotel the next morning and go to visit one of the factories.

Once the arrangements for the trip had been made, including calling up Sue, her independent translator—Jen had quickly learned that translators provided by Trade Winds took the good of the company to heart when deciding what to translate—Jen decided to give herself an hour or two off from business concerns before things became impossibly late in California.

The indefinite extension of her stay weighed heavily, and she felt the need to talk to someone back home, but as she sat staring at her phone, she found herself hesitating over whom to call. Other than Katie, who was left to struggle with bills and other condo maintenance in her sister's absence, there was no one, she realized, who would find it particularly unusual not to hear from her for a month or more at a time.

She flipped backward and forward through her contacts and at last called Dan Fischer. It stretched to three rings, and she was on the point of canceling the call when he picked up.

"Jen. Are you back in the States?"

"No. I'm stuck. Aspire just canceled my tickets and extended my visa again. There's no leaving China for me till these folks can get the bags right."

"That's harsh."

"Anyway . . . I'm sorry, I should have asked: Can you talk now? I just wanted to hear a familiar voice."

"I can talk for about ten minutes," Dan said, a barely detectable hint of reserve in his voice. In the background, Jen could faintly hear traffic.

"Where are you going?"

There was the slightest of pauses before he replied. "Picking up a date for dinner."

"Oh. I'm sorry. I didn't mean . . ."

"Don't worry about it. Right now I'm just stuck in traffic. It's you or Terry Gross."

"My conversations aren't so renowned."

"But you said you wanted to talk to me, and I don't think Terry knows whether I'm listening or not."

"Well . . ." She found herself suddenly without anything to say. Then they both spoke at once.

"Who's the date with?"—"How's China?"

They laughed.

"Let's not talk about China," Jen said. "How's California? How's the law practice? Who's this date with?"

"One of Mom's 'nice Jewish girls'. First date, but she sounded nice when we talked the other night. So I guess I could use a little distraction to keep me from feeling nervous."

"Wow. I can't imagine being set up by my mom."

"It's a little weird. But she's not just any mom; she's a Jewish mom. It's different. Besides, it's not like I've had a stunning dating life on my own the last few years."

"Yeah, but . . . Does she do this often? Does she do a good job? Pick girls you're interested in, I mean?"

"Three or four times over the last few years. They've all been really nice girls. I did date one of them for almost six months. But I'm single right now, so it hasn't been as successful as Mom would like."

"I suppose, with my mom and dad getting all religious again, they'd love it if I found some 'nice Catholic boy', but I can't imagine trusting my mom to pick a date for me."

"It depends on the mom. And being Jewish is different anyway. It's not just something you do; it's something you are. I'm not as observant as my parents right now, but I can see why they think it would be important to marry someone Jewish."

Jen was not sure how to respond to this, and Dan cut off the silence before it could stretch for long.

"Anyway. I'm getting off the freeway and will be there in a minute. I hope your stay goes well. If you get lonely again, feel free to call me."

"Thanks, Dan. It's good to hear your voice. Hope the date goes well."

She had intended to call Katie next—hear another voice from home—but the first call had soured the experience, and she felt the need to do something else and purge her mind. She began putting on her running clothes. There was time to get some exercise before lunch and afternoon work.

What sat badly was that she had called Dan with no particular thought of how he might be spending his evening. Indeed, now that she cast her mind back, she saw that since their Stanford days, she had seldom contacted Dan unless motivated by some reason of her own—something that she wanted. He kept up with her: sent invitations, called to ask how things were going, all the small elements that constitute friendship. But unless she had some specific object in mind, it was always he who made contact. Nor, perhaps due to reclusiveness on his part, perhaps due to lack of interest on hers, did she normally learn much about his personal life when they talked. Here he was on his way to a date. He'd had a girlfriend for six months, someone he met through his mother. Had she seen him during that time? When had he been single or dating?

All this came painfully into view because she had called him, not out of any real desire to know what was occurring in his life, but to give her a distraction from what was happening in her own. She'd sought to use him as a reminder of the home to which he formed a background element.

Her running clothes on, she resolved that she would make a change. If she had to live in China, she would live there. She would go down to the street and take a real run in the open air, rather than repairing to the treadmills in the gym. She took the elevator to the lobby, where the young man behind the desk seemed to give her an appraising look as she passed. She went out through the doors and found herself among the press of humanity. The sidewalk was crammed. Even though Guangzhou's motorcycle ban removed the usual developing-world sight of innumerable bikes zipping between the cars in already crowded streets, cars were packed fender to fender in the street, honking insistently at one another. All around was the faint, background buzz of a language that remained impenetrably foreign to her.

Suddenly she yearned to be back in the impersonal and sheltered silence of the hotel. She plunged back in through the lobby doors and took the elevator back up to the gym, where she mounted a treadmill and ran to the sprightly though incomprehensible tones of a pretty young television announcer on Xinhua. She ran until her body was tired and sweaty, and her mind was at last clear, then retired to the showers.

The expedition, when it left the next morning, was not without certain comic undertones. Eddy had brought a young female assistant with him. Sue, Jen's translator, had arrived as requested, and in addition, Jen had all of the prototype bags to bring with her: six designs, each in a variety of materials. Eddy's S-series Mercedes was spacious, but it also came with a driver. There was some question of bringing a second car, but at last the prototype bags all went into the trunk, the three women into the back seat, and Eddy sat in front with the driver—the glassed-off front compartment gradually clouded with cigarette smoke.

With traffic, the trip took nearly two hours, though it was

only seventy miles to the smaller city in which the factory was located. None of the car's occupants were the more cheerful for their journey, nor was the guard who stopped them outside the chain-link-fence surrounding the factory visibly glad to see them. He argued for a while with Eddy and the driver. Then the three reached a compromise that involved standing around smoking together while the car idled. At last, the guard opened the gate, Eddy and the driver returned to the car, and the guard waved them through.

The factory was a large structure of corrugated metal. Jen, Sue, and Eddy and his assistant were met outside by a middle-aged woman in a navy-blue suit who assured them repeatedly that they could call her Tina. She led them into the factory, where perhaps a hundred workers were busy. At one end of the hanger-like building (brilliantly illuminated throughout by the blue-white glow of fluorescent lights) was a bank of cutting tables at which a dozen workers were cutting out shapes from huge rolls of imitation leather. Most of the building was filled with sewing tables, at each of which a man or woman in an identical white uniform bent over a heavy-duty sewing machine, assembling pieces.

Accustomed as she was to the electronics factories she had visited while working on the PocketDJ Player, Jen was surprised at the lack of complexity. There were only four stages to the building of each bag: cutting, assembling the external pieces, inserting and attaching the lining, and attaching the straps, buckles, and other fittings. Nonetheless, progress seemed rapid and efficient.

After they had toured the production area, with perfunctory explanations of various points by Tina, they were led to a back room that was dim in comparison with the brilliantly lit factory and furnished in relative luxury with deeply piled carpet and overstuffed leather couches. An assistant brought in a tea service, and Tina served them with some formality.

The tea was drunk, and some small talk was awkwardly attempted through the mediation of Sue's translation. Then Tina summoned an assistant, who brought a selection of production samples for the bag that this factory was making: a satchel-style design made to fit a fifteen-inch laptop and emblazoned with a brass-finish buckle in the form of the Courier brand's "CR" logo.

Jen retrieved the relevant prototype from the car and set it next to the production-run samples.

Tina pointed proudly at the bags.

"She says that they look very good. You will sell a lot of them," Sue translated.

Jen pointed out that the strap on the production bag was not the same as that on the prototype. It was made of fabric rather than leather.

Tina considered the strap for some time, until Jen began to think that she would refuse to respond. Finally, she countered, explaining that the fabric strap was stronger.

Stronger or not, Jen objected, it was not what Aspire had requested. The exterior of the bag was to be entirely leather.

The bag *was* entirely leather. This was only the strap. A strap must be strong. Tina would not build a bag that did not have a strong strap.

They circled the topic and considered it from every angle. Tina sang the praises of a fabric strap. She denied that the original design had specified the nature of the strap. She suggested that a leather strap would look ugly. When all this failed, she warned that the bags would cost more.

This, Jen advised, was something she would have to take up with the senior vice president of Procurement when he arrived to sign the final purchase orders. Jen's job was to ensure that the production bags were like the prototypes.

But the production bags *were* like the prototypes.

Exactly like the prototypes.

Tina waved her hand in dismissal of this detail.

Nearly twenty minutes had now passed, and Jen was fully ready for the interview to be over. Unfortunately, the bag presented more sources of conflict.

Why had the piping been removed from the edges of the flap?

What piping?

Jen pointed out the feature. Tina insisted that she could see no difference. Time passed, voices were raised. The piping was at last admitted.

There remained only the matter of a pocket. The prototype had four pockets on the inside of the flap: two sized for pens and two larger ones. The production sample had a single large pocket and two sized for pens. Jen needed the missing pocket to be restored to the design.

Tina threw up her hands. Why so many pockets? Did she want her customers to lose things?

Jen remained firm. The design had four pockets; the bag must have four pockets.

Would she not prefer three pockets?

She would not.

Would she prefer three pen pockets and one large one? People had many pens!

No, even this generosity in regard to pens would not do.

Very well. If what Jen wanted was pockets, she would have pockets. Did this satisfy her?

If it matched the prototype, it did.

This round of negotiation finished, Tina sat back and surveyed her customers with evident pleasure.

It was clear they worked well together. Would they like to see another bag her factory could produce? It would go well with their other bags.

No, Jen explained, their line was already set. They had designers in the United States who created their bags. They needed only to have them manufactured exactly as designed.

Tina waved this away. They would like this bag. She was sure of it.

She called an assistant in, spoke briefly to him, and a moment later, a leather satchel was brought in and presented to Jen.

The first thing that Jen noticed was the Coach logo on it. No, she could not buy this bag. This was a Coach bag.

That was not a problem, Tina assured. The Courier logo could easily be substituted for the Coach one. Did she like the bag? It was a very popular bag. People would like it.

Jen turned on Eddy. Did this factory make pirated bags?

He shrugged.

Were Courier's designs being shopped to other companies the way this Coach design was?

He told her this was impossible.

How was it impossible?

Eddy shrugged.

Returning the Coach bag to Tina, Jen suggested that it was time for them to go.

Did Jen want to have the bag herself? As a gift?

She did not. She wanted only to get out, though she hesitated to express the feeling so bluntly. Sue, she noticed, was casting longing glances at the rejected Coach bag. Jen considered briefly accepting it and giving it to her, but she was sure that any compromise on this point would result in problems later.

Hands were shaken all around, and Jen and her entourage gradually made their way out of the factory to the car.

This visit was followed by others, similar in outline but each excruciating in its own way. One factory had produced a bag that looked, to the naked eye, exactly like the prototype but had been reduced slightly in dimensions such that it no longer fit a fifteen-inch laptop. At another factory, the Courier design had been abandoned entirely and replaced by one that the factory already had patterns cut out for. (It was a very popular bag, the owner assured her. Jen remained unmoved.) In the most extreme case, not only did the design presented not match the prototype at all, but the factory they toured clearly did not manufacture bags at all. Under heavy questioning, it was eventually admitted that the bags were being provided by the factory owner's cousin. "From where?" was a question that no one was willing to answer. Jen provided Sue with cash and sent her off to see if anyone could be convinced to venture an opinion. "I heard a rumor", several were willing to suggest, when neither management nor Americans were in sight, that the bags were being produced in Vietnam. The outsourcers had outsourced in their turn. Despite Eddy's objections, Jen insisted that this factory be wholly terminated and the business given to another.

The last two bags in the product line were manufactured at a factory so far from Guangzhou that it was necessary to make an overnight trip. The drive was long, the roads dusty. The factories themselves were primitive, but the results were, in fact, some of the most faithful to the original designs. After several hours of negotiation, the owner had committed to correcting what small issues remained.

With her two weeks of factory visits behind her, Jen felt a glow of accomplishment that was only slightly dampened as they pulled up in front of the hotel in which they would stay the night. It was not a gleaming tower on the model of the one in Guangzhou, but so long as it had a soft bed and a hot shower, Jen was willing to be forgiving. If it had a hotel bar, she was willing to be downright enthusiastic.

The bed, when she was shown to her room, was indeed soft. She turned on the water for a hot shower, undressed, and returned to the bathroom in a bathrobe, only to find that the water was no hotter than it had been before. She waited and checked again; the water was still cold.

Jen got dressed again and called the front desk. A woman who spoke surprisingly fluent English expressed her apologies and promised that the water problem would be rectified immediately. Some moments later, there was a knock at the door. Jen opened it to find the woman from the front desk, a young man in a porter's uniform, and an elderly maid. Jen led them into the bathroom and showed them the problem. They contemplated the shower and discussed among themselves in quiet tones. They turned the water off and then on again, tried the sink, then tried the shower again. Time passed. At last they emerged from the bathroom. Jen was sitting on the bed, knees together, arms folded, feeling tired and miserable.

"You will have the hot water now," the woman from the front desk advised. She began to leave the room, the porter and the maid following her.

Relief flooded Jen, but it was immediately followed by sickening doubt. She went into the bathroom, turned on the shower, and felt the water. It was cold.

She called out for the delegation of hotel staff to stop.

The woman from the front desk folded her arms and regarded her with an exasperated expression.

"The water still isn't hot," Jen explained.

The woman from the front desk led the way into the bathroom. She turned off the shower faucet and turned on the hot water tap for the tub. Water came out. She pointed.

"Hot water," she said.

Jen put her hand in the stream. "But it's not hot."

The woman put her hand in as well and considered.

"It takes time to get hot," the woman advised. She turned on the sink's hot-water tap and dipped a finger in it. "See. Hot water. There is hot water here. It takes time."

Jen objected that she had given the water plenty of time and it had gotten no hotter.

The woman tested the water again with her hand. It was, she pointed out, not entirely cold. Indeed, it was a little bit warm. Could Jen be satisfied with this?

It occurred to Jen at this juncture, after the last two weeks of intensive negotiations with factories, that the Chinese solution at a time like this would be to secure some kind of compensation: money back, a discount, some sort of free room service. An accommodation was being offered. She did not, however, want accommodation. The only thing she wanted was a hot shower. She remained firm: while the shower might not be as cold as it could be, it was not hot.

Her interlocutor now fixed her with a suspicious glare. Why was it that only Jen's room lacked hot water? No one else had complained. What had Jen been doing to it?

Jen was on the point of losing her calm completely at this accusation, but she saw the chance to make her own switch in tactics. Was this, she asked, not the largest and best hotel in the town?

The woman from the front desk drew herself up with pride. It certainly was.

Did she not then think, Jen asked, that the best hotel in the town *ought* to have hot water?

She felt almost cruel when she saw how the woman sagged under this attack. Yes. It should have hot water. She was sorry. She did not know why it did not have hot water. What could she do? The water was cold. She shook her head sadly and made her way toward the door. At the door, she stopped and turned back. The hotel did have an engineer. He was responsible for things like pipes. He was on his dinner break right now, but if Jen would like, she would send him up when he returned.

This renewed hope was unlooked for. Suddenly, the hotel seemed less dingy, the town less remote, the world better. Jen thanked her with real warmth. Then she shut the door behind her erstwhile helpers.

She contemplated waiting till later for a shower, in hopes

that the engineer would appear and work wonders with the water temperature, but she simply felt too grubby and tired after the long hours in the back seat and the tour through the hot, stuffy factory. She resolved to take the briefest possible shower now and then, if the engineer appeared and was successful, to luxuriate in hot water later.

Some minutes later, still shivery but feeling freshened by clean self and clean clothes, she ventured downstairs to investigate questions of food and drink.

Eddy and his assistant had gone off in search of a karaoke bar. Sue had expressed an intention to eat in her room and go to bed early. Jen had thus expected to eat alone—either truly so or alone in a crowd. The hotel restaurant had only a few customers in it when Jen entered, and she was surprised to see, sitting by herself, eating a bowl of noodles, a blonde woman about her own age who looked vaguely familiar.

Jen approached her. "Hi. My name's Jen Nilsson. With Aspire Brands. Do you mind if I join you?"

The woman looked up and replied in a reassuringly American accent, "April Holland. No, go right ahead. It's quiet here tonight. And it's not every day I see someone from home."

They discussed the menu and the town. Jen ordered. Discussion of home—which, for April, was Seattle—followed. Jen couldn't shake the feeling that she looked familiar, but they could not definitively nail down any common acquaintance or milieu. Talk centered on home, and once dinner was done, Jen suggested drinks. She had been determined on at least a drink or two after her long day, and April was not opposed. Katie consulted the bar. It featured a few expensive brands but not a very wide selection. She ordered a bottle of Johnnie Walker Black Label, and over it the two women became increasingly effusive. April was an "old China hand" and provided story after story of factories, hotels, and street vendors.

"How about you?" April asked. "Is this your first time in China?"

"No. But it's the longest I've been here. I'd never been for more than a week before, and now it's been almost five. And this is the first time I've been here for Aspire. You wouldn't believe it. I hadn't even started yet. I'd accepted their offer and I get an e-mail from Bryn: 'Do you have a passport? I need you to go to China next week.' Hoo!"

"Aspire Brands . . . Are you working on the Courier brand relaunch?"

"That's me."

"How's it going for you?"

Jen rolled her eyes. "I've learned a lot. I can certainly claim that. I hadn't realized how protected I'd been, working with huge electronics manufacturers. On this project, we've seen all kinds of things."

"Getting your own share of China stories?"

Jen demonstrated that she was, indeed, becoming a "China hand" with her own trove of stories, concluding with the factory that had so very obviously not been designed for making bags at all, and the detective work that had revealed the Vietnam connection.

"It's almost enough to make you wonder sometimes," observed April. "Are we actually gaining anything by manufacturing here? By the time we deal with the cultural barriers, the intellectual-property issues, the quality fade . . . What do you think?"

Fortified with a second glass of Johnnie Walker and a sense of comradeship with her fellow businesswoman, Jen was prepared to consider herself an expert. "Look, there's a huge amount of drive and entrepreneurial zeal here. It's inspiring to see. But it's true: by the time we deal with all the cultural barriers, the tendency to focus on the short term of getting orders rather than the long term of being known for quality, the double- and triple-checking . . . I don't know if the savings we get by manufacturing here always make up for the unresponsiveness, the quality issues, and the lack of stake in the company. You have to ask yourself: Is following the dollars—not even the dollars, the cents—always the right thing to do?"

April raised a glass. "I'll drink to that, sister."

5

Jen dragged herself out of bed at five o'clock the next morning. She now had cause to regret both the late hours and the quantities of Johnnie Walker that had vanished during them. It was Thursday morning in China—Wednesday afternoon in California—and it was just over five weeks since Jen had gotten off the plane for what was to have been a one-week trip. She wanted to lose no time in alerting Bryn that she had now resolved all the factory issues.

"That's a huge relief," Bryn said. "The Macy's and Saks account teams have been after me all week, wanting to know if we'd have the sourcing secure in time for their line reviews for next fall. The last thing we want with a newly relaunched brand like this is to have to dump the first year's product line on the channel partners because we were too late for the big players."

"So . . . where do we go from here?" Jen asked, deciding that the time had come for directness. "My understanding had not been that this was a China-based role. I'd like to be able to get home soon."

"I know. I know. We all really appreciate your flexibility, Jen. We'll get you back as soon as we can."

"I hate to push, Bryn, but . . . when?"

"Well, we need to get Todd Williams out there from

Procurement to sign papers with Trade Winds. You should be there for that exec meet and greet. This project has been your baby, and everyone recognizes you made it happen. I'll call his admin and see if Todd can fly out Monday. That would put him in . . . what? Late Tuesday or early Wednesday. You can have the meet and greet on Wednesday and Thursday. Tie up any loose ends and be ready to fly home sometime the next week."

"Seven weeks," said Jen dully. Long-ingrained instinct told her this was the moment for some more optimistic statement about pride in getting things done, but with the full body ache and sour taste of too much alcohol and too little sleep, added to the prospect of at least another two weeks of what she was beginning to think of as "exile", she could not muster up any business enthusiasm.

"Hey, hang in there." Bryn offered a sympathetic smile. "I know this trip has been tough, but you've accomplished something not a lot of people could, and you're recognized for it. Okay?"

Jen nodded.

The next week passed slowly. It was difficult to stay in the loop with work in the San Francisco office due to the time difference, and Trade Winds did not wish her to be overly involved in their work.

"This is your chance to be the tourist!" Katie told her, when Jen complained. "Go look at something. Go shopping. What do people do in China anyway?"

"Run factories and repress political dissidents."

"Well, do some of that. Or visit the Great Wall. Is that near you?"

"It's north of Beijing. About a thousand miles from here, I think."

"That's kind of far. How about the terra cotta warriors?"

"I think that's pretty far away too. Look, Katie, I'll find stuff to do. How are things at home?"

Katie looked down, then sideways, seemingly unwilling to meet Jen's gaze even through the webcam. "Ummm. Things are fine. Just, you know, work and stuff."

"Have there been any more issues with bills that weren't on autopay?"

"No. No problems. Nothing to talk about. How's work? How are the bags?"

Jen sighed. "I don't want to talk about work. That's why I called you."

Though she had at first ignored it, Katie's advice to be like a tourist and go shopping stuck in Jen's mind. Given that she had originally expected only a short trip, she had brought only a limited selection of work clothes. The insufficiency of these clothes grew in her mind until, on Tuesday afternoon, with the office in California closed and Todd safely in the air en route, she resolved to blow off what little work remained and go shopping. Surely for the big closeout meeting she deserved a new outfit. She consulted the hotel desk, and they arranged for a car to drop her off at one of the city's glittering downtown shopping malls. It proved a good thing that she had allowed all afternoon for the expedition. She did find several things that she was very pleased with—though she was surprised to discover that the elite shopping experience in China was not much less expensive than in California.

Next morning, she got up early, dressed in one of her new suits, put on new shoes, and dialed in to her daily conference call with Bryn in a significantly better frame of mind than usual. A call down to the desk revealed that Todd had arrived in the small hours of the morning. He was doubtless sleeping in late. That afternoon, they would have their first meeting with the Trade Winds executives, then go out for a tour of the nearest of the factories.

Looking at her image in the Skype window, it suddenly struck her how much her highlights had grown out since she had been in China. It was clear that she had dark brown roots, the highlights beginning nearly an inch out. If it was obvious in a fuzzy, two-inch video image, it certainly detracted from the polish of her in-person appearance. She went to the mirror and contemplated the situation, quickly confirming her conviction that it looked terrible.

She went down to the front desk. Were there any openings in the hotel salon this morning? The young man behind the desk briefly consulted a ledger of some sort, then shook his head sadly. There were no openings till the afternoon. She was about to turn away, resigned to looking like "warmed over businesswoman who has been in China too long", when the man behind the desk called after her. The hotel salon did not have any openings, but he knew of a salon nearby, a very good salon that many Americans went to, that might have openings. Would she like him to direct her to it?

Jen hesitated a moment. Leaving the shelter of the hotel typically meant abandoning the precincts in which everyone could be relied on to speak English. But if the salon had many American customers . . . Why not? How hard could it be to explain that she needed her highlights touched up? She accepted the man's offer with gratitude, and he drew a map for her on a piece of paper and wrote down the name. The name was in Chinese characters, but he assured her that the sign was big, and she was sure that she would be able to recognize it from his note. She set out.

The salon was indeed easy to find. Inside, it was modern, white, and gleaming, with impressive banks of hair products along the walls and giant mirrors hanging above new chairs and sinks. It was also surprisingly empty. Perhaps this was not a time when many other people were free to visit a salon.

A young woman in a brilliantly white uniform greeted her, but her command of English seemed limited to such standards as "hello", "okay", and "yes".

Jen attempted to explain what she wanted in the traditional fashion of those who know themselves to be confronting a language barrier: by speaking louder and more slowly. "Highlights." She held one of hers up. "I want to have my highlights touched up." Again she held up one of the blondish locks of hair.

The young woman nodded. "Okay. Yes. Fine, fine."

Wanting to be doubly sure, Jen sought out a large photo book in which models with a variety of hairstyles and colors could be seen. She paged through it until she found one with blonde highlights. She held the book out to the young woman and indicated the highlights. "Highlights. Can you do that? Mine are growing out. The roots are dark." She indicated the roots.

More nodding. "Yes, yes, yes." The young woman led her back to one of the stations. Jen closed her eyes and relished the relaxing sensation of a professional working on her hair.

"Jen," objected Katie in a sleepy voice. "It's late here. I have to be at work in a few hours."

"I can't believe I did this to myself," Jen wailed.

"Did what to yourself? Are you okay?" concern began to overcome sleepiness in Katie's voice.

"I'm blonde!" The adjective was drawn out into something very near a cry.

"What?"

"I'm blonde."

"This I have to see," Katie said, now sounding fully awake. "I'm heading to the computer. Call me up on Skype."

"Are you laughing at me?"

"No, but if you call and wake me up on a work night to tell me you're blonde, the least you can do is let me see. Come on, log in."

The relief of sharing the misfortune was greater than her annoyance at Katie's attitude. Jen raised the lid of her laptop and logged in to Skype, still holding the phone to her ear.

Katie's image came up bleary-eyed and tousled, wearing an old tank top. "Wow," she said. "You really are blonde. I didn't know you could *be* that blonde."

"I'm not supposed to be. I was trying to have my highlights touched up and—and this happened."

Her hair was not quite platinum, but it was very close. Not even a streak of brown remained.

"Did you try to do it yourself or something?"

"No, I went to a salon. It was a nice salon. I don't know

. . . Maybe she thought I wanted all my hair the color of the highlights. Or maybe Chinese hair takes much stronger bleach. Or . . . What am I going to do?"

"I don't know. It's kind of cute. It might grow on you."

"It doesn't grow blonde on me, and I don't want it to."

"Can't you just have it dyed brown? Or how about red?" She mimed thoughtfulness. "I could see you red."

"Shut up!" Jen considered but shook her head. "There's no time. I have a big meeting in less than two hours. The senior vice president of Procurement flew out to sign contracts, and I have to meet with him. Getting the highlights touched up was a last-minute idea, so I'd look more professional. Besides, now I'm terrified to go into a Chinese salon again. What might they do next time?"

"Dye it black," Katie suggested, giggling.

Jen snapped her laptop closed, cutting off the video connection.

"All right, all right. I'm sorry," said Katie over the phone. "Look, does this guy you're meeting with know that you're *not* blonde? Just play it cool."

"I met him once before, at the main office. I suppose maybe he doesn't remember me, but . . . No. Anyone can remember that I'm not blonde. I'll look silly."

"Just brazen it out," Katie advised. "Don't think about your hair. And really, if you don't know it was an accident, it looks kind of good. You always impress people."

Aspire had taken a penthouse hospitality suite in the hotel for the two days of meetings with Trade Winds—a venue designed specifically for such business-entertainment purposes, featuring a conference room, dining room, and several large open rooms with scattered seating and panoramic window views. Jen went up slightly before the appointed time in order to see that the hotel staff had everything ready. The largest of the panoramic sitting rooms had been selected for the meeting, and two young women, each wearing a uniform that consisted of a mandarin-collared variant of the "little black dress", stood ready with an elaborate tea service to provide refreshments.

Todd Williams made his first appearance with the slightly antic vigor one sees in someone who is attempting to overcome severe jet lag by sheer force of will.

"Great venue here," he observed. "The view . . . Don't do things halfway. Is the tallest building in the world somewhere here in China now? No, no. I guess not. Dubai or something. Still . . ." He trailed off for a moment, extreme tiredness showing through for a moment, then shook himself. "Right. So, what's the plan? They're due shortly. Is it paper signing and business first, then dinner and getting-to-know-you kind of things?"

"I've lined things up to go a little bit more Chinese-style, so we'll start with a tea service, and typically that initial conversation is fairly social. Then we have a tour of one of the factories and dinner. So today is primarily social. Tomorrow morning is the business session, starting at nine in the morning. Then dinner again in the evening to close things up."

"Socialize first, then business, then socialize again. Got it. Glad I've got an old China hand to guide me through this. You seem to know all about it."

The Trade Winds delegation arrived exactly on time. It was led by the husband and wife who owned the company, along with the chief of sales and Eddy, their account manager. A half dozen other men and women, whose functions within the company were never made clear, followed in their wake to round out the party.

Tea was served, hands were shaken. Todd showed a video produced by the Aspire Brands communications department, which sought to express the overall brand character and culture of Aspire—complete with buzzword-bedecked executive sound bites, a pounding soundtrack, and plenty of wildly camera-angled runway footage relating to Aspire's fashion brands.

One of the owners of Trade Winds, who insisted that people could call her Amy, stood up and gave a brief speech of thanks. She handed out glossy brochures that showed the Trade Winds and Aspire Brands logos intertwined, with a background collage that included images of a factory floor more glistening than any that Jen had seen, the Great Wall of China, and the Guangzhou skyline.

She and her husband, Amy explained, thought of Aspire Brands as part of their family. They were grateful for Aspire's business and were proud of their partnership. Her husband gave a slight bow of agreement and said something sufficiently unintelligible as to make it unclear whether it was intended to be in English or Cantonese. Amy then produced a camera and insisted that her assistant document the event: Amy and her husband flanking Todd; Amy planting a matronly kiss on Todd's cheek; Amy, her husband, Todd, Eddy, and Jen all arm in arm; finally, everyone was ordered to crowd into the frame, and one of the young women from the hotel staff was asked to take the picture.

Once this photographic ritual was completed, Amy and

her husband led the group down the elevators to a small fleet of waiting Mercedes-Benzes to drive to the factory.

The factory was owned by a heavyset, middle-aged man who went, inexplicably, by the name of Uncle. It was his factory that had, on Jen's initial tour, provided her with production samples that were visually perfect but reduced in size such that laptops did not fit into them.

Uncle greeted them at the factory gate. Jen immediately noticed that a large "Joint Venture" sign had been mounted above the gates, showing the names of Uncle's company and Trade Winds and that of Aspire Brands as well, for good measure. Todd seemed impressed by this detail.

After greeting them with a brief speech on how pleased he was to be working with Trade Winds and Aspire Brands, and how his greatest priorities were product quality and providing good conditions for his workers, Uncle called in an assistant with a bottle of whisky and a tray of glasses and proposed a toast.

The tour itself was fairly brief. Jen's more practiced eye noticed that while the workers were all busy with Courier bags, one side of the factory was busily removing piping from the bags while the other half of the factory was taking these denuded bags and sewing the piping back on again. Todd, however, did not seem to absorb this detail, and since these were doubtless the undersize bags that did not fit Aspire's spec anyway, Jen felt no need to bring it up either.

"This place is so clean!" Todd marveled. "Look at the white uniforms and new sewing machines. I'm glad we're partnering with someone top-notch."

"Top-notch," assured Uncle. "Very top-notch. Everything top-notch."

He bragged that his workers had more room and better light at their work stations than those in other factories, and that he had had an Internet cafe and karaoke lounge installed for them.

"Do you have a system for dealing with worker complaints?" Todd asked. "Our customers are very concerned to know that the workers who make our products are treated well."

Uncle shrugged. "There are never any complaints."

"Never?"

"Of course not. My workers know there are lots of peasants who would be happy to make as much as they do. No complaints."

Having shown them the wonders of the factory, Uncle led them into his showroom, where all of the products his factory was capable of producing were on display. Jen briefly wondered if this would cause concern, since a number of these items were, in fact, pirated designs from other, more famous bag designers. On the contrary, however, Todd was very much impressed. He pulled Uncle aside and explained that he had promised to bring his wife a thing or two from the famous pirated merchandise markets. Could Uncle advise him where he could find his wife something that would impress her?

In response to this, Uncle cheerfully loaded Todd down with a half dozen of his best pirated merchandise. What did his wife like? Uncle knew many other factory owners who produced products with the very best brand names. Shoes? Clothes? Watches? Jewelry? What was her size? Todd demurred at this offer but accepted a purse and a wallet to take to his wife. Uncle then provided everyone with another round of whisky and another toast, and the whole group loaded back into the cars (Uncle joining them now as well) and drove off to a restaurant for dinner.

Dinner ran long and concluded with round after round of whisky.

Near the end of the evening, Todd leaned close to Jen —indeed, through some minor accident of balance, found himself leaning *on* Jen—and explained in what was meant to be a whisper, "There's a lot of drinking going on around here."

Jen nodded. Whether through some notion of politeness or due to personal preference, Todd had been alternately accepting rounds from Uncle and Amy's husband, making him by far the furthest-in of the party.

"Luckily, I have a pretty strong head," Todd confided. "And most Asians can't hold a lot of liquor. Or I might find myself getting into trouble."

"I don't pretend to be an expert," Jen advised, "But the factory owners I've met over here are all accomplished drinkers."

"But not quite in my weight class!" Todd countered, giving his gut an appreciative pat. "I'll be fine."

Not long after this, a suggestion was made that the group decamp to a karaoke bar. Jen had no desire to sample the delights of Guangzhou karaoke and knew that the primary focuses of such an expedition would be alcohol and karaoke hostesses, so she excused herself. She reminded Todd that they had a nine o'clock meeting the next morning to negotiate purchase orders, but he was bent upon getting the full Chinese business-entertainment experience. Amy was leaving too and offered Jen a ride back to the hotel.

With Todd in China, the usual five o'clock call with Bryn was canceled. Jen allowed herself to sleep in until the seemingly luxurious hour of 6:30. Showered, hair blown out, made up, dressed, she arrived at the hospitality suite twenty minutes before the meeting and availed herself of the coffee and American-style breakfast that had been provided.

At five minutes to nine, Amy arrived, her male staff in tow, though looking a little tired and puffy about the eyes, but her husband not in evidence. Greetings were exchanged. Amy politely enquired whether Todd was perhaps suffering from the time difference. Jen professed ignorance and excused herself for a moment, dialing Todd's cell number as soon as she cleared the door.

"Whuh?" asked a sleepy voice after several rings.

"It's nine o'clock, Todd. The Trade Winds team is here. Are you not up?"

Todd let out a burst of profanity that suggested rapidly increasing consciousness. "I must have set the alarm wrong. I'll be up in ten minutes."

Jen hung up, reflecting that it was among the insurmountable inequalities between the sexes that a man could somewhat credibly make it from bed to business attire in ten minutes.

It was, in fact, closer to fifteen minutes later that Todd burst into the hospitality suite, hair damp, suit somewhat wrinkled, as if it had reposed on a chair overnight rather than being hung up, and a large dollop of shaving cream behind one ear. Jen tried to indicate the problem to him, but her look and gesture only caused him to look wildly over his shoulder as if he expected to see someone or something sneaking up behind him.

"Hold still," Jen ordered. She retrieved a tissue from her purse and removed the shaving cream. "Come on."

"Thanks," said Todd, rubbing the now clean spot behind his ear from which Jen had wiped the shaving cream. "Guess it takes a woman's touch."

The Trade Winds team was quietly sipping coffee. Jen and Todd each grabbed a cup and led the way into the conference room.

The negotiations that followed were hardly worthy of the name. Amy had a sheaf of notes meticulously documenting all of the changes Jen had required. Each of these became a point of negotiation, with Amy insisting that the changes that were requested would cost more money, and thus required that a higher per-unit cost be passed on to Aspire Brands. Todd was alternating sips of coffee and ice water and seemed to be struggling even to understand the objections Amy raised, much less counter them.

Although it was, in theory, Todd's responsibility to deal with all cost-related negotiations, Jen became frustrated to see Amy winning every point and at last opened up her own front in the campaign, repeatedly pointing out the ways in which the production samples Trade Winds had provided had failed to match the prototypes they themselves had produced.

Amy was little pleased to find a less pliable person entering the fray but was equal to it. She began to lay out the difficulties faced by Trade Winds and their manufacturing partners at ever greater length, explaining why it was a simple business necessity that they be compensated for meeting such detailed and unreasonable demands. Indeed, she hesitated to state things too bluntly, but if things became too difficult for them, they might simply have to pass on the business entirely. They did not want to do this, for they felt deeply the awkward position it would put Aspire Brands in if their China partner backed out so late in the process. Why, they might not be able to launch the Courier line on time. Trade Winds was mindful of these things, but if they were pushed to the brink, what could they do?

Amy then re-presented her demands, this time as a middle ground between some unthinkably painful concession and Jen's unreasonably inflexible position. She appealed to Todd to intervene and see that this middle ground that she had selected was ideal, was really the best for all involved. Todd, whose grasp of the situation had not improved during the flood of verbiage, followed his most basic instincts and aligned himself with the middle. Surely both Amy and Jen should compromise, and it did indeed seem as if the middle ground that Amy described was the best place to meet.

Outmaneuvered on ground not of her own choosing, Jen elected to abandon the field of battle and leave Todd to his fate. She fell silent and allowed Amy to display her ability both to lead Todd to metaphorical water and to make him drink.

The negotiations finally concluded in the midafternoon, and all parties decamped to a restaurant for a celebratory meal.

"Bad luck feeling under the weather for something like this," Todd confided as he and Jen got into one of the cars. "It's a good thing Amy was willing to be so reasonable. She seemed eager to meet in the middle on everything."

Jen refrained from comment and instead asked about the night before.

"I didn't realize that the Chinese took karaoke so seriously. The bar they took us to was *very* nice. Like a private club. And they're all just really into it. I'd thought Amy's husband was a pretty quiet guy, but he was belting out songs. And there were these girls there who were huge karaoke fans: jumping up and down, and cheering, and hanging on guys like they were pop stars."

"Those are karaoke hostesses. They're paid by the bar to act that way."

Todd looked affronted. "No, I don't think so. If they worked for the bar, I don't think they would have been so . . . I mean . . ."

"This isn't the U.S., Todd. That's what they're paid to do. Treat the customers like pop stars."

"Oh." Todd lapsed into silence for the rest of the drive as he contemplated this.

Amy's husband rejoined the group for the celebratory dinner. Whatever ill effects of the evening before might have kept him from the morning's negotiations, he seemed now in a boisterous temper, though his remarks were primarily delivered in Cantonese, and the other members of his party were not always forthcoming with translations.

The dinner seemed almost planned to include as many things unknown to the American palate as possible. Todd seemed convinced that it was necessary at least to sample every dish that was put before him. Jen had no such qualms. As the courses progressed, whisky was brought in between each offering, and toasts were offered aplenty.

As the dinner finally drew to a close, it was proposed that they adjourn to a nightclub.

"The American Club," Amy's husband explained. "Everything American style."

Unlike the night before, Amy was clearly going too, so Jen assumed that this was not a male-only venue. They piled back into Trade Winds' trio of black Mercedes-Benzes and tooled out through the glittering Guangzhou night.

The cars stopped and let them out before a fairly typical-looking skyscraper, with a revolving glass main door and a marble-floored lobby. The group crowded into an elevator glistening with brass fittings, and Amy pushed the button for the twenty-second floor.

The lobby they stepped into was specific to the American Club, as indicated by a sign with the name of the club in giant block letters, above which flashed outlines of the Empire State Building, the Hollywood Sign, and Mount Rushmore in glowing neon. In the center of this lobby stood a ten-foot-tall statue of Marilyn Monroe, garishly colored as if in technicolor made real, holding down her plaster skirt in a vain attempt to keep it from blowing up to expose her famous legs.

Amy's husband and Eddy insisted on Todd's posing with them for a picture in front of the statue. The three men stood arm in arm, with Todd in the middle, with the oversize Marilyn's skirt billowing around them at shoulder height. "Okay, ready? Ready?" Just as the picture was being taken, Amy's husband reached a hand back to tickle Marilyn between the legs. "For luck!" he shouted. The attendant who had taken the picture rushed forward with it, and the three men examined the preview on the camera's screen, Eddy and Amy's husband doubling over laughing and slapping each other on the back.

At the entrance to the club itself, they were greeted by a hostess wearing daisy dukes and a cowboy hat, and a waiter sporting a football jersey, a sideways baseball cap, and a large gold chain bedecked with a dollar sign. A cacophony of memorabilia covered the walls. The immense room was round and shaped somewhat like an amphitheater, with semicircular tiers descending toward a wedge-shaped dance floor opposite the entrance. The wall beyond the dance floor was all glass, allowing the dancers and those seated at the tables arranged along the tiers a view across the glittering downtown Guangzhou cityscape. At various points, larger pieces of Americana stood on platforms: a finned, pink, Cadillac; a stuffed Texas longhorn; a Harley Davidson motorcycle; a plaster Statue of Liberty.

At the lowest level, in the very center of the club, between the tiers of seating and the dance floor, stood an immense round bar, above which slowly rotated a replica of the General Lee, its resplendent orange body and Confederate-flagged roof reflecting the lights of the disco ball that hung from the ceiling above it.

Their party occupied a booth, and a waitress dressed as a low-necklined Dorothy from *The Wizard of Oz* arrived to take their orders. Eddy asked Jen and Todd what a good American whiskey would be, and Jen reeled off the names of the most expensive bourbons she knew, determined that some aspect of the night would be to her taste.

After several rounds of bourbon had been consumed, the Trade Winds contingent suddenly decided it was necessary that more pictures be taken to memorialize the occasion. The various *objets à l'américaine* seemed the obvious venue.

They converged upon the Cadillac. After some argument, Amy and her husband climbed into the front seat. Eddy took control of the camera and boisterously shouted instructions in Cantonese. Amy's husband, still clutching a highball glass with a generous portion of bourbon, first mimed wild driving, swinging the steering wheel back and forth, while Amy leaned back against the seat impassively. Eddy shouted some instruction, and Amy's husband let go the wheel, turned, and planted a huge, drive-in-movie teenager-style kiss on Amy, flinging bourbon across the back seat as he did so. The camera flashed, the image was shown around, backs were slapped. Amy smiled benevolently over the increasing pandemonium.

Next, Eddy and Trade Winds' head of sales were to be photographed with the Statue of Liberty. Several poses were tried, with Amy's husband manning the camera, and at last they settled on each kissing one of the Statue of Liberty's cheeks. As the camera flashed, Eddy grabbed one of the reproduction's overly prominent breasts, to the hooted approval of the assemblage.

Then Todd, urged on by the others, mounted the Harley Davidson. He gamely cranked at the throttle and made motor noises, to the amusement of the others. This, however, did not seem to fit the spirit of the evening. Eddy had the necessary inspiration. "Biker girl!" he exclaimed, indicating Jen. "Get on the Harley with him and be biker girl."

Jen demurred.

"Have some fun," Eddy urged. "Biker girl. Just for fun."

"You should relax a bit," advised Amy, with a smile that lifted only one side of her mouth.

"Come on," said Todd, with an "aw shucks" grin. "What happens in Guangzhou stays in Guangzhou."

"Nope." Jen returned to the booth and poured herself another glass of bourbon instead, angry at having been persuaded to join the expedition, though considering that with a certain liquor-induced distance, it might have its amusing side, so long as she remained strictly a spectator.

Looking back toward the Harley Davidson, she could see that the group had persuaded one of the hostesses, this one wearing a *Mad Men*–era dress with flaring skirt, to sit astride the motorcycle with Todd as Eddy gleefully took pictures. This accomplished, the group milled around briefly, and Jen feared that they might return to the booth, but at that moment, the lights dimmed, garishly colored spotlights began to search the room in dizzying circles, and a sequined Elvis impersonator took to the dance floor to lead the assembled masses in a set of rock 'n' roll favorites. This proved more than any of the Trade Winds group could resist in their current state, and Jen was left in her preferred solitude.

Time passed. Another club emcee took to the dance floor. Dressed in hip-hop pastiche and waving a golden microphone around, he led the crowd in a spirited Chinese cover of "Jump Around".

Jen had begun to slip into a half-waking state, so it was a feeling of movement next to her rather than sight that alerted her that Todd had slipped into the booth with her.

"It's late. I've been sitting here zoning out," Jen said.

"What?" Todd leaned in close to hear her over the thumping music.

"I'm tired. I wouldn't mind getting back to the hotel soon," Jen said more loudly.

"Me too."

"I wonder if we could commandeer the car that took us here. The Trade Winds folks may want to dance all night, but I'd rather go to bed."

"That sounds good."

"You must want to get to bed at a decent time too. What time is your flight out tomorrow morning?"

Todd did not respond, and Jen became aware that he was leaning closer to her only a moment before she felt the unwelcome presence of his hand exploring her thigh. She pushed his hand away sharply.

"Todd! Stop it!"

"Oh, come on." He didn't return his hand to her leg, but he was leaning over her, hands planted against the booth-back on both sides of her shoulders. "First you lead me on, being all couple-y with me this morning. Then you play hard to get over the motorcycle. We don't have time for games; it's my last night here."

He lurched toward her, and his lips briefly made sloppy, bourbon-tinged contact with hers. Jen shoved him away hard, and his head hit the booth back with an audible thud. She extricated herself from the booth and left the club rapidly without looking back to see what effect her rebuff had had on him.

It was fully dark outside in the street, and there was a chill in the air. The Trade Winds cars that had brought them there were nowhere in sight. Several taxis were idling by the curb, however. She climbed into the nearest one and showed the driver the card for the hotel. He nodded and swerved off into traffic.

When Jen's alarm began to sound, less than four hours after she had gone to bed, her first thought was to get another hour's sleep and drag herself out of bed with mere moments to spare before her five o'clock call with Bryn. Her second thought was to send Bryn some sort of curt e-mail declaring that she was unavailable that morning. The first she rejected as a matter of personal standards, the second because she didn't want to have to wait till after the weekend before enquiring about when she would be returning home. Despite this triumph of will over exhaustion, however, the call was not particularly satisfying on any front.

"How did the purchase-order negotiations go?" Bryn asked, after they had covered various pieces of immediate urgency.

"Frankly, I thought we came off worse than we had to. The Trade Winds team came in demanding price increases in response to all the manufacturing errors I'd insisted that their manufacturers correct, and Todd didn't seem able to keep up with the detail sufficiently to rebut all their demands."

"Were you able to help him with the facts?"

"I tried where I could. But I couldn't do the negotiating for him, and there was a limit to what I could do. I was already working beyond my scope trying to cover for him."

Bryn shrugged it off. "Well, it's commendable you tried. At the end of the day, it's Procurement that'll take the blame if they don't hit their cost targets. Anything else interesting? Did you at least get a good dinner out of it?"

Jen was tight-lipped and shifted the conversation to her return.

Bryn sighed. "I want to get you back here as soon as possible. It's awkward having had so little real time together since you started. And I would think things should be on a good footing for a while now that Todd has finalized pricing and placed purchase orders for the first season's inventory. But the cross-functional team wants to wait till we get Todd's full report on Monday before scheduling your return. I'm sure we'll have you back sometime soon."

"Is there a point when it starts to be a bad use of company money to keep me sitting around here just in case there's something for me to do?" Jen demanded, exasperation causing her professional demeanor to slip for a moment. "I'm supposed to be a product-line director, not a babysitter for the Chinese side of the operation."

"Look, I hear you," Bryn said. "Don't think I like having one of my line directors stuck outside the country either. There's lots I'd rather have you doing."

"Thanks."

"You know, honestly, what with having to wait through another weekend, go take yourself out on the expense account and break the monotony a bit. So long as it's not totally insane, I'll make sure that it works out okay with Accounts Payable when it comes through. And there's no benefit to having you go nuts over there. Soak up some culture or something."

Jen reflected on the examples of culture and soaking that she'd seen the night before but remained silent. "I'll come up with something. Honestly, though, I just want to get home. This is getting excessive."

"I hear you."

"Well, make the cross-functional team hear me. If this goes on another week without a good reason, I will call them up individually to tell them what they can go do with themselves."

"Jen, I get it. Chill."

"The only expense-account indulgence I want is a ticket home, okay?"

"Well, go get a massage or something. Take the weekend off. Relax. And I hope I'll have some good news for you on Monday."

They closed the call.

Over the weekend that followed, Jen attempted to give the expense account some exercise, but her heart was not in it. Back in her room, she tried calling Katie, but Katie seemed oddly preoccupied. She tried calling Dan, but he did not answer his phone.

Tuesday morning—Monday afternoon in California— Jen woke easily at four o'clock, eager to find what news the new week brought in relation to her return. Instead, she found an e-mail from Bryn waiting for her: "Some things have come up, and I can't make our call this afternoon. Feel free to catch some 'me time'. I should have updates shortly."

Irretrievably awake, Jen went down to the hotel gym to work out until the breakfast buffet opened. When she got back to her room and checked her laptop, she found that Bryn had canceled their morning meetings for the next three days.

She spent Tuesday and Wednesday in anxious inactivity, woke up on Thursday to find an e-mail from the travel department with a travel itinerary for her to fly home the next day. She tried calling and e-mailing Bryn but received no response. The tickets themselves, however, were an undeniable fact. She packed her bags and scheduled the hotel car to take her to the airport.

It is a strange fact of travel that if you fly from Guangzhou to San Francisco, you arrive at almost exactly the same time that you left. This "no time at all" takes fully twenty hours. Conscious of this, Jen paused in the airport to stock up on reading material. Although her boarding pass told her that she would spend all of three minutes by the clock in the air, she knew that these three minutes would provide her with plenty of time to experience boredom.

Over the timeless expanse of the Pacific, while reading an English-language newspaper that was already two days old when she picked it up in the airport, Jen found herself regarding a familiar face.

"The Chinese Manufacturing Game", read the headline. And next to it, April Holland's byline and blonde visage.

She read the article with a growing feeling of expectation, and these expectations were fulfilled when she obediently "continued on page D6" and found herself quoted at length.

"Jen Nilsson, product-line director for the revived Courier brand, currently in the midst of sourcing its new product line in Guangdong Province, spoke with me about the difficulties of sourcing in China."

There followed a number of her comments from the evening spent with April over the bottle of Johnnie Walker

Black Label, which, read in the sober, if somewhat cramped, light of a transoceanic flight, seemed all the more blunt in their force.

She had, in the days since communication from Aspire had ceased, wondered whether perhaps Todd had returned to the office in full confessional mode and informed HR of his behavior the night before he left. Were that the case, the silence and then sudden return home might be an artifact of Legal trying to decide how best to deal with the situation and advising others not to communicate with her until they had resolved the question. Now she wondered if, instead, it was the result of the company trying to decide how to respond to her extensive quoted comments in this newspaper article.

As she contemplated these two alternatives, she felt a sudden sense of freedom. She knew what it was that she would do, and there remained only a feeling of peace unlike any she had known in some weeks. She closed the newspaper, reclined her seat, and slept.

The plane landed in San Francisco slightly early, with the amusing result that the passengers arrived before they left. Few seemed refreshed by this bit of trivia as they stumbled tiredly down the jetway. Having slept unusually soundly, Jen strode off the plane with purpose, her bag rolling behind her. Once out of the initial press of the crowd, she found a seat and pulled out her cell phone. She considered briefly the satisfaction of simply sending an e-mail, but she called instead. Bryn answered.

"Jen. Hi! You must have just landed."

"Yep. Just stepped off the plane."

"How was your flight?"

"It was good. I got some clarity at thirty thousand feet, and I'm quitting."

"Ummm . . . What?"

"I am resigning my position, effective immediately. I will not be coming in today. I'm going to go home and rest up a bit."

"Whoa. Jen. Hold on. You're tired. Is this about—"

"Actually, I'm rested. I slept very well on the plane. I'm happy to tell you what this is and is not about. It is not about Todd. If you don't know what I'm talking about, ask him."

"Jen—"

"It is not about the newspaper article, either. I stand by everything I said there. To the word."

"Hold on, we—"

"Thinking about this job, this industry, this company, this past seven weeks, I've decided that I'm done. When I took this job, I was convinced that anything would be better than being jobless. I see now that is not entirely the case."

"Can we just—"

"I will be in tomorrow afternoon to drop off my laptop, company credit card, and any other company property. I will turn in my final expense receipts then. I do not think it would do either of us any good for me to stay on for two weeks."

"I know that you must—"

"Goodbye, Bryn. I'll see you tomorrow." She hung up. For a moment she sat looking at the phone. It began to vibrate with an incoming call. It was Bryn. She turned the phone off.

She collected her checked bag and then her car. Highway 101 was traffic-free. Midmorning on a Friday. Everyone was at work. Two months before, this feeling that everyone else was occupied while she was not had been paralyzing. Perhaps in another month or two, it would be paralyzing again, but at this moment she felt utter bliss.

Back in the South Bay, nearing home, she pulled off two exits early and stopped at her usual salon.

"I know I don't have an appointment, but I was wondering if you have an opening. Normally I see Amanda, but anyone will do."

"Actually, it looks like Amanda has an opening at 10:30. Do you mind waiting fifteen minutes?"

"Not at all."

She settled in one of the chairs and pulled out her phone to check her e-mail, then stopped herself and returned it to her purse. She skimmed a few articles in Us. It seemed that Angelina could not resolve her babysitting issues but had a new beach body. Nicole was settling into motherhood. In the auditory background, the women of The View discussed the issue of the day. All of it was somehow glorious.

Amanda came out and greeted her at 10:30.

"Jen! It's been a long time. How have you been?"

"I got sent to China for seven weeks for a new job. I tried to get my highlights touched up and . . . well, you see."

Amanda, having now been given permission to be critical of the hair, nodded sympathetically. "Oh, you poor thing. I was wondering!"

"After the bleach job, I didn't trust anyone in China to try to fix it. I haven't even been home yet. I came straight here to see you."

"We'll get you fixed right up. No one will even know. What happened in China stays in China, right?"

"And how . . ."

"So, you want it back the way it was before, sweetie?"

"You know, I'm thinking maybe my natural color. I just want to look normal."

"Natural color . . . All right, let's see what we can find for you. Let's start out with a nice relaxing wash, okay?"

Amanda led her back toward the sinks. Jen's mind went back to her conversation with Katie after the bleaching. "Do you think, maybe just a little bit of red? With my natural brown?"

"Oh, sweetie, you would look great with just some little hints of red. I know exactly the right thing."

An hour and a half later, feeling relaxed and slightly red-headed, Jen sat giving herself a final look over in the rearview before starting the car. Then, out of long habit, she pulled out her phone to check e-mail.

She hesitated, then turned it on. There were several e-mails in her work mailbox, but she ignored them and checked her personal box instead. Among numerous pieces of junk mail, LinkedIn updates, and other detritus that had accumulated during her hours in the air was an e-mail from Lauren Baird at Search Solutions:

"Jen, I know it's been a long time since we last talked, but I wanted to check and see if you're still available and potentially interested in the Schneider and Sons opportunity."

Jen sent back a single word response: "Yes."

6

It was with a feeling of comforting familiarity that Jen drove down her own street and turned into her own driveway, the garage door opening to meet her. Then she slammed on her brakes as hard as she could, stopping with an audible screech. Katie's car was parked in the garage. She was preparing her rebuke over this as she backed out of the driveway and parked on the street when it came home to her that she had been gone for a month and a half. Of course, with the condo to herself for so long, Katie would have become used to parking in the garage.

She was wrestling her bag out of the trunk when she heard her sister's voice, "Jen! You're back! Oooh, hey, I like the hair."

Katie ran the last couple of steps down the driveway and gave her sister an enveloping hug. "I heard the garage door opening, and I knew you must be back," she said in a rush, still not releasing Jen from the hug. "I'm sorry I forgot and left my car in the garage. I'm so glad to see you! Do you want me to move my car so you can park in the garage?"

"Whoa. Calm down, kiddo," Jen said, prying her sister off. "No, don't worry about the car. Just help me haul this thing in, okay? I'm glad to see you too."

They lugged Jen's bag up the stairs and deposited it just

inside the door. Jen found herself casting a quick appraising eye around the condo to see how well Katie had been keeping the place. It was surprisingly neat, counters clean, several new potted plants sitting in the kitchen window.

"How have things been here?"

"Good. Quiet. I've been trying some new cooking stuff."

"That's it? Nothing exciting? New job? New boyfriend?"

"Um, no . . ." Katie looked away briefly.

Jen snagged a bottle of wine off the counter and was about to pour herself a glass. There was an unsettling feeling of energy running through her and perhaps a drink or two would take the edge off. Then she stopped. "Sheesh, it's not even noon yet, is it? This time change is going to take some getting used to. It feels like evening." She went into the living room and flopped on the couch instead. "Well, I've got news if you don't. I quit my job."

Katie's look of incredulity was so comic that Jen, in her current adrenaline-based state, laughed aloud.

"You quit your new job?" Katie finally got out. "But . . . you don't *do* things like that!"

"What do you mean I don't do things like that? I just did."

"But you—wow. I could never do anything like that."

"What you are talking about? You do all kinds of stuff. You moved out here on the spur of the moment without even telling me. You nearly lost your job at Starbucks because you stayed out all night."

"I moved out here because I couldn't take dealing with Mom anymore, and I didn't call you because I was scared. And that time . . . Starbucks is a stupid job anyway. You've got a great job, and you make all kinds of money, and you love it. And you just quit?"

"Yeah, I quit. Best thing I've done in weeks. You wouldn't believe . . . Their manufacturers were a mess. The VP of Procurement they sent out was a complete idiot. He let the Chinese distributor get him trashed the night before negotiations, got walked all over at the negotiating table, and the creep got drunk again that night and hit on me. And then they just clammed up and left me stranded for a couple days. To top it off, I was on the plane, and I read this article—it turns out this woman I spent an evening talking with was actually a reporter, so now there's this article with me ripping on Aspire's Chinese manufacturing strategy. So I quit. And I feel great about it. You know, I think I will get that glass of wine. It's after noon in China."

Jen returned a moment later with a glass in hand, sat back on the couch, and draped her legs over the arm.

"But you hated being out of work," Katie said, still sounding concerned and a little confused. "What are you going to do?"

"Look for a better job. I got a note earlier . . ." Jen pulled her phone back out and checked her e-mail. "Ha! I've got an interview."

The e-mail from Lauren read, "Great to hear you're still available. They'd like to get you for a phone interview. What's your availability?"

Jen tapped out in reply, "I'm available any time. Just let me know."

"You quit your job this morning, and you already have an interview?" Katie asked.

Jen pulled up the e-mail and tossed the phone to her.

"What is with you?" Katie demanded. "No one has that happen!"

Jen shrugged. "It happened to me." She threw back the rest of her glass of wine. "No, look, I'm sorry. That sounds arrogant. I don't know what it is. I feel really punchy right now. I'm getting some more wine. Do you want something?"

"No," said Katie flatly. "It's not afternoon in China for me."

"I'm thinking maybe I should get really drunk," said Jen.

"I'm thinking maybe you should go to bed," responded Katie. "You're tired and all wound up, and if that company suddenly says they want to call you, you don't want to be drunk."

Jen paused on her way to the kitchen. "Oh, that." She looked doubtful. "Let's check!" She consulted the phone. Nothing. "What is up with that?" she demanded.

Katie got out of the easy chair and wrested the wine glass from Jen's hand. "Jen, you need a nap. And even I can see this isn't the best way to self-medicate stress." She took her sister by the shoulders and guided her to her room. "Seriously. Get some rest."

Jen obediently sat on the bed. "Okay." She kicked off her shoes and lay down. Katie pulled the blanket up over her. The maddening sense of excess energy drained away, and she felt the full force of the exhaustion that had been lurking behind it. She closed her eyes and slept soundly until midafternoon.

When she woke, she found an e-mail waiting for her:

"Sorry for the short notice, but can you talk tomorrow (Friday) at 9 A.M. Central? Let me know."

Seven A.M. Well, why not? All times were out of joint at the moment. "No problem," she responded, and provided the cell number at which they should call her.

Having slept off the worst of her jet lag the day before, Jen felt comparatively fresh when she sat down, dressed in business clothes and with notepad and résumé before her, to await her phone interview on Friday morning. She pulled up the website for Schneider and Sons: hardware store founded in 1873 by Gustav Schneider. Under Gustav's sons, turned into a purveyor of tools known for quality. Original logo (a German eagle with two blackletter S's) modified in 1941. Now a maker of power tools known for exceptional quality (and price). Located in a small town south of Chicago.

Her phone rang and she answered.

"This is Jen. . . . Good morning, Brad. Good to talk to you."

The interview seemed to go moderately well. Near the end, when Brad, the hiring manager, asked the usual "Do you have any questions for me?" Jen responded with a brief summary of the business aspects of her China trip.

"What I found particularly disturbing was the company's willingness to put up with chaotic sourcing and mediocre quality in order to get out the gate fast. There was a lot more concern about being in time for seasonal sell-in and about product appearance than there was about brand integrity or good business practices. There may be a place for that, but I chose to quit rather than continue to be a part of it. So, I just want to put my cards on the table and be clear about what kind of business environment I'm not willing to work in. If you choose to move forward with me for this role, I don't want either of us to be set up for an unpleasant surprise."

The interview closed shortly thereafter.

Jen took the time to make herself a hot breakfast, then gathered up her things and set out to make her final visit to Aspire Brands. She had considered a last conversation with Bryn, but as she approached the inverse fountain and the tangle of steel beams that stood above it, she realized she had neither the desire nor the patience to revisit any elements of her time there. She went down to the HR offices instead, dropped off her equipment and expense reports, and signed a few forms. Within half an hour, she was back out on the street again, happily unemployed.

It was as she was riding Caltrain back south, away from the City, that she got the call from Lauren.

"They'd like to bring you out for in-person interviews next week. What's your availability?"

"Next week? I'm completely free. Just have them send me an itinerary."

"Well, that makes it easy."

"Any feedback from the interview?"

"Brad said he was particularly impressed by your integrity. Don't let your game slip. You still need to win over the rest of the interview panel, but I don't think I'm spilling any secrets to say you've got a fan in Brad. I'll get you a prep document later today with profiles of everyone you'll be meeting with there. And you can expect to hear from their travel department with an itinerary. Okay?"

"Okay. Thanks, Lauren."

Jen ended the call and sat back. The speed of this progress was as dizzying as the dysfunction that she had dealt with at Aspire, but somehow with none of its unsettling aspects. By the time she pulled into her garage, there was an e-mail waiting for her from Schneider and Sons' travel department, showing her flights and accommodations for the interview. Fly out Tuesday morning, return Wednesday evening. She would be there and back before she had been home from China for a week.

Katie was still not back from work, and the condo was silent. Jen's first instinct was to bustle around and do some sort of work, but there was none to do. The dishes were washed, the counter clean, the carpets vacuumed. Katie had clearly settled fully into the responsibilities of living on her own during the time Jen had been away. And yet this left Jen with the feeling almost of living in someone else's home, a feeling oddly similar to the daily alienation of hotel living that she had become so used to.

She thought briefly of running, or of going out, but what she most wanted was to interact with someone familiar. She scanned through the contact list on her phone, but, of course, it was the middle of the workday. She continued to flip idly through the names and at last found herself calling her parents.

"Hey, Mom, it's Jen."

"Jen! How are you? Are you still in China?"

"No, I got back last Thursday. No, wait—yesterday. Yeah. It was yesterday morning. Things have been happening fast around here. I'm going to be flying out your way next week to interview for a job."

"But, honey, didn't you just start your job?"

"Yeah, but I quit. This trip, Mom—by the way, I'm sorry I never had the chance to call you guys; it was really crazy over there—this trip was terrible, and it made me realize I really didn't want to work for Aspire. So I quit. But I have this interview out near you. So, who knows, maybe I'll be moving back out there."

"That would be wonderful. We never see you! And Katie, will she be moving back too?"

"Well, keep in mind, Mom, this is just an interview. I haven't talked with Katie about whether she'd move with me. I guess so. She seems happy living with me."

"Is Katie doing all right?" her mother asked in a worried tone.

"So far as I know. Why?"

"She called us a few weeks ago to tell us about you in China, and I thought she seemed worried or unhappy about something."

"Did you ask her about it?"

"Yes, of course, but she told me that everything was fine. Maybe she's lonely out there. Does she have friends?"

"I think she knows some people at the Starbucks she works at."

"But is she happy? I think something that makes Katie unhappy is that she's not good at making friends, but she really needs to know that people care about her. I think she's lonely—but she would never talk to me about it."

"I don't know, Mom. She seems more organized. She's keeping the condo really clean."

"Jen." Her mother's voice was stern, almost scolding. "Don't you girls talk?"

"Well, yeah. But just, you know, about stuff."

"She's your little sister, Jen. Watch out for her a bit. There's no one else to do it right now, I'm afraid."

"Sure, Mom. Don't worry about it. We're fine." She was on the point of ending the call, but a memory tugged at her. "Mom, do you remember a time when Katie got locked in a trunk at Grandma's old house?"

"Oh goodness, yes! The poor thing. She woke up screaming at night for weeks, and for a long time she was terrified of enclosed places."

"Really? I'd forgotten all about it until she reminded me, and even then I only remembered the fuss at Grandma's. I didn't remember it having any effect on her."

"You were fifteen. You were off in your own world."

Jen was chagrined to think that "off in her own world" was how she would have described their mother when they were young. That wasn't without justice, but she had been less conscious of her own defects than those of others.

"Well, I'll see if there's anything on her mind. I might take her out to dinner tonight. It would be nice to talk after having been gone all this time."

"Yes, do that. Will you have time to come see us when you're out here?"

"I don't think so, Mom. It's going to be pretty busy. I'm only in for two days and one night."

"Well, let us know how it goes."

"Is Dad around? Can I say hi to him?"

"He went out to play the back nine before people got off work and the course filled up. He'll be sorry to have missed your call."

"Oh well. Give him my best. Goodbye, Mom."

"Goodbye. And good luck. Your dad and I will keep your interview in our prayers."

"I was talking to Mom today," Jen told Katie later that afternoon. "She said she thought something was bothering you. Is everything okay?"

Katie looked momentarily apprehensive. "Jen, you know Mom is nuts. Why do you even listen?"

"She sounded like she cared and was worried about you. Hell, she sounded like she pays more attention than I do."

"I don't want to talk about Mom," Katie announced.

"Okay. Well, here's what I was thinking: How about if we go out to dinner? I've got a job interview next week, and we might as well celebrate."

"Okay."

As they drove up into the City to enjoy one of the better restaurants, Jen found herself reflecting on differences in perception. Her mother, who both she and Katie were used to assuming, with reason, had missed a lot of their lives, had somehow noticed more than she. And if Jen had missed so much even as it went on around her, how did others see her?

Tuesday came, and Jen got up early to make her flight. As she dressed, she began to hear sounds from the kitchen and smell food cooking. When she left her room, she found Katie standing before the stove.

"I didn't expect to see you before leaving this morning. Isn't it your day off?" Jen asked.

Katie shrugged. "I thought you'd want a good breakfast before your flight." The smell of fried onions, bacon, and bell peppers rose overpoweringly from a plate where Katie had set them aside. She cracked eggs into a bowl and whisked them vigorously. "Besides, it was awfully quiet here with you gone. It's nice to be kind of a family again."

The eggs having cooked to a certain firmness, Katie slid the bacon and vegetables on top, sprinkled cheese over all with a flourish, then let it all cook while she returned various ingredients to the fridge. It was as Katie turned back to her cooking that Jen found her attention taken, indeed assaulted, by Katie's shorts. That Katie was wearing cropped pink sweat shorts with her signature pajama tank top Jen had seen before. What had somehow failed to register until this moment was that, emblazoned across her bottom in large, black, collegiate letters was the word *ASS*.

"What," demanded Jen, "are you wearing?"

"Aren't they awesome?" Katie asked. "I saw an ad for them on Facebook, and I had to have them."

"Awesome? No. Exploitive? Demeaning? Juvenile? Quite possibly."

"Oh, come on. They're *ironic*."

"Once you're wearing them, they're literal."

"No, wait, get this: They come in a set of three. The pink shorts say 'ASS'. The white ones say 'MY', and the blue ones say 'KISS'."

"Wait—a set of three? Do you mean you own all three?"

"Of course! You can borrow them if you want to. They're really comfy."

"Katie, sometimes I wonder if I don't treat you like enough of an adult. And other times . . ."

"What?" Katie asked, handing her a plate with half the omelet.

Jen took her food to the table, shaking her head. "Katie, I'm not your mother, but I'm saying this anyway, and I mean it: Don't let me ever see you wearing those outside the house."

"Sheesh. What do I need two moms for? One was enough trouble."

"At this rate, you need three moms: one for each pair of shorts."

Jen had described Schneider and Sons as "just south of Chicago", and on a map, that was indeed the case. The translation from map to reality, however, could make even small distances large, so even after Jen had cleared the tangle of traffic and toll stations around Chicago and was driving through farm fields, the GPS assured her that she was still forty minutes from Johnson, Illinois.

Upon arrival, she checked into the hotel that Schneider and Sons had booked. It was one of those business-focused hotels: Please enjoy our complimentary WiFi and hot breakfast! The workout room and pool are open twenty-four hours to accommodate the needs of busy professionals.

Walking the halls, she could have been in any of her usual business destinations. It was only when she looked out her room's window and caught a view of cornfields that she was reminded of how far from home she was.

Despite this rural view, however, the city information flyer in her room assured her that Johnson was one of the growing business centers of central Illinois, boasting not only the Schneider and Sons headquarters but also one of the nation's largest casket companies and a newly built Nestlé plant. It was still early in the evening, and her interviews did not begin until 9:30 the next morning, so Jen set out to "Discover Historic Downtown Johnson" and have some dinner on the Schneider and Sons expense account.

Her interview the next morning began with a tour, conducted by a young woman from HR named Stephanie.

"It's a beautiful day out," she said. "Let's take the bicycles. That'll be much faster."

Sure enough, outside the employee entrance was a large collection of black touring bicycles.

"Actually, I suppose we shouldn't really have you on a bike when you're not on the company insurance," Stephanie said, hesitating. "Let's take a pair of the trikes to be on the safe side."

Jen took this for a joke and laughed appreciatively, but further inspection revealed that there were indeed several adult-size tricycles off to one side. Stephanie cheerfully threw a leg over one and wheeled it onto the path, and Jen, not knowing what else to do, did the same. A moment later, the two women were cruising down the gravel path, past the corporate pond, and between rolling lawns.

"We have a big emphasis on health here at Schneider and Sons," Stephanie explained. "The bikes are to help encourage exercise, but they're also handy for getting around. It takes fifteen minutes to walk to the factory and ten to the R&D building, but with the bikes, it's much faster."

With Stephanie cheerfully pedaling and talking, and Jen trying to maintain some degree of interviewee dignity despite riding an adult-size tricycle while wearing a suit and heels, they visited the factory, the employee health center, the R&D building, the workshops—employees were encouraged to do projects using Schneider and Sons tools, and an annual furniture and woodworking contest offered substantial prizes—and the distribution warehouse. In passing, they admired the corporate lake; the tennis, volleyball, and basketball courts; and the helipad where Gus Schneider IV landed on the days he flew to work rather than driving.

Jen could not help marking the odd similarities between this 139-year-old company and the tech firms that had not yet existed as many weeks back in the Bay Area. She had never thought of the foosball tables, bike trails, and squash courts of which previous employers had bragged as being a revival of an older approach to combining business and recreation.

After an hour, she and Stephanie returned to the main building, and Stephanie turned her over to Brad, vice president of product marketing and her potential boss. Jen was feeling slightly windblown and disarranged, but Brad—who proved to be a balding though fit-looking man in his mid-fifties with a penchant for company golf shirts and cargo pants—was setting no intimidating standard in dress and neatness.

She and Brad talked for an hour. Jen then progressed through four thirty-minute interviews. Last of all was a late lunch with Andrea Gomez, senior vice president of strategy.

"I don't know why they put me on the interview list," Andrea announced as they got into her VW to drive to lunch. "I don't tend to say no to interviews, so I get stuck with a lot. And they seem to like to assign me to interview all the woman candidates. I'm not Hispanic, in case you're wondering," she added, shaking her long blonde ponytail. "My husband is Captain Jesus Gomez, U.S. Marine Corps.

If you come work here, I'll be the one who's always circulating the office e-mails about donations for care packages to send out to his base when he's on deployment. So, what are you thinking about Schneider and Sons so far? Big change from California?"

Three hours later, Jen was sitting in O'Hare, waiting for her flight, when she got a call from Lauren at Search Solutions.

"So," the recruiter asked, "how were the interviews?"

"I would have thought you could tell me that."

"Well, how did you feel about them?"

"I thought they went well. They're a distinctive company, and at first I was a little thrown off by some things like taking a tour on a tricycle, but I enjoyed the interviews, and I thought they went well."

"I'm glad you enjoyed your visit. They enjoyed having you. As you guessed, I've heard back from them. The whole team is very impressed with you. They did have some questions about whether you'd entertain an offer. Going from the Bay Area to small-town Illinois would be a big change. Are you interested in making it?"

"I think I need to think about it on the way home, talk to my family, and see an offer, but if they're prepared to make a fair offer, I think I'm pretty likely to accept it. Remember, I'm from this area. I'd be within two hours of my parents, and that would be nice."

"Okay. Thanks for the candid feedback. I'll pass that on to them. You keep an eye on your e-mail. I think you can probably expect to see something fairly soon."

"I will. Thanks."

"They're offering you the job already?" Katie asked.

"Yeah, I've got an offer letter. It's less money than the Aspire Brands job, and it's a manager role rather than a director one, but it does seem like a good company. And it would be a lot cheaper living in small-town Illinois than it is here."

"How soon would you have to go?"

"Pretty soon. They want me to start within three weeks. They'll move us out, of course. There's a relocation package."

Katie sat on the couch, hugging her knees and looking worried. "Jen, I can't leave the state."

This odd claim brought Jen out of her thoughts and caused her to focus her attention on Katie. "Why can't you leave? I thought we were getting along really well together. Wouldn't you want to come with me?"

"No, you don't get it. Jen, I—" She looked desperately around, but finding no relief, plunged on. "There's something I haven't told you."

"What?"

The pause stretched on long enough for Jen to have expected the next words before she heard them. "Do you remember that time I was out all night? The day before you got laid off?"

"Oh my gosh!" Jen's mind was running far faster than her words. In a moment she had already envisioned the future: she and Katie drawn ever closer together as they struggled together to raise Katie's child—a daughter, surely. The late nights. The time away from work. The crying and toys and diapers, but the small face with its pale blue eyes looking up at her aunt. Jen had never felt the attraction of a baby before—she had on many occasions expressed the opinion that she lacked any mothering instinct. But now she saw that helping to care for Katie's child would give her life a new sort of meaning. "Why didn't you tell me you were pregnant, Katie?"

"What?" Katie squawked. "I'm not pregnant. How could I be pregnant?"

"But, you said—"

"I'm not pregnant, Jen. I'm going to jail!" This last came out in something very near a wail, and Katie buried her face in her arms.

Katie's claim was so utterly unexpected that Jen could not yet even make herself alarmed. "What? Wait. Katie, what are you talking about?"

"I can't leave the state. The papers from the court all said that," Katie said, sounding close to tears. "And I think they're going to send me to jail."

"Katie, this isn't making any sense. Explain from the beginning," Jen fetched the box of tissues, handed one to Katie, and sat down next to her. "What happened? Why do you think you're going to jail?"

Katie blew her nose thoroughly, wiped her eyes, and pulled Jen's arm around her more tightly, then began. "You remember that I went out with Abby and Myra from work, and I met a guy named Brian?"

Jen nodded.

"Well, we'd all been drinking a lot. And then, after a while, Abby and Myra went home, so it was just me and Brian. I had had a lot to drink, and we were going to go over to his place, or maybe he was taking me back here—okay, to be honest, I don't really remember where we were going. We got in his car, and he said he could still drive, and we took off. But the cops pulled us over. They were making him do a Breathalyzer, and they were both being such assholes. Well, okay, I mean, I think they were. To be honest, I was really drunk. I was telling them that they should leave us alone, and that we were just trying to get home, and they should be out protecting people, and . . . you know. Like I said, I was really drunk. And I guess I was yelling at them a lot or something after they told me to stop, because the next thing is, they handcuffed me, and they took us *both* to the police station. And I think I kind of passed out or fell asleep for a while or something. But when they let me go the next morning, they gave me a ticket for $500 for 'interfering with an officer at a crime scene'. And I didn't have the money, so I filled out the paper saying I wanted a court date instead and mailed it back, so I'd have some time. But now they keep sending me court dates, and the papers say that I owe $500 plus costs, or else I'll go to jail for six to ten days. And it doesn't say what the costs are, and I don't know how much longer I can keep delaying the court date, but I don't know what to do, and it says if I leave the state, they'll issue a warrant for my arrest and— oh, Jen, I'm sorry!''

After having gradually increased in energy and speed, her explanation finally devolved, upon this apology, into tears.

"Katie. Katie, it's okay," Jen comforted, stroking her hair.

"It's *not* okay. I know it was stupid of me to get drunk and yell at police officers, but I don't want to go to jail."

"Don't be silly. You won't go to jail. Katie, this is easy. Let me call up my friend Dan. He's a lawyer, and we'll get this all sorted out. No one is going to jail. It'll be fine. Why didn't you tell me about this back when it happened?"

"I guess . . . I didn't want to admit it. Lots of people hook up at bars and have one-night stands. It's not like spending the night in jail."

"Oh, I don't know. I know a lot of people who've landed in the drunk tank for a night. This is not that big a deal, Katie. I wish you'd told me the truth and not left me thinking that you'd slept with some guy you'd never met before."

"Have *you* ever spent the night in jail?" Katie demanded, shrugging her sister's arm off her shoulders.

"No."

"And have you ever hooked up with a guy you didn't know?"

"Well . . . sort of. Once or twice. That was a long time ago."

"Then why are you being all judgmental with me?"

"I'm not judging you, Katie."

"Yes, you are! You're *glad* to hear I ended up in jail instead of sleeping with Brian. How is it not judging me to want me in jail instead of sleeping with a guy?"

"Katie, look—" Jen paused. "We should have this conversation, but I need a drink. Do you want anything?"

"No," Katie responded sulkily.

Only with that refusal did Jen see the basic tactlessness of the offer, but she still wanted the calming effect for herself. She went into the kitchen and poured herself a generous tumbler of bourbon, then returned to the living room. She had a momentary instinct to sit in the easy chair, across from

137

Katie, but instead sat back down next to her on the couch and pulled her sister close.

"Here's the thing. You get drunk, you yell at a cop, you spend the night in jail. That's humiliating and upsetting. I understand that. But look, all we have to do is put on some nice clothes, go to court, pay your fine, and it goes away. You don't have any ties to it. This just becomes a funny story to tell people about the kind of dumb things that we've all done when we were drinking. If you'd slept with this Brian guy, where would you be now?"

Katie tried to turn away from her sister, but Jen kept her arms around her.

"No, really. Like you said, I've had one-night stands a couple times. What do you get afterward? You still would have dragged yourself home all hung over, but every time your phone rang for weeks, you would have been wondering if he was calling you back, and in the meantime trying to think what was wrong with you when he never did."

"How do you know he wouldn't call?" Katie asked.

"Has he called you?"

"No, but that night was so bad . . . Maybe if we'd had that connection, something would have happened."

"Katie, do you know of any good relationships that started with a hookup with a stranger in a bar?"

"Well . . . I don't know. I guess not." After being sullenly passive since the topic had come up, Katie suddenly shifted to the conversational offensive. "Look, it's easy for you to be all righteous about this stuff. You had your hookups when you were young, and now you're older and successful and have everything you want. What am I supposed to do? Just sit around wishing I was like you?"

"Katie, what are you talking about? I don't have everything I want. I haven't found a boyfriend or had sex since Kevin and I broke up three years ago. Do you think that's what I want? To be alone at thirty-three and not know if I'll ever find anyone again?"

"But you've got your job, and this place, and . . . you have everything so together."

"Yeah, I've done okay with my career. I dunno. Maybe I've done great. So what? I got to call myself a director for two months while I was stuck in China getting hit on by some married forty-five-year-old freak of a senior vice president. Is that so great? I mean, yeah, I've been lucky. If I'm going to be lonely, I'd rather be lonely with a nice condo and a BMW. But I don't have everything I want."

"Really?"

"Yes. And you know what?" She pulled Katie closer. "One of the best things about the last three months has been having you here and starting to feel like a little bit of a family. I didn't realize I'd been missing out on that until after you came."

Katie leaned back into her sister's hug. "Thanks," she said.

The next morning, Jen printed out the offer letter from Schneider and Sons, signed it, scanned it in, and e-mailed it to the company's HR department. Then she looked up Dan's law-office number and called it.

"Fischer and Plumm. Can I help you?"

"Good morning. May I speak to Dan Fischer?"

"Who may I say is calling?"

"Jen Nilsson."

"Just a moment."

Jen waited, reflecting that, once again, she was calling Dan only when she needed something.

The secretary's voice returned, "Thank you for holding, Ms. Nilsson. He'll speak to you now. I'll put you through."

Dan's voice greeted her. "Jen, what's up? Why are you calling on the office phone? You've got my cell."

"Hey, Dan. I know, I just—this is a professional call, and I want you to go ahead and bill me, so I figured I should call on the business phone."

"Oh, come on, Jen. If you need a hand with something, you don't have to pay me. What's the problem?"

"No, Dan, seriously: I want you to bill me for this, just like you would anyone else. Okay?"

"Jen, is everything okay? This doesn't have anything to do with that newspaper article, does it?"

"Oh, you saw that? No. Nothing to do with that. Here's the deal: My sister Katie needs to go to court. She was out at a bar a couple months ago and drove home with a guy who got pulled over on a DUI. She got into an altercation with the cops, spent the night in jail, and she's got a ticket for 'interfering with a police officer at a crime scene'. She'd filed for a court date in order to put off paying the ticket, so she's up for $500 plus costs, and she's got a court date coming up. I figured you would know how to deal with this so that she keeps her record clean and doesn't pay any more than she has to. Let me pay whatever your normal rate would be plus any fines or expenses. I just want to make this go away for her."

"Okay, well, honestly, this should be pretty easy. Basically, she just comes into court—I'll go with her and bill you for a couple hours; e-mail me the date, and I'll put it on my calendar—and we explain that she's really sorry, she's never been in trouble with the law before, and we ask them to suspend the prosecution. If the judge is in a good mood and thinks she looks like a nice girl, the judge suspends the case, and so long as she stays out of trouble for the next three years, the whole thing just goes away. If she does end up in legal trouble again, she has to deal with both charges. Now, if that's not working, we offer to plead guilty in exchange for having the charge reduced to something harmless (jaywalking would be good). Then we just pay the fine and she's good. Either way, it's not a problem."

"You mean, chances are we just ask them to drop it and they do, and we don't even have to pay a fine?"

"That, my friend, is the unfair advantage of having legal representation. And knowing what to ask." Dan now shifted audibly from business voice to chitchat. "So, how're things at Aspire? You're back from China, I discern?"

"Uh, yeah. We haven't talked in a while. Well, actually, it's been only a few days, but—I quit Aspire as soon as I got back last Thursday. It was . . . it was just bad. I had to get out."

"Wow. Are you okay?"

"Yeah. Yeah, actually . . . I just got back from central Illinois, where I had an interview, and they offered me a job."

"Illinois?" Dan sounded taken aback. "That's far from home. Are you thinking of taking it?"

"It seems like a good company, and it's near my parents and—you know, what we need is to have dinner. When are you free?"

"How about Saturday?"

"That would be great."

Jeff's Fusion Bistro described itself as having "a casual yet intimate ambiance" and "a menu drawing from the best of every continent". It rambled through several small dining rooms, with small, high-backed booths and low lighting. The wait staff, however, dressed casually—clearly under orders to express their own style as wildly as possible while never straying from the company approved black-and-white palette. The menu, too, claimed a certain casualness by focusing almost exclusively on small portions and exhorting customers to create a meal out of a selection of dishes to suit their mood, yet the prices and the exhaustive wine list made it clear that this was no mere light dining venue.

Dan and Jen had arrived separately, and the first ten minutes after they were seated were taken up with discussion of the food and wine options. Their server—a young woman named Skye with short, spiky, black hair, a fitted black silk blouse, and white pants—took down their choices with apparent calm derision and left them to themselves.

Silence stretched on for several moments. Jen laughed awkwardly. "I wish they'd bring the wine. I just can't get the balance right. Last time we saw each other in person, I was being too loud. Now I say we should meet, and I don't have anything to say." She shook her head. "Thanks, by the way, for helping with Katie's legal problem."

"No problem. It's what I do. Really, it's going to be very simple. Just make sure she wears some conservative, 'nice girl' clothes when she comes for her court date next week. It'll be easy."

"I didn't know what to do, but I was sure that it would be a lot easier than she was thinking. I guess you just have to know the way these things work."

Dan shrugged. "As with anything. There's a heavy tax on not understanding how the legal system works. And a lot of people just freak out anytime they have to deal with a judge or a lawyer. That's why I have a job."

Jen nodded.

"So, speaking of jobs: The last I'd heard from you, you were stuck in China trying to fix bags. What happened?"

"Oh, sheesh. Where to begin? So, you remember I was product-line director for this line of expensive, women's laptop bags, right? There were supposed to be six different bag designs. The U.S. design team had come up with the styles, and they'd sourced the bags from China. The prototypes looked great, but then once I got there and saw their production samples, I found out the contract manufacturers had been changing designs and materials and taking shortcuts."

Having embarked on the kind of narration that came easily to her, Jen described the whole China adventure in detail —which proved far more amusing in the retelling than it had seemed at the time. When she reached "So then I see myself in the mirror for the first time as she's drying my hair, and *I'm blonde*", Dan choked explosively on a spoonful of bisque and apologetically began to mop up the table.

"Not just lighter. Not dishwater blonde. Nearly platinum blonde!" Jen continued with triumph.

"I'm having trouble picturing that. I kind of wish I'd seen it."

"There are pictures, but I don't think the people who have them will share them."

"Sounds like there's more story to come. Go on."

Dan was more serious as Jen closed the story with the newspaper article and her decision to quit as soon as she landed.

"Now, I'm the lawyer friend, so let me give you the quick lecture here: You did not knowingly speak to a reporter, and you didn't divulge any proprietary information to the person you thought was just another business traveler, so you have grounds to take action against this reporter if you wanted to, and Aspire does not have grounds to discipline you for appearing in the article. Further, since one of their executives made a pass at you on a business trip, you have very strong grounds for a sexual harassment claim against him and the company, and if they took any kind of action against you —regardless of what they claimed the reason was—you'd have a good case that they were punishing you for reporting the harassment."

"Dan, honestly, I'm just glad to be out. It may sound funny now, but that China trip was one of the worst business experiences I've had in my life. The company culture is toxic. I just don't want to work there."

"I get that, but if that's partly because of the harassment, that's something you could sue to remedy. You're letting them off easy by just walking away. A lot of people would say you have a duty to other women to sue so that they'll clean their act up in the future."

Jen looked away for a moment. "Look, maybe I'm a bad person for this, but honestly, I just don't want to deal with these people again. Yes, Todd was an entitled jerk, and I imagine he'll hit on some woman on a business trip again. But it's not the first or the last time I've had to deal with some drunken slob trying to start something with me. Maybe I'm not doing my part for womankind, but I'd rather just never see any of the people involved again—even if that means forgoing some level of justice."

"You don't have to defend it to me," Dan assured. "I just wanted to make it clear that if you want to get some justice and teach Aspire a lesson, you can do so really easily."

Jen shrugged.

"All right. So you got off the plane and quit. But since you lead a charmed existence, you already have another job in the wings. Tell me about that."

"Hmm." Jen poured herself a second glass of wine, enjoying the loquaciousness that came with it. It let her talk the way she wished she could naturally, silencing the mental editor that at other times kept her quiet lest she say the wrong thing. "I didn't have anything waiting in the wings when I called Bryn and quit. I just wanted to be out of Aspire as soon as I had my feet planted safely back on U.S. soil. But on the way home from the airport, I stopped at my salon and had my hair put back in something like its natural shade."

"Depriving my sense of curiosity."

"Oh, hush. It wasn't all that. Anyway, by the time I got out, I had an e-mail waiting from a recruiter I'd talked to weeks ago about this job at Schneider and Sons, asking if I was still available. I said yes, and next thing I know, I've got a phone interview, and then they ask me to fly out for in-person interviews."

"You make these things sound so easy."

"You know, it was pretty easy. I feel like I ought to feel bad about it, with so many people having such a hard time

145

finding jobs. But for whatever reason, it keeps working out. Though, you saw me before I got the Aspire job. I was a mess about being unemployed. And I suppose if I hadn't landed the Aspire job, I would have been tearing my hair out for the last two months, waiting for something to come along."

She trailed off, poking bits of food around her plate and contemplating this other possible existence, then shrugged it off. "So, I flew out to O'Hare and drove down to Johnson, Illinois, where Schneider and Sons has their headquarters. It's about an hour and a half from Chicago. Definitely a small town.

"Schneider and Sons makes high-end tools, mostly power tools. Most of their customers are construction companies, contractors, and other professionals who are willing to pay more for tools that will last way longer than the brands you see in Home Depot or Lowe's. But the line I'm being brought in to manage is 'Schneider', their consumer line. It's still more expensive than mainstream brands, but it's not as overengineered as the professional grade. Right now, it's only sold directly through their website and through a few woodworking chains, but they've been working to try to get it into the big-box stores. What?"

Dan was shaking his head and smiling slightly. "We've known each other for what—six years? When I look at you, I don't exactly picture power tools and Home Depot."

Jen shrugged. "I didn't use the PocketDJ app or carry a designer laptop bag either. Product management is a skill totally separate from using the product."

"I know, I know. I just . . ." Dan paused, swirling his wine in his glass and clearly considering his words carefully.

"I've seen you in, what, four different jobs since you got your MBA? I know how you thrive in a fast-paced environment and how ambitious you are. Are you really going to be happy living in some small town in the Midwest and working at a company that makes power tools? I have trouble picturing you working with a bunch of middle-aged guys who drive pickup trucks and shoot deer. Are you sure you're not just reacting to the bad experience at Aspire Brands? Looking for the farthest thing from that kind of frenetic dysfunction that you can find?"

"In some ways, the company isn't as different from the tech companies I've worked for. I mean, they've got a fleet of company bicycles for getting from building to building —because the campus is big and they want to encourage people not to drive too much. And they've got tennis and volleyball courts and stuff—though the woman from HR told me that those date back to the fifties, when there was the whole 'company town' kind of thing, and people would come down to the campus on weekends and have barbecues with their families.

"So yeah," she concluded, "it'll be a huge change from the Bay Area and from the companies I've been working at lately. But it does seem like a fairly dynamic company— for all of being 130 years old—and maybe it's time for me to try a change anyway. Illinois is where I'm from, and the Bay Area hasn't been treating me so well lately anyway."

Dan nodded. "Hey, maybe so. You remember how fast I burned out on corporate law and went off to write wills and dispute speeding tickets. So, it's not like I have any credibility to tell someone to stay on the fast track."

Conversation turned, for a while, to Dan's activities and

then to those of others they had known from graduate school at Stanford. This flow of conversation was finally punctuated by the server appearing beside their table to glare darkly at them and inquire if they would be having dessert tonight.

"What exactly is the molten cocoa torte?" Jen asked.

"Basically chocolate cake."

"I'll have that."

The server retreated and left them looking at each other in silence.

"So," Jen asked after a moment, "how's the 'nice Jewish girl' thing going?"

Dan shrugged. "She was nice. I'm still single."

"I just can't get over that whole idea. Your mom setting you up, that is."

"Yeah. It kind of makes sense, though. She has friends who have single daughters my age. And it's not necessarily all that much more awkward than the first date with someone I found on JDate."

"But why is it so important to find a woman who's Jewish? I mean, aren't there much more important things to agree on?"

Dan gave his crooked smile. "Well, like what? Following the same sport? Having gone to the same school? You always first meet someone because of some shared characteristic, and often it's something pretty shallow. It's not as if I'd just go off and marry someone just because she was Jewish. But if I'm going to start somewhere, it's not that bad a place to start, is it?"

"Maybe it's just because I'm not Jewish, but religion just seems like an odd thing to be so fixated on when looking for a girlfriend."

"I don't know. None of my college girlfriends were Jewish, and those didn't work out either. So at least I've got consistency across creeds."

"But why the big emphasis on finding a Jewish girl now? Have you really become that religious?"

"I'm a bit better than I was when we first met, but no, I'm not what you could call a 'good Jew'. I believe in God and everything, but somehow I just don't follow many of the rules most of the time."

"I really don't get it then. So, most of the time you don't do that much about being Jewish, but you're saying that if you met some woman you really hit it off with, but she happened to be agnostic or Methodist or something, you'd take a pass because you really need to find someone who's Jewish? That just doesn't seem *like* you."

"No, I'm not saying that. But let's be honest: I don't have lots of women just wandering into my life who seem perfect for me. I'm thirty-five, and I'm not getting any younger. So, if I want to ever get married, I have to search. And if I'm searching anyway, I need to pick some criteria to determine who I look for. The fact is that being Jewish is defining: racially, culturally, religiously. At least we start out with certain things in common. And if things did work out, it would give us commonalities on which to build a family life."

Jen considered this as she ate her dessert and drank her coffee.

"You know," she said at last, her sense of honesty overcoming her reluctance to bring a subject back up merely to concede it. "That makes a lot of sense. You've thought about this more than I have. Maybe because there were a couple times I really thought everything would work out—with

Kevin when he first moved in with me, with Adam back when I was at Stanford—I always thought about marriage in very specific terms: Is *this* the guy? Maybe that's enough for a lot of people. But obviously, for people like us, mid-thirties, no prospects, we need to have *something* going for us, some first spark. If being Jewish means so much to you, I can see how it would be that common thing you'd look for."

Once such topics had been brought up and their depths plumbed, it was hard to return to small talk. Soon after, they requested their checks. The server had evidently not expected this, and so they found themselves confronted with a single bill. Dan offered to pay the whole thing, but when they'd just spent time discussing their separate ideas of dating, this hardly seemed just. A series of negotiations followed, but between them they had enough cash and enough flexibility to reach an amicable arrangement, and after a few words in the parking lot, they went their ways.

The next week brought a quickening stream of change. Jen's start date would be the last Monday in September, two weeks away. The transfer of her life from the Bay Area to Johnson, Illinois, was entrusted to a "relocation specialist" named Carla, working for a company based out of Omaha. Clearly practiced in the details of moving people across the country, Carla set to work with an efficiency that made large decisions pass almost without notice. E-mails would arrive laying out some detail of Jen's coming life and providing two or three easily chosen options.

How many people were in her household, and what relation did they bear to her? She lived with her sister. Would the sister be moving too? Yes. This was nonstandard, but since there were no other members of the household, the company would probably approve it. She would check. Yes, they did approve it. Did Jen want to have the company buy out her condo if it didn't sell in three months, or would she prefer to keep marketing it herself as long as necessary? Take it off her hands if it doesn't sell. Following please find links to three residence communities in which furnished apartments are available in or near Johnson, Illinois. Let me know which one you would like to have for your three months' company-paid temporary housing.

Decisions about where to live, when to move, and how to sell her condo were made so quickly and easily that it seemed hard to credit the fact that such major changes were occurring at all.

Katie's court appearance, which had loomed darkly over the week, proved something of an anticlimax. Having been told that all that was required of her was to dress conservatively, say she was sorry, and be polite, Katie had invested the first of these with perhaps undue weight. After spending significant amounts of time contemplating her own closet, she secured Jen's permission to plumb the depths of hers. From this she emerged, well satisfied, wearing one of Jen's best suits.

"How about this?" Katie asked, turning around for inspection. "Muted colors. Very conservative. Low heels. Does this say, 'Don't send me to jail; I won't do it again'?"

Jen's first—though, she recognized, not kindest—instinct was to try to calculate whether Katie looked better than she did in the outfit, due to being younger, or worse, due to being less in shape, but she quickly drove these unwelcome considerations from her mind.

"You look good, and it's a conservative look, but that's an expensive suit. If the judge knows anything about clothes, it'll make you look too well off for your age, and spoiled rich kid is probably not the look that helps."

"Are you saying I look too good?" Katie asked, with a hint of a smile—an encouraging change, given how obviously nervous she had been all day.

"Yeah, I guess so. We probably want you looking a little young and inexperienced—the sort of girl who never found herself yelling drunkenly at a cop at a traffic stop before."

"I *am* the sort of girl who never found herself yelling drunkenly at a cop before," Katie replied with a touch of sullenness.

"Well, then we just have to make you look like you, right? Would you have gone out and bought that suit for $1,200?"

"You paid $1,200 for this? How can you *wear* that kind of money?"

Jen shrugged. "I've worn it to the interviews for my last three jobs, and I got the job each time, so I guess it worked. For you, however: How about if you pick out a skirt and top you like rather than a suit? Or, if you feel more comfortable with another layer on, pick a cardigan or a jacket. If you really like that suit, you can borrow it some other time."

Katie snorted as she headed back into Jen's room. "I'd be terrified I'd *spill* something on it."

Jen laughed silently and wished that she could see, other than in her mind's eye, what she had looked like riding around the Schneider and Sons campus on the adult-size tricycle while wearing the suit.

The fashion crisis having been resolved to the satisfaction of all—after Katie had found an outfit she felt radiated "let me off with a warning", Jen decided to exercise her concerned-older-sister prerogative and wear the interview suit for luck—the two sisters drove to the courthouse together the next morning with plenty of time to spare and met Dan there.

Dan gave them a brief description of the judge Katie would be in front of, then excused himself to continue reading a stack of legal briefs he had with him.

After what seemed like hours of anxious waiting, it was all over very quickly. Dan conveyed Katie's contrition and resolution not to make such a mistake again. The judge asked Katie several questions in a severe tone. She responded meekly. The judge agreed to suspend the prosecution and explained that this meant that if she were charged with another crime within three years, she could face both charges, but if she avoided trouble, she would have no crimes on her record. Dan thanked him and guided the sisters out of court.

"See? No problem at all," Dan said.

"I feel like I'm shaking all over," Katie confessed. "I need to go sit down."

Dan looked mildly nonplussed. "Is she okay?"

"She's not used to dealing with this kind of thing like you are," Jen said. "Thanks. This really was a huge help. I'm glad I didn't have to worry about it at all, with all this relocation stuff going on."

"No problem. You can expect my bill shortly." Dan grinned. "Everything going all right? You staying sane while you get ready to move?"

"Yeah. Actually, they make it amazingly cushy for you.

It's easier than planning a business trip, until you start to think about everything that's happening. The guy who came out to look the condo over for the moving company said, 'Now don't pack anything. Any boxes you pack yourself won't be insured. We'll get it all done when the time comes to pack and load.' "

"So, are they packing all your stuff before you fly out?"

"No. I fly out next Saturday with basically just luggage. They've got a furnished apartment for us in Johnson and a rental car while they bring the cars out on a trailer. Katie's going to stay another week to tie up loose ends, and then she'll fly out too. Our stuff stays in the condo while we find a permanent place out there, and then they pack it up and move it for us."

"Crazy. Are you worried?"

"Oddly not. I'm still waiting for that to set in."

"Well, good luck. Am I likely to see you again before you leave?"

"I don't know. I was hoping to do some kind of a going-away thing."

"Well, in case you don't: Good luck. Keep in touch."

There was an awkward pause. Dan extended a hand to shake. Jen started to take it, then reached out both arms and hugged him instead.

For a moment, some faint whiff of sexuality, unwelcome, unlooked for, passed through her at the feeling, so long absent, of a male body held close against her own. Briefly—so briefly, she hoped afterward, as to have registered only with her—she pulled him tighter, soaking up the physical closeness. But almost as soon as she felt it, she pushed him away, sensing the violation of using someone so long a comrade, whom she had never sought to make anything other than a comrade, to fill the long unsatisfied need for touch. She released him with a couple of "just pals" slaps on the back.

"Thanks, Dan. I'll be in touch. I'm going to miss having you to watch out for me."

"All right, well . . ." There was an awkward pause during which Jen wondered if her briefly fierce hug had been more obvious than she had hoped. "I better get going. More cases to deal with today. Good luck."

He left, and Jen turned to her sister. "How're you feeling, Katie? Want to go pick up some lunch?"

7

"Our last night together here," Katie announced. The condo showed little sign of it, aside from Jen's luggage sitting near the door. "I should have planned something special for dinner."

"Let's go out," Jen said. "I could go for some sushi. That seems a fitting way to say goodbye to the coast."

Katie agreed.

"Should I call an Uber?" Jen asked. "We could make it a sake night. Big send-off."

"No. I can drive. I may be crazy, but I'm not crazy enough to mix raw fish and hard drinking."

In the end, it was a quiet night that ended early.

The next morning, they both got up early, and Katie made breakfast.

"I could just call for a ride," Jen offered one last time. "You'll get stuck in all kinds of traffic."

Katie shrugged. "I've got the time."

It was good to have the company. Up to this point, the move had hardly seemed real. Now the reality of leaving her home and the city in which she had built her career came down with crushing force.

At the airport, as she unloaded her bags curbside under the watchful eyes of airport police, who blew their whistles and waved on any cars that tarried long, the immediacy of their household dissolution gripped Jen. She tapped at the driver-side window.

"Did you forget something?" Katie asked, as the glass rolled down.

"No, you idiot. Come here." Jen reached in and enveloped her sister in a hug. "I'm going to miss you."

A policewoman whistled loudly at them and waved the car on.

"Sorry. I'll see you in a week." Jen stepped back and waved as Katie pulled away from the curb.

The furnished apartment in Johnson was a sort of architectural white noise, drowning thought. The possessions she had unpacked from her two suitcases did nothing to make it homelike. The effect was so lonely that Jen turned on the TV for company.

The kitchen provided no comfort. Under Katie's care, her own cupboards had become packed with ingredients, the shelf stacked high with cookbooks. The few items here were studiously generic: salt, pepper, a package of microwave popcorn, and a Snickers bar in the cupboard; in the freezer, a lone turkey-and-mashed-potato microwave dinner and a pint of mint 'n' chip ice cream. Did they expect the resident to dine on turkey and Snickers her first night, or were these items merely intended to avoid the offense of a completely bare shelf?

She consulted the phone book and discovered she could order Mad Jack's World-Famous Wings, pizza, or Mamma Ming's Chinese food. For a moment, she contemplated getting back in the car, driving to Chicago, and abandoning small-town life and her new job. But that would be failure.

Not long ago, an evening alone with a frozen dinner or takeout had been a normal routine. Had she become so dependent on Katie in the last few months?

The question, as it formed, had an offensive sound to it. Why not be dependent on her sister? Who else should she depend on? But Katie would be there soon enough. In the meantime, she needed to eat and get ready to begin her new job. With a new feeling of determination, she put the turkey dinner in the microwave.

On Monday morning, Jen was just heading out the door, feeling commanding and ready for new things in a grey wool skirt and blazer, and heels that brought her up to five foot ten inches, when her cell phone rang with an unfamiliar number.

"Hello?"

"Hi there. Jen?" asked a vaguely familiar voice.

"This is she."

"This is Andrea Gomez. We had lunch when you were out interviewing."

"Yes! Hi, Andrea. I was just heading out the door."

"Good, I'm glad I caught you. Getting the kids off to school, I almost forgot to call. Did anyone tell you about the orientation this morning?"

"Uh, no," Jen replied, fighting down a sudden feeling of panic.

"Figures. I don't know if it's the gals or the guys who find it funny, but somehow everyone forgets to clue the new girl in. There's an in-depth factory tour as part of the orientation. Do not wear a skirt, and do not wear heels. You'll be up and down ladders, and there are a bunch of those anti-fatigue rubber mats. Heels get stuck in them something awful."

"Oh. Okay. Thanks for the warning."

"Aw, poor thing, you probably had something real cute picked out. Well, have a good orientation. I'll try to drop by your office this afternoon and say hi."

"Thanks, Andrea. See you then."

Jen swore as she ran back to her room, shedding clothes as quickly as she could. Orientation started in twenty minutes, which, even though the Schneider and Sons campus was only five minutes away, gave her far too little time.

Somehow, within ten minutes, she was walking out of the apartment again, this time in pants, a fitted oxford with pale pink and gray pinstripes, and flats, but with her sense of composure somewhat rumpled.

With only a moment to spare, she presented herself to the front-desk receptionist and was directed to join a half dozen other new hires milling about the lobby. For all her worry about the time, however, it was not until almost ten minutes later that a harried man from HR, looking barely old enough to be out of college, rushed in, apologized for his lateness, and announced they would start by getting their pictures taken for their security badges.

The orientation was necessarily less flattering than the interview process had been. Then she had been the center of attention and known to be interviewing for a fairly senior role; now she was just one of the unfamiliar faces being shown where the cafeteria was and advised on the workings of paid time off. A friendly, fiftyish-looking man named Shin, whose newly made badge marked him as belonging to Engineering, sidled up to her and asked, "Is this your first role?"

Jen blanked at the incongruous question. "Uh, here at Schneider and Sons? Yes."

"No, no. First or second role out of college?"

"Uh, no," Jen said, unsure whether to take this as an insult or a compliment, except that it was so clearly unintentional that any reaction seemed out of place.

"Sorry. Sorry. You looked so young. Don't feel bad! Get to be my age, it's not so bad to look young."

"Thanks."

The orientation and tour left the new hires off at the cafeteria at noon. The lines were long, though most people seemed to be taking their food back to their desks. Those who were sitting and talking at tables in groups of two or three were mostly not eating: meetings unable to secure a conference room.

Jen ordered a salad, which, in keeping with the company's sustainable convictions—so the tour guide had explained—was served in an opaque compostable container that would not have been out of place back in California. She seated herself at a table to eat and watch the ebb and flow of people move through. As she was finishing, Andrea appeared and waved to her.

"Did you have a good orientation?"

"Yeah. Thanks for the tip about clothes."

"Did they take you through the workshops too?"

Jen nodded. "I got to use an industrial bolt tightener."

"You laugh now, but pretty soon you'll want one of your own," Andrea deadpanned.

"I'll make sure I find a house with a big garage."

"See? You're going to get along fine here. Now, I just ran into Brad on my way down here. He got pulled into a pre-read for the IBP meeting this afternoon, so he asked if I could catch up with you and get you to your desk. He'll meet you at 1:30. Let me just grab a salad."

"Okay."

Andrea returned a moment later. "All right. Walk with me, and since I've got you in my clutches, I'm going to tell you how I think the world works while we go. So, you've got the Schneider line. You know why you were the one picked?"

"If it's going to be a reason besides the obvious, please have it be a flattering one. It is still my first day."

"No first-day privileges, sister," Andrea warned, but then flashed her a smile. "What you need to understand is that the Schneider line *ought* to be a big seller. Too many of the consumer brands have spent the last twenty years engineering quality out of their products so that you can buy a drill driver for thirty dollars at Walmart. Which is great if you want to use it a couple weekends a year and throw it away after four years when the battery won't hold a charge anymore. But it's frustrating for home-improvement enthusiasts who want a tool they can actually love, not just put up with. See, we have that credibility and quality, but what we don't have is enough of a sense of urgency in the company about what is seen as a stepchild product line to actually make it work. That's why I advocated so strongly for you (and Brad has this religion too, so don't worry), because you are a pro, but you're an outside player who doesn't have this institutional sense that the Schneider line is a backwater that people are sent to for bad behavior. All of which I tell you —have they told you I talk a lot yet? I do, but I make people listen—because one of your challenges is going to be overcoming that institutional inertia and indifference about the line. Forewarned?"

"Yes. Thanks."

"Okay. And remember, don't let it bother you. I'm going to get you sent off to the LeadFirst training. Have you heard of this one?"

"No. I don't think so."

"No, I guess you wouldn't have. It's not a very Bay Area kind of thing. You'll enjoy it, though!"

Exhausted by her first day, Jen promptly abandoned her standards on the way home and picked up dinner at Mamma Ming's: deep fried and syrupy Chinese takeout of the guiltiest sort. If it was utterly unlike any food she had eaten while in China, the flavors held memories of meals eaten out of folded cardboard boxes on busy nights when she was growing up.

At the end of the week, Katie arrived, and Jen was so glad to see her that, in a reversal of recent roles, she made dinner for her younger sister. She was so glad, in fact, that she did not feel frustration boiling up when Katie used her free time to install the Xbox and begin playing *Mass Effect*.

Sunday saw Katie rooted to the console for much of the day, until she got up and made enchiladas and a pitcher of margaritas for dinner.

The next morning, a full-body ache and the empty pitcher

sitting on the counter accused Jen as she drank a hurried cup of coffee before heading out the door to work. But the tangle of gaming technology on the floor in front of the TV and Katie's closed bedroom door at last made the apartment seem homelike.

So great was the pleasure of reunion that it was not until near the end of the week, as Katie's Xbox binge continued unabated, that Jen threw a real estate catalog at her sister. "If you can't find anything better to do with your life than blow up virtual bad guys all day, go look at some houses and find us a real place to live. Some of us are busy with work and stuff."

"The problem with this place," Katie announced Thursday night, indicating the apartment in general, "is that it's all white walls and newness and has no character."

"Do you say this because you've been looking at places with character, or places without character, or simply because you're cultivating a new aesthetic sense and need to practice your discernment?" Jen asked.

"I say this because it's soulless," Katie explained. "Why is it that we have beautiful old houses just five minutes' walk from here, and those massive apartments above the old storefronts on Main Street, and yet what they're building is white soulless boxes with green lawns in front of them? What's wrong with our world?"

"I think the old places are sometimes a lot of work," Jen offered.

"Don't you think that would be more real, though?" Katie pressed. "To really work on your house? Fix things. Do things. I dunno . . . paint things?"

"Katie, have you ever done any home-repair work?"

"No. But you work for a tool company now. It would be good practice for you. And we'd be rooted and stuff."

"Whence all this? Did you find a realtor who specialized in old houses or something?"

"Well . . . no. But I did walk around a lot with my iPhone and pull up listings on Zillow. And some of the old houses around here are really, really cool. Not old like Mom and Dad's place. Really old—like a hundred years old or more. Seriously, after dinner let me show you some of these listings."

Jen called a realtor connected with the relocation company and arranged for them to spend the next Saturday looking at houses. The realtor, a generously proportioned older woman named Carol, arrived at the apartment at nine o'clock on Saturday morning and presented Jen with an elaborately constructed binder with flyers for all the houses they would be visiting.

"Since this is our first time out, I thought we should look at a range of options in your size and price range," Carol explained.

"That sounds great," Jen replied.

The sisters piled into Carol's spacious Jaguar XJ. "This back seat is amazing, but it seems like it should come with a mimosa," Katie announced. Jen handed her the binder instead, and she began paging through their choices.

Jen had not been much in sympathy with Katie's excitement over old houses. When Carol led them through Victorian foursquares, Katie rhapsodized about woodwork and tightly spiraled back staircases, while Jen noted damaged paneling, peeling paint, old-fashioned radiators, and the probable lack of insulation. At the same time, newer houses all seemed to come in little subdivisions so manicured that one almost expected a giant hand to reach down from the sky and arrange plastic people on the lawn. The open floor plans and white walls that had seemed so cleanly natural in California here looked shallowly false.

"Have you discussed what you want before today?" asked Carol, as they returned to the car after yet another house to which the sisters had expressed clashing reactions.

"*I've* talked and researched," Katie said. "But someone was too busy at the office to think about it much."

By the time they stopped for lunch, tempers were beginning to shorten, and Jen considered suggesting that they call off the rest of the day. However, by the time she allowed for thirty to forty-five days to close, plus time to move, she figured it was necessary to find a house within the first month. And how quickly would Carol put them on her schedule again if they did not find at least one house they could at least compliment?

The next house was in the old part of Johnson, a neighborhood of two- and three-story Victorian houses presiding over tree-lined streets, where several houses had already charmed Katie but not Jen. This one, however, was a single-story bungalow, its gently sloping roof covered in deep-blue tiles. The walls were brick up to waist height, and then light-brown stucco.

"When was this built?" Jen asked. "It looks like some of the old houses back in California."

Carol consulted a sheaf of notes. "Nineteen nineteen. It's a Sears kit house. Two bedrooms. Kitchen needs a little work, but it has a new furnace and air conditioning, and it's priced to sell."

There were touches aplenty to warm Katie's heart, beginning with the sinuous brass-lizard door knocker on the heavy, green front door. Jen noted that the windows, though wood-framed, were new, and that the heating and cooling systems did indeed look modern. These practicalities ensured, she could allow her heart to be warmed by touches such as the deep-set, finished-wood window seats in the identically sized bedrooms—the more so when Carol pointed out that the window seats lifted to reveal built-in cedar-lined chests.

"Look at the fireplace!" crowed Katie from the other room. Art nouveau tiles set off the smallish firebox, surmounted by a carved wooden mantle on which lizards like the one on the door knocker frolicked among stylized leaves.

The kitchen, and, to a lesser extent, the bathroom, were the sticking point. The appliances were old, rust beginning to show through white enamel, and no concessions had been made to a more modern taste in layout and storage.

After spending nearly an hour in the bungalow, the women moved on to see the rest of the houses on their itinerary, but Katie's heart was clearly won, and every subsequent house was assiduously, and unflatteringly, compared with the bungalow.

"You would hate that kitchen," Jen pointed out that night, as Katie was making dinner in the apartment.

"It's pretty bad," Katie conceded. "But we could get a new fridge and stove and fix it up, couldn't we?"

"The asking price isn't much more than the equity I can get out of my condo back in California. It would be easy to keep out enough money for renovations and still have a pretty tiny mortgage," Jen conceded. "Still, I can't think of anything I'd like less than having to supervise a bunch of contractors all the time."

"I could help!" Katie assured her.

Through the weekend, the hold of the bungalow on their minds remained firm—Jen's as well as Katie's, despite her calmer approach to the matter. When she went running on Sunday morning, she unconsciously directed her steps in that direction and found herself standing outside the low, wrought iron fence, looking up the walk.

Tuesday, over lunch, she called Carol and asked if they could see it again that night. The sisters took their time wandering all over the house. An hour and a half had passed, and Jen was sitting on the window seat of what she couldn't help thinking of as "her room": her legs pulled up, her arms wrapped around her knees, her eyes looking out on the secluded backyard in the gathering gloom.

Carol entered, saw Jen, and observed, "It's such a pretty view. The yard would be just right for you: large enough to have a garden but not so big that it would be hard to manage."

Jen nodded. For several moments she remained silent. "All right," she said. "I want to make an offer on it."

Over the next two weeks, paperwork ebbed and flowed: inspections, loan paperwork, proof of employment, equity advance from the relocation company for the California condo. Katie, in a burst of enthusiasm, got a library card and returned home with what appeared to be the entire home-improvement and decorating section. Jen gently mocked this development, especially when Katie brought her new passion into the modern age and started a Pinterest account, but this aloofness did not prevent Jen from quietly contemplating the relative brand value of Wolf versus Viking ranges. Carol assured them that they should be able to close within thirty days. "You can be in by Thanksgiving if you want."

Their parents, Tom and Pat, were enthusiastic at the news and promised a visit, which occurred on the second weekend after the offer had been placed. The four of them walked down to view the house, Jen and Katie pointing out its many virtues with the consciousness of impending ownership.

"I'm glad to see you and Katie getting along so well," Pat said, as she and Jen were cleaning up the apartment kitchen together that evening. Katie, having made the dinner, had retired to the living room, where Tom was watching the football game. "I was real worried about her when she picked up and moved out, but you seem to have been a steadying influence."

This we-are-the-adult-women-talking-together-about-your-sister dynamic was not a familiar one, and Jen was not sure she liked it. "I've enjoyed having her with me," she replied blandly.

"I keep looking back to those couple months when she was with us after graduating and trying to think what I did wrong," Pat confided. "How did you get through to her?"

"I did yell at her to go get a job after she'd been sitting around for the first couple days she was with me," Jen conceded. "But honestly, she's matured a lot on her own over the last few months. I can't take credit for it."

"You must be doing something right," Pat persisted.

"When she was staying with us, she was staying out late without telling us, coming in drunk some nights. I was terrified I'd get a call from the police some night that she'd been pulled over DUI."

"Nope, I never had that happen," Jen said, having no intention of telling her mother about Katie's court appearance. "I think after she had some space for a while, and thought about things, she found her own reasons to mature," she added, with truth.

"I feel sometimes like I failed her as a mother. But it's so hard to make up that ground now. I wish I'd done a better job when she was younger. I wish I'd known the sort of things that go on at secular colleges these days. Maybe if I'd pushed her to go to a Catholic college, she would have had better influences. You were so responsible in college, but not everyone has the strength to resist peer pressure like you."

Jen shrugged, divided between the drive to argue with her mother and the desire to move the conversation on to another topic. "You know, Mom, I probably did a lot of stuff you wouldn't approve of when I was in college and afterward. It's just that I kept my grades up and never moved back home. Honestly, Katie's a good kid. It'd be easiest on both of you if you stopped trying to bring her up and just tried to know her better the way she is."

Pat dashed at her eyes with an elbow as she finished loading the dishwasher, and Jen feared the conversation was in danger of taking a maudlin turn. "How have you and Dad been doing?" Jen inquired. "It's good to see you guys. I know I'm terrible about calling."

"Oh, we're doing all right. Actually . . . I was wanting

to tell you . . ." Pat looked around as if guilty over imparting something that was supposed to remain secret. "The latest contract negotiation at your father's work hasn't been going well. You know how things are these days. They've announced a buyout for people between fifty-five and sixty-five who are willing to take early retirement, and Dad's been thinking about it very seriously." She nodded sagely.

"Wow. Is Dad really thinking of retiring? He's not that old."

"Sixty-two next year, honey. That's not *old*, but he'd be glad not to have to go out with the trucks anymore. And his knee has been giving him a little trouble lately. He says if he's going to keep working, he'd like it to be on something he cares about. If he took the retirement offer, he could look into something like teaching a shop class part-time at the high school or the community center."

"Wow. Dad retired and teaching shop classes part-time. I guess I really am a grown-up."

"Well . . . And I'll tell you something else." Pat paused dramatically. "Your father's been talking for ages about what a big yard we have for two empty nesters. And the house is really bigger than we need and so much work to keep clean and decorated. With you girls back nearby, we've been talking about whether it's time to put the house on the market and move somewhere smaller. Maybe even somewhere nearer to you girls. You know that nice young priest we had at our parish for a couple years? Father Larry?"

"Mom, I haven't been to your place in three or four years."

"I must have told you about him on the phone, though, hon. You should hear him speak. He gave a Bible study on the Epistles last year, and there were a hundred people crowding into the parish center every Tuesday night just to hear him talk. Well, we were all so sad when he got reassigned this spring. But where do you think it was they sent him? Saint Anne's, right here in Johnson. I told him when he left, 'It'll be a long drive, but Tom and I will come out and see you sometime.' So when Katie told me the job you were interviewing for was in Johnson, I knew it was meant to be. And here you are!"

Jen did not venture an opinion on the providential nature of this coincidence. Pat tried to entice her to come to Mass with them the next morning with the promise that she would be able to meet Father Larry and that his sermons were short but always made her think, but Jen passed on the opportunity, slept till eight, and got in a run while her parents were gone, returning in time to help Katie make breakfast.

The closing date for the house was set for the Friday before Thanksgiving. The sisters were united in their desire to host Thanksgiving dinner at the new house, both to show off their new home and as an act of independence. This deadline created certain logistical difficulties, but these were solved by sending Katie back to California to supervise the movers' packing up the old condo while Jen stayed in Johnson to sign paperwork and meet office deadlines.

Left to herself, Jen succumbed to her own form of house fever and visited a kitchen showroom to order glistening stainless-steel replacements for the old stove and refrigerator. The prices would have drawn shocked indignation from Katie, but Jen assured herself she was investing for the long term and that the savings of picking a KitchenAid fridge over the Sub-Zero justified the expense of the Wolf stove in all its red-knobbed glory.

The great day came. Katie, jet lagged from her trip back the night before, dozed in a chair while Jen went through the rituals of assuming ownership.

"This document says . . . Please initial each page and sign here."

At last, they left the title agent's office, Jen carrying a large, legal-size folder full of papers and the keys to the house. They drove straight there, let themselves in, and wandered slowly through the empty, echoing rooms.

"Let's stay here tonight," Katie said, bursting into Jen's room, where she had been sitting on the window seat, quietly daydreaming.

"There's nothing to sleep on," Jen pointed out.

"We could get a couple sleeping bags or air mattresses or something."

The idea had an unquestionable allure. The next day, their furniture would arrive, but the house was hers now, and Jen couldn't help seeing a night spent anywhere else as a waste.

They went out and laid in cleaning supplies, a pair of air mattresses, and a six pack of beer. They spent the afternoon cleaning the house—hard, grubby work, which neither of them had ever enjoyed as much before, nor would again— and at last, tired and feeling far less fresh than the newly scrubbed house but deeply gratified to look around at the glistening floors smelling of Murphy Oil Soap, they sat on the floor of the empty dining room and relished a dinner of pizza and beer.

"Was it like this when you bought your condo?" Katie asked.

Jen tried to turn her mind back to those days. She and Kevin had started dating during the weeks she was waiting to close on the condo, and he had helped her move her things from her old apartment. There had been no need for a day of cleaning then; the newly built condo had been utterly pristine when the agent at last gave her the keys and showed her around. Still, there had been a headiness to placing furniture and unpacking boxes together, which, no doubt, had speeded her invitation that he move in.

"No," Jen said, dismissing the memories. "The condo was different. I was excited, and it's always fun the first time you go into your new place, before the furniture comes. But it was brand new and perfect, like being shown into a hotel room. I ran around barefoot so I wouldn't get anything on the new white carpet and showed my boyfriend where each piece of furniture would go."

"I wish I was doing that," said Katie with a gusty sigh.

"What?"

"Showing a boyfriend around the empty house. Running into every corner. Kissing. You know . . ."

Jen laughed. "Sounds a little awkward with me here."

"Well, of course I mean if it was my house, and my boyfriend, and I had my life together. Sheesh, fine—make a joke of it. Maybe you're just way too together to ever feel this way, but sometimes . . ." Katie trailed off for a moment after this outburst, assessing whether she wanted to go on in this confessional vein. When she spoke again it was a quieter tone, and she drew her knees up and wrapped her arms around them defensively as she spoke. "It's just stuff like this that makes me feel so desperate to be living a real life in a real relationship. And then I wish I could just grab some guy and—" She paused again. "In my head it's always just some random guy. Which I guess is how I know it's just desperation talking, because with any real guy I knew I'd be thinking about him as a person and I'd be nervous and never just *grab* him . . . unless I'd had an awful lot to drink first to give me courage."

Jen laughed again, but this time her laughter had a wistful edge.

"What?" Katie demanded.

"You won't always be the bundle of hormones you are at twenty-three. The loneliness stays, though. Loneliness is worse."

"Oh, Jen, I'm sorry!" Katie gave her sister an impulsive hug. "I don't know what's wrong with me. Sometimes I just say whatever comes into my head."

It grew dark outside. The evening was cold, and the furnace gently growled in the basement, exhaling warm air through decorative brass grilles. Jen had picked up a case of fire logs at the store. They lit one in the fireplace and sat talking in the living room until late. At last, each went to her own room, where they had made up the air mattresses using bedding borrowed from the apartment.

Jen snuggled under her blanket and looked up at the unfamiliar ceiling. The moon was nearly full, shining its blue-white glare in through the curtainless window, and the trees in the backyard cast strange, dancing shadows across the walls. She heard the click-click-whoosh of the furnace starting up again in the basement. Then, as the ducts warmed, the sighing of the air moving through the house, and the pingings and creakings of the ducts changing temperature. A floorboard creaked. There was a strange, quiet rattle somewhere in the house. Jen pulled the blanket up over her head like a child and felt wide awake. She found herself wondering if anyone had ever died in this nearly hundred-year-old house. This line of thought only magnified every sound in the empty house, and she found herself wishing very strongly that they had waited until the furniture arrived before spending their first night in it. Her furniture would tame it. The still-bare house still owned itself, with all its history and secrets, the two of them as yet just a tolerated intrusion in the structure.

She heard footsteps, and the door creaked open.

"Jen?" said Katie in a very quiet voice.

"What?"

"I know this sounds really stupid, but the empty house sounds spooky. Can I get in with you?"

Sharing an air mattress with another adult did not promise a very comfortable night, but the ominous sounds of the house had already receded to nothing with the arrival of another person.

"Sure."

Katie crawled in under the blankets next to her, curled up, and fell asleep almost instantly. It was some time before Jen drifted off, but with the warm presence next to her, the night held no more fears.

The movers came early the next morning, and all was chaos from there on out. The truck arrived from the kitchen showroom, and yet another set of workmen entered to carry out the old appliances and bring in the new fridge and stove. Such was the madness at that point that neither sister had time to stop and wonder at the glistening stainless-steel appliances until the movers had gone.

Nothing is quite as comforting as breakfast, and so, when they were alone at last that night, Katie fried up bacon and scrambled eggs while Jen unpacked dishes and put them in the cupboards.

By the end of the weekend, they had most of the everyday accoutrements of life unpacked.

Jen went back to the office for the three days before the holiday, while Katie laid in extravagant supplies for Thanksgiving dinner and simultaneously embarked upon painting her room. She finished in the small hours of Thursday morning, and Jen (who had nurtured reservations about Katie's do-it-yourself abilities) was forced to admit that it looked professional.

"It's not hard," averred Katie. "You just have to be patient and do it like on YouTube."

The Thanksgiving dinner, too, was a success. Katie devoted herself to the turkey, which she had brined for two days. Jen took charge of the mashed potatoes. Tom and Pat arrived just after noon, bearing the two signature family dishes: green-bean casserole topped with french-fried onions and a concoction involving Cool Whip, green Jell-O, and marshmallows. Conversation was ebullient. The sisters showed off their new house, and the parents were in the throes of their own real estate excitement, having put their house on the market three days before.

"The way the market is these days," Pat explained. "You really can't list too soon. If we're lucky, it'll sell within the next six months or so. After New Year's, we'll get into doing some serious looking for a new place closer to you girls."

The moment, however, that all would remember in years to come did not come until late in the evening, after the dishes had been put in to wash and the football game was concluded, when Pat and Tom were making noises about getting on the road. Pat's cell phone rang, and as she answered it, her shock became obvious to all those in the room.

"Yes? Oh. Really? Well, that's—"

She turned off her phone at last and tucked it away carefully in her purse before facing the rest of her family. "That was Susan, our real estate agent. A couple emailed an offer on the house to her this morning. A full-price offer. I never —I don't know what we'll do. I hadn't even thought we'd start looking till after Christmas, but they want to close as quickly as possible."

Silence reigned for a moment, and then Jen heard herself saying, "Well, you're always welcome to stay here for a few weeks until you can get into a new place."

8

"What were you thinking?" Katie demanded later that night, after their parents had left. "They're a lot easier to get along with as visitors than they were as . . . as parents, but that's no reason to invite them to move in."

"They'd just be staying for a couple weeks between when their house closes and when they get into a new place," reassured Jen, who was reclining on the couch while drinking an after-dinner Manhattan. "They wouldn't be running the place."

"No, Jen, you don't get it. You haven't lived with them in more than ten years. It's going to be terrible."

"You won't be living with them. They'll be visiting us. It's my house, and I'm sure they'll be mindful of that."

"You'll see," Katie predicted darkly. "I'm going to go get a beer before the Gestapo moves in."

"Oh, come on. You want any melodrama with that beer?"

Katie returned with a bottle and sprawled on the easy chair. "Where are we going to put them?"

"That," Jen conceded, "is a much better objection. I feel like we have all kinds of space because I've never had a stand-alone house before. But with two bedrooms and one bathroom, it will definitely be tight."

"How about that little room you set up as your office? We could put them in there."

"That's awfully small to put a full-size bed in."

"If we put them here in the living room, we could never do anything at night."

"I think we'd have to give them your room, and you'd have to move in with me."

Katie made a humphing sound.

"Look, it's nothing personal. I just don't see what else we could do."

"I just painted that room."

"It'd be for only a week or two, if it even happens. Trust me, they're not going to be eager to be crowded into this house with us for any longer than they have to be. And remember, it may not even happen. This is just if this offer goes through and they close before they're able to get into a new place. And if they want to. Heck, they may be talking in the car right now about how they don't want to be crammed into this tiny house with us."

"I bet they're not," Katie prophesied darkly.

Perhaps as a distraction from her fears, Katie spent the rest of the long weekend throwing herself into her next project, the bungalow's one bathroom, which had both the charm and limitations of not having been visibly updated since the fifties. She took Jen's credit card to Sherwin-Williams in downtown Johnson and bought paint at the Black Friday sale, then braved the crowds at Home Depot to return with a new showerhead and what seemed, for such a small room, a vast array of drop cloths, tapes, caulks, fillers, and other supplies.

"Will I be able to take my shower in here tomorrow

morning?'' Jen demanded Sunday night, as Katie was re-caulking around the bathtub.

"That's why I'm doing this now," Katie explained. "It has to cure overnight before it can get wet."

"Okay. I'm happy to fund all these projects, and you're doing great work, but keep in mind that we have only one bathroom."

"How about if while I keep that in mind, you go get me a can of Coke," Katie suggested, carefully smoothing the line of caulk with one finger.

Jen considered a retort but instead fetched her the Coke.

It was thus with concern but not complete surprise that Jen received a text from Katie on Monday afternoon: "make sure you go to the bathroom before leaving work".

She called Katie instantly. "Katie, what happened?"

"Uh, this isn't a good time," Katie informed her. "Don't worry. Everything will be okay. Just make sure you use the bathroom before leaving."

"Katie . . ." Jen warned.

"Bye!" Katie hung up.

When Jen got home, she went straight to the bathroom to see the damage. Katie was sitting on the edge of the bathtub, doing something on her iPhone. In the center of the room stood the toilet, resting on a pile of newspapers. Where the toilet had stood, was a disturbing hole in the tile.

"What is this?" Jen demanded.

"It's not as bad as it looks," Katie said defensively.

"But . . . why did you take it out?"

"I was going to caulk around it. But then it was bugging

me that it rocked a little bit. I tried to tighten the bolts, but they were really rusty, and one of them broke. And the book said replacing the bolt was really easy."

"And it wasn't?"

"Once I got it off, the connection wasn't like the one in the book."

"Katie, this is serious. What are we going to do? Crouch over the hole?"

"It'll be fine: I've already got a guy coming. He promised he'd be here tonight."

Jen relaxed slightly. "So, who's the guy you've got coming?"

"I'll show you," Katie said, leading the way into the kitchen. "I couldn't find anyone good online here in Johnson. There are plumbers, but this isn't exactly a plumbing problem. But then I found this." She held out a church bulletin from Saint Anne's that their parents had left behind.

"You called the church?"

"No, look, there are ads on the back. See? This one." She pointed to a larger square that said, in a chiseled font that would have seemed more appropriate to a classical ruin, "Paul Burke, handyman" and then noted in smaller letters, "Bathroom and Kitchen Renovations; Cabinetry and Carpentry; Painting. Historic home specialist. Fair prices. (Parishioner)."

"He said he's finishing up another job, but I told him we had nothing but a hole in the floor for a toilet, and he said he'd come tonight. He doesn't think it'll take long to fix."

Jen was not sure what she had expected—perhaps a heavy man in his fifties—but when she answered the door about an hour later, what she found was a man her own age, or perhaps a little younger, with black hair and a full beard, battered work boots, a flannel shirt tucked into paint-spattered jeans, and suspenders.

"Hello, my name is Paul Burke," he said. He spoke slowly, but in a way that conveyed an instinctive formality rather than a dull wit. "I believe we spoke earlier about a toilet?"

"That was my sister, Katie. She went out to pick up dinner and find a bathroom. I'll show you the problem."

She led him to the bathroom and pointed to the toilet and the gaping hole. "Katie said she was trying to tighten the bolts, and one broke, so she decided to take it off and replace the bolts like in the Home Depot book, but it wasn't put together the way she expected."

Paul nodded and bent down next to the hole to look more carefully.

"Yes. I see. The floor under the tile is cement, and the bolts are set into that. You see that often in houses this age. Nineteen twenties?"

"Nineteen nineteen. It's a Sears kit house."

"Those are good. Very well laid out." He poked at the remaining bolts. "None of these are very solid. They ought to be replaced. That will take some time, however. Let me show you what I can do."

He pulled a round package out of his bag and unwrapped a ring of black rubber and some disgusting yellow compound.

"I can put a new wax ring on it tonight and set the toilet on it with the remaining bolts. It will be stable enough for you to use if you are careful with it. Tomorrow afternoon I can come back with a brass plate that will fit this hole and put that down with epoxy. Then I can slot modern bolts into that and fix the toilet down permanently."

183

"So long as we can use it tonight."

"It will be fine. The work tomorrow will take a couple of hours to dry, but you will be able to use the toilet tomorrow night."

"That would be great."

Paul pressed the ring into place over the hole, then set the toilet down on it and replaced the nuts on the remaining bolts.

"Thank you so much for coming tonight," Jen said. "I was ready to kill Katie when I saw the toilet up and that hole in the floor. How much do I owe you for tonight?"

"You don't need to pay anything until I finish," Paul assured her. "Let me give you one of my cards."

The card was magnetic and featured the same classical lettering as his ad, in this case complemented by a line drawing of a Doric column. Jen put it on the fridge.

"May I ask how you heard about me?" Paul inquired.

"My parents brought home a church bulletin from Saint Anne's when they were here visiting a few weeks ago, and my sister saw your ad on the back."

Paul nodded.

"It says that you do kitchen renovations. We have one of those in our future. Katie was talking about trying to do it herself, but after this fiasco with the toilet, I don't want to let her try to build cabinets."

Paul looked around the kitchen with consideration. "What kind of renovation do you have in mind?"

"It seems like it should have an island, to be a little more modern. And new lights and maybe replacing these old cabinets. I left aside a fair amount of money for working on the kitchen when I bought the house."

Paul moved around the kitchen, opening cupboard doors, trying the drawers, peering at the plumbing under the sink. "It would be an interesting project," he said. "I see you have new appliances. Do you want to make a place to put in a dishwasher?"

"Yes!" said Jen. "I don't know how the previous owner never had one. Do you work on designs as well as doing the work?"

Paul nodded.

"I'd love to get an estimate on all this."

"The kitchen will require some planning. I can help you with that for free."

"I'd be happy to pay. I'm sure the design is a lot of work."

Paul shrugged. "I'm not a professional designer. I think of drawing plans as a sort of detailed estimate. I am happy to just charge for the actual labor. We could talk about it after I finish with the toilet."

"If you're putting work into making a plan, it seems like you should charge even if you don't call it 'designing'. There's no reason to be providing value you don't monetize," Jen said, her work instincts kicking in.

"What do you do?" Paul asked.

"I'm a product-line manager at Schneider and Sons."

Paul nodded. "That's a very good company."

"Do you use their tools?" Jen asked.

"I would if I could afford them."

Jen thanked him again as she showed him to the door. Katie was coming up the walk, balancing several bags. Paul stopped on the porch to hold the door open for her.

"Was that the repair guy?" Katie asked. "He's younger than I expected from the phone."

Jen nodded.

"Kind of cute too," Katie added in an undertone. "In a hipster kind of way."

Paul was finishing up work in the bathroom by the time Jen got home from work the next day.

"This should be pretty well set up," he said. "I used a fast-drying epoxy and let it sit for two hours before bolting the toilet to it. I told Katie to give it a day or two before caulking it."

"Jen," Katie interjected. "Paul does electrical work too. I want to get a nicer light for this bathroom, and he could put it up for us. Do you mind? And he says it would be easy to replace the old two-prong outlets with three-prong."

"Do you mind?" Jen asked.

Paul shrugged. "It's an easy job. If you pick up the fixture and outlets you want, putting them up is a matter of a few hours."

"When would be a good time for you?"

Paul's brow furrowed slightly. "This week I am very busy. And I will need to turn the power off, so it should be during daylight. Would you mind if I came Saturday morning?"

"I certainly don't mind," Jen said. "You don't have to work the weekend just for us, though. Next week is fine if that's better for you."

Paul shrugged. "I usually work six days a week. This time of year especially, people are in a rush to get projects done before Christmas. Then there will be a few weeks when no one calls unless it is an emergency, until the new year."

"Well, if you don't mind Saturday, that's fine with us. Let me get you a check for this job," Jen led the way into the kitchen and got her checkbook out of her purse. "How much do I owe you?"

"Seventy-five dollars." Paul pulled a yellow receipt pad out of his bag and wrote out a bill, which he handed her.

"Is that all? You had to come two times."

"It was really a small job."

"Okay. No wonder you're busy. People must love your rates. I was sure it would be at least a few hundred."

Paul spread his hands. "Too many people overcharge. It isn't right to charge people more than it's worth just because they don't know how to do the work themselves."

"Well, there's a lot that we don't know how to do, and I'd be happy to have you back for lots more hours. Let me give you my phone number." Jen retrieved one of her business cards from her purse and wrote her and Katie's cell phone numbers on the back of it. "Let me know if your schedule changes, and otherwise we'll expect you Saturday morning. No matter how lazy we are, we'll be up and about by nine."

"I will see you then."

Katie spent the week doing an impressive job of painting the bathroom—creamy-white beadboard and cabinets, pale teal walls—as if determined to redeem herself after the toilet incident. By Saturday, it was finished and pristine, except for the box sitting on the floor with the new light fixture she had picked out.

Jen awoke early Saturday and went for a run in the frosty, early-morning light of the first day of December. When she got back, Katie had the coffee on and was mixing muffin batter.

"You better go get your shower now," Katie advised.

"You don't want to be tying up the bathroom when Paul gets here in half an hour. I'll have these muffins in the oven in a few minutes. Do you want chocolate chips or blueberries?"

"You're hopeless," Jen complained. "I get out of bed early to try and stay fit, and you're mixing up muffins."

"If you want to go gnaw on some celery instead, be my guest. I don't see you passing up anything I cook."

"I can't! It's so good."

"Then why are you complaining? You're thinner than I am."

"Only because I work out and watch what I eat. At my age, if I ate like you, I'd look like Mom. Genetics bite, kiddo, and I'm not ready to settle into a comfortably soft middle age."

"And if I knew what was good for me, I'd get in shape now because it's harder later. Blah, blah, blah. Blueberries or chocolate chips, Miss Taut Thighs?"

"Blueberries." Jen stalked off toward the shower, feeling that moral victory had somehow remained elusive.

Paul arrived just when the muffins had gotten cool enough to come out of the papers cleanly.

"We're having a late breakfast," Jen explained. "Can we get you anything? Cup of coffee? Muffin?"

"I already ate," Paul excused himself. "Really, I can just start work."

"Oh, come on," objected Katie. "You must at least want coffee." She poured him a cup. "Here."

Paul accepted the cup that was thrust into his hands, and Katie put a muffin in front of him, which he eyed speculatively.

"I'm sorry there's nowhere to sit in here," Jen said. "That's one of the things I want to change with the new kitchen design. Right now, we just kind of stand around if we don't go to the dining room."

Paul took a bite. "Mmm. You make them from scratch?" he asked.

"Always," said Katie with some pride.

"You said things are usually slow for you during the holidays," said Jen. "Would that be a good time to work on some kitchen plans and get started on that?"

Paul nodded. "In another couple weeks, people will stop calling, and I will have a lot of time on my hands. That would be a good time for planning a big project. The last few years, I've just used that time to catch up on projects around the farm if the work isn't too bad."

"You have a farm?" Katie asked.

"A very small one: seventy acres. Eventually it will be a full-time sustainable livestock farm, but right now, I just have a couple dozen goats and some chickens. I want to get cows, but cows take a lot more attention."

"So, is the handyman work just until you can get the farm running full-time?" Jen asked.

"It's hard to say. I like working on old houses. And I think it's important for farmers to be integrated into the community, not just treating farming as a business. That is how we got to the point where we eat corporate food that is grown in ways nature never intended."

"So, did you start the handyman work or the farming first?"

"After I left seminary, I came out here to stay with a friend and sort out what to do with my life. The job market was terrible, and I was helping Joe's father lay down some flooring and do other things around their house. He was telling me what an absurd quote he'd got from a contractor to do the work. I thought, 'There must be a need for honest guys who are willing to do this work.' So, I took out an ad and started doing work. After a year and a half, I was starting to feel bad about staying with Joe's family for so long. I heard about this farm for sale, twenty miles out of town. It was going cheap, and there was a farmhouse on it, though it was in such bad shape that you could count the stars in some rooms at night. I had a little money in the bank from the insurance when my father died. So, I bought the place and started fixing it up."

"Wow," said Katie. After a moment's silence, she asked, "You said you were in a seminary?"

Paul swirled his coffee thoughtfully, then shrugged. "I became convinced during college that I had a calling to the priesthood and transferred to a pontifical college halfway through. Then I went on to seminary for the Chicago Diocese. It pretty quickly became clear that it wasn't my vocation. But I'm stubborn, so it took me a while to drop out. You said you saw my ad in the bulletin. Do you two go to Saint Anne's?"

"Oh no," said Jen, then felt a sharp kick to her shin from Katie. "We were raised kind of Catholic," she added, "but our parents didn't really go to church except on Christmas and Easter until a couple years ago, when they got religion. They're big fans of this priest named Father Larry, so they went to Saint Anne's when they were visiting and brought the bulletin home."

"Father Larry." Paul shook his head. "Sometimes I think I should just go find a Latin Mass." After this inexplicable comment, Paul drained the rest of his coffee and gathered up his things. "I didn't mean to spend all this time talking about myself. I had better get started."

Katie led the way to show him the light fixture she had picked out while Jen gathered up the plates and mugs and bore them away to the sink.

It was midafternoon by the time Paul was done replacing all the electrical outlets.

"The nice thing about Sears houses," he observed, "is that they are very compact, so it is easy to run wire."

"How did they work?" Jen asked. "Did people just order them from the catalog and a truck dropped off all the supplies?"

"Almost. All the supplies would come out in a train car. The lumber was precut, and the instructions were included. The buyer had to put up the frame, plaster, all of that. But the design was done, and the measurements were precise. The materials were quite good, too. A house like this would have sold for a couple thousand dollars in 1919, and all you would need was the labor to put it together. It really was an amazing feat. The quality was far better than modern mass-produced houses."

"Amazing. I had no idea. I always just thought of the Sears catalog as cheap family clothes."

"It was a different world back then. A more human economy."

Once again, Paul's bill was less than seemed to Jen a normal price. Katie tried to persuade him to stay for dinner, but he refused. He did, however, promise faithfully to call in a few weeks when he was available to start planning the kitchen renovation.

Katie continued her progress through the house, painting, repairing, and refinishing. Jen was impressed at the workmanship, though silently disappointed over the dearth of homemade meals. On a few of the nights when she came home to find Katie tired and spattered with paint, she resorted to her old standbys of salad or frozen entrées. But generally on these evenings, they survived on a diet of pizza or Mamma Ming's.

"This is amazing work that you're doing," she told Katie one night. "But I hope you don't feel like you have to knock yourself out like this all the time. Unless you're enjoying yourself."

Katie looked up from the masking tape she was applying to the window frame.

"I enjoy it. I've never done this kind of work before. I hadn't realized how satisfying it is. Besides," she added. "I've tried looking for a job around here, but the local kids have it sewn up tight. The girls who work the Corner Café all went to high school together. I didn't want you to think I was sitting around doing nothing since I don't have a job."

"Sheesh, Katie, I wouldn't think that. I hadn't even noticed you weren't working. You never just sit around anymore."

Katie flashed her a crooked smile. "I *think* that's a compliment. Or is it?"

Jen shook her head. "We all have to take what we can get. How long before you have that prep done?"

"Another hour or so."

"After that, you're done for the night?"

"Yep."

"How about if I go make us one of your cookie recipes and we watch a movie when you're done?"

"I thought cookies made you fat."

"Shut up."

Their mother called on the tenth to discuss the house situation.

"The buyers are set to close on the twentieth," she told Jen. "And they want to move in before Christmas, so there's no renting it back from them. Your father and I have found an apartment we can rent in Johnson month to month, but we can't move in until after the first. Now, some friends invited us to stay with them for a few days. Our parish is giving us a send-off dinner on Saturday the twenty-second. So, if you still don't mind having us, what I was thinking is that we'll have everything moved into storage, spend those couple days with our friends here in town, and then come down to your place on the twenty-third and stay till just after New Year's."

"Family holidays! It's going to be just like old times."

"Are you sure you don't mind, Jennifer? I hate to be a burden on you two. I know the house isn't huge."

"It's just a week, Mom. It'll be fine. We're glad to have you."

"Really? Because we can stay in a hotel if that would be better."

"Only if you want to, Mom. Katie will move into my room with me, and you and Dad can have her room."

"Okay. Well, thank you girls so much. It's going to be so nice to have the whole family together for Christmas again."

After a few more minutes of conversation, they ended the call.

Katie, who had been eavesdropping avidly, pronounced, "We're doomed."

"Katie, it's going to be fine. This is the kind of thing families do."

"Wait and see if you still think that way when you're having a sober New Year's," Katie predicted gloomily.

Paul's call later that week to inform them that he was available to start working on the kitchen was greeted with significantly more enthusiasm. He came over on Saturday and spent an hour taking every possible measurement of the kitchen, noting his findings down carefully on graph paper. The two sisters then took turns reeling off all the things that most appealed to them about a kitchen.

"There has to be an island," Jen said. "All modern kitchens have islands."

"The thing I really liked about how her island in California was laid out," Katie said, "is that I could get things out of the fridge, put them on the island without taking a step, prepare things on the island, and then turn to the stove without taking a step. I feel like I walk all the time in this kitchen."

"That's called a work triangle," Paul explained, noting the phrase down on his pad.

"I also want there to be room for people to come in and talk in the kitchen without getting in the way," Jen added. "Whenever there's a party, people gravitate to the kitchen, because that's where the food and drinks are coming from. There needs to be room for them to hang out without tripping over each other."

"If we replace these cabinets, I think it would look good if we had wood-finished ones instead of painted like these," Katie said.

"Oh, yeah, and those cool little racks under the cabinets for hanging wine glasses upside down. I've always wanted those. And a wine rack built in. Do you think we could have granite countertops, or would that look wrong in here?"

"Tile would look more period," Paul replied. "But it's hard to clean. You could have butcher block on the island and then finished wood on the rest. I'll get you some samples of different counters."

After this sort of conversation had run on for some time, and Jen and Katie had run out of ideas, Paul promised that he would think all these over and come back Monday evening with plans and drawings for them to discuss.

At this juncture, Jen pulled out her checkbook. "I want to write you a check for all this planning work that you're doing," she said.

Paul shook his head firmly. "I'm a handyman, not a designer. This is just my way of making sure you get the work that you want."

"That's silly," Jen said. "This is work. It's something that we don't know how to do and you have the skills to do for us. It takes time. I want to pay you a fair rate for it instead of taking advantage of you."

"This is just how I work." Paul gathered up his papers, stacked them carefully, and put them into a battered leather satchel. "When I've got a hammer or a drill or a saw in my hand, I'm working, and I charge a fair rate for that. I think of this as just earning your business. Lots of people do free estimates."

"No." Jen was adamant. "This isn't just a free estimate; this is free work. That's just not good business. Look, I've dealt with pricing and profitability issues for years, and this just doesn't make any sense. Now, you seem to charge about twenty-five dollars an hour. That's another thing. You charge too little. That's why you're so busy all the time but don't seem to get ahead. If you charged more, the amount of business you got would even out, and you wouldn't have to work so many hours. So," she started writing in her checkbook, "I'm writing you a check for four hundred dollars. I'm sure you'll spend at least ten hours on this over the weekend and Monday. And forty dollars an hour is the least you should be charging. Really, we should get you up to sixty or a hundred. Here."

She handed Paul the check. He accepted it, tight lipped, folded it carefully in half, and put it in his shirt pocket.

It seemed as if they might part in silence, but Katie spoke up, feeling the tension more than her sister.

"What time will you be coming Monday? Do you want to come for dinner, and then we can talk afterward? We'd love you have you."

Paul hesitated just a moment, then nodded. "All right."

"Come at six. Jen's home from work by then, and I'll have something good for dinner."

Shouldering his satchel, Paul nodded to both of them. "I will see you ladies at six, then."

Monday saw the first snowfall of the season, though a light one. Katie matched the weather with a thick, rich beef stew, which had been simmering on the stove all day, and fresh-baked bread.

Conversation was slow at first, leaving Katie to recall Jen's warning that "it's super weird to invite the handyman over for dinner." Refusing to admit defeat, she filled the silence with a series of crazy-things-that-happened-at-Starbucks stories. Eventually she prevailed on Jen to recount some of her China adventures, and at last Paul contributed several strangest-handyman-emergency calls.

His plans, when he produced them, were meticulous: both graph-paper schematics of the kitchen layout and surprisingly artistic elevation and detail drawings, showing what each wall would look like as one faced it.

"You see?" asked Jen. "How could you say this isn't work? This is amazing."

Paul nodded but turned away, unwilling to meet her gaze.

Katie served coffee and freshly baked cookies as they discussed changes to the plans and materials. It was ten o'clock by the time Paul left, with a meticulous set of notes and a promise to return the next night with revised plans as well as wood and countertop samples.

Conversation began and flowed more easily the second night. It was nine o'clock before they turned from social topics to the kitchen and eleven before they finished. The notes this time were fewer, and the materials Paul suggested were accepted with enthusiasm. He cautioned as to the cost, but Jen didn't bat an eye and promised to pay for all the materials up front.

On Wednesday night, the conversation was even more relaxed, and discussion of the business at hand was restricted mostly to the question of when to begin the work. Paul expressed concern that it would be too disruptive for him to start work on the kitchen while their parents were staying there. Katie said that so long as he didn't begin until after Christmas, and the big dinner it necessitated, she could get by with feeding everyone even while the kitchen was in the throes of renovation. Jen closed the matter by saying that if he was available to work, she had no intention of wasting perfectly good time, when he was likely to become busy again after New Year's.

"We can eat out some of those nights if we have to," she said. "Besides, having someone outside the family around will keep us all on our best behavior. And you'll like Mom and Dad."

Katie rolled her eyes at this last, but it was resolved that work would begin on the twenty-seventh.

"Thank you," said Paul rather formally as he was preparing to go. "I hope I haven't seemed too forward in socializing with a customer. But I still don't know many people my age in town and this has been a real pleasure."

"Us too!" Katie exclaimed. "A pleasure, I mean."

"We know even fewer people in town," Jen said. "So we've been glad of the company."

Friday night was a night of angst as Katie contemplated the impending arrival of their parents and would allow nothing to calm her. She alternately cleaned frantically and harangued Jen because she *just didn't understand* what they were getting into.

"Katie," said Jen, at last, taking her by the shoulders. "You have got to stop. You've just vacuumed this room for the second time, and it was already clean. Calm down."

Anger and tears seemed to vie for control of Katie's face for a moment, and then her features suddenly cleared. "You know what we need?" she asked. "We need a party. A night-before-parents party."

"We don't know anyone to party with," Jen pointed out. "And Johnson isn't exactly full of hopping clubs."

Katie was downcast, but only for an instant. "I'll call Paul! He can come over. I'll get a case of beer. You can make those fancy drinks you're always making. We can crank the stereo."

"If it makes you happy, Katie."

Katie pulled out her cell phone and rushed to the fridge, where Paul's business-card magnet hung. "Hey, Paul! It's Katie. Are you doing anything tomorrow night?"

Paul arrived the next night with a guitar case in one hand and a six-pack of Guinness in the other.

"I didn't know you played," Katie said as she opened the door.

"Only when I drink," Paul promised.

Katie had made a dessert of astonishing indulgence, which Jen had insisted repeatedly she would be completely unable to partake of, but did. Jen mixed up a Manhattan for herself, but Paul would accept only straight Bourbon. Katie was making rapid progress through a case of Little Kings and dancing slightly to the music that blasted from the stereo.

The evening was, afterward, a somewhat fractured one in Jen's memory, whether due to the succession of Manhattans or the selectivity of strong impressions. She remembered talking vivaciously over dinner but remembered very little of what she had said. Deeply marked, such that she could call it up easily years later, was the image of Paul sitting in the armchair, a fire burning in the fireplace, the lights dimmed: his bearded head leaning back against the chair while he played Johnny Cash songs with his eyes half closed and a bottle of Guinness by his side.

His singing voice was deeper than this speaking voice. She would not have thought to describe a sound so very masculine as "beautiful", but she could think of no other word. Katie had curled up at the other end of the couch, a beer can still cradled in her hand, and fallen asleep. Jen, however, was happy to sit and watch Paul singing in the firelight.

She wished that it would never stop.

9

For all of Katie's concerns, Tom and Pat's arrival proved a very quiet event.

The party had reached its quiet end just after one in the morning, when Paul put away his guitar and Jen made him a mug of hot coffee for the road. After seeing him out and shutting the door, Jen contemplated Katie's sleeping form on the couch for a moment, deciding in the end to leave her there.

Jen woke not long after her usual time, feeling that slight ache throughout her body that signified too little sleep and a not-quite-hangover. The house was silent, and when she reached the living room, she found that Katie had, at some point during the night, taken herself to bed.

The morning solitude, contrasted with the remains of the previous night's party, served to emphasize that this morning would be the last time she would have her home wholly to herself until after her parents left. With this feeling giving her energy, she changed into winter running clothes, took a thirty-minute run in the biting, early-morning air, and then set about cleaning the kitchen and the dining room. By the time Katie roused herself, the house was ready for parental visitors and Jen was enjoying some late-morning relaxation over a cup of coffee and the Sunday paper.

Tom and Pat arrived in the midafternoon. Their "moving

in" consisted of two suitcases, a cardboard box full of meticulously wrapped presents, and Tom's snowblower, which he deposited in the garage along with a gas can.

"Haven't had a decent snow yet this year," he complained, "and we won't need it in the apartment. I thought you girls might get some use out of it this winter."

Katie, who had been close to moping throughout the day, roused herself to poke at the snowblower, staying in the garage with her father for some time while he explained its workings, virtues, and quirks.

As evening drew on, Pat offered to make dinner. Katie agreed to this, but then went to supervise the use of the kitchen. Jen gave it fifteen minutes, then ventured in on the pretext of getting herself a drink. Whatever difficulties may, at first, have occurred seemed to have been overcome, and mother and daughter were making the family macaroni casserole recipe in apparent harmony.

That night, the sisters lay side by side in Jen's bed while their parents inhabited the next room. The situation seemed to call for slumber-party confidences.

"Well?" Jen asked.

"Well what?"

"You and Mom seemed to be getting along fine in the kitchen. Are things better than you expected?"

Katie considered, staring up into the darkness. "I guess so far, it's a lot better than I expected. She hasn't tried to rearrange anything. It still feels like the parents coming home in the evening, though. No more after-school fun."

"What, were you thinking we would paint our nails and discuss boys if they weren't around?"

"I'm just saying that we haven't tried to have any fun

yet. And even if they're not throwing their weight around, it doesn't feel like it's just our house anymore." Katie rolled onto her side, putting her back to her sister, and settled down under the blankets. "One more thing," she added darkly. "Mmm?"

"Your feet are cold. Keep them to yourself." She gave the blanket a mighty tug.

The next day continued in family harmony. Jen had Christmas Eve and Christmas off from work. For breakfast, Tom got out his ancient Tabasco Sauce apron and made his signature chocolate chip waffles, which had adorned many a weekend morning when the sisters were young. Pat complained that there were no Christmas decorations, and in the end, she and Katie set off to see what remained in the stores, as well as to collect additional provisions for the holiday meals.

When the mail arrived, Jen found, among the usual assortment of items, a Christmas card–sized envelope from Dan. Opening it, she found a card that showed a cow wearing a Santa hat. Inside was inscribed:

Jen, I saw this card, and since you don't seem to answer your e-mail anymore now that you live in the great Midwest, I thought more old-fashioned greetings might be in order. Happy Hanukkah, Christmas, Solstice, Holidays, and New Year. Things are much as usual at the office, as we brace for the New Year's rush of people who follow up resolutions to write wills or get divorces. My Mother made another valiant attempt at finding the Nice Jewish Girl™, but though she is certainly nice and Jewish and a girl, I don't think either of us sees any future in it. I hope you and your sister are doing well. Have you tipped any cows or met any farm boys? Best wishes, Dan

The card caused a twinge of Jen's conscience. Following the well-established course of their past interactions, Dan had sent her several e-mails since she had moved away, and each time, she had thoroughly meant to reply. Each time, it had seemed that he deserved a longer response than she had time to write at that moment, but as she had not had any pressing reason to contact Dan, she had never made the time to write those lengthy responses.

Her first instinct was to pick up her phone and call him. But, of course, it was Christmas Eve. No one made random social calls on Christmas Eve. The day was for events and for sitting around with family.

As she thought about this for a moment, however, it occurred to her that Katie and her mother were still out shopping, Tom was napping in the easy chair, and Dan himself was unlikely to be involved in any Christmas activities. She picked up her phone and called him.

"Dan. Hi, it's Jen."

"Jen," replied the familiar voice. "I wasn't expecting to hear from you today. Is everything okay?"

"Yeah. Yeah, everything is fine. I got your card. And I was thinking about how I keep meaning to write or call you and not doing it. So, since everyone else was busy with one thing or another around here, and I thought you might not be busy, I thought I'd call. Is this an okay time?"

"Sure. I'm at the office, but no one is coming in and there's not much work. In the evening, I might fulfill a few stereotypes by getting Chinese food and watching a movie."

"Sounds relaxing. I think Katie and I will probably end up going to vigil Mass with my parents. Christmas and Easter are the two times going to church is so traditional that I don't feel like a hypocrite going along."

"Ah, but that's how it starts," warned Dan, his tone half joking.

"I figured it was the one bit still clinging on. Going to church on holidays seems like it's just acknowledging traditions and some general sense of order to the year. Going every week would be pretending to be holy—and I'm just not."

"I can't pretend to understand how these things work for Catholics, but in my experience, when I started going to temple more than just on High Holidays, it wasn't because I thought that people who went every Saturday were especially holy. It's a way of keeping the week rooted in order and tradition, not showing off."

"I don't know," Jen said, striving to close out the topic. "It's not something I really think about much when I'm not around my family."

"How has it been back near your family?" Dan asked, accepting the change of subject. "Have you enjoyed seeing your parents more?"

Jen offered a comic summary of the events that had led to their parents' moving in with them for a couple of weeks. This led to an exchange of anecdotes about family gatherings, quirks, and tensions. After a while, the conversation lagged.

"So," said Jen, feeling the irresistible urge to take some-one far away into her confidence. "The mention in your card of your Nice Jewish Girl problems reminded me that I've been thinking of taking a page out of your book."

"You've decided to look for a Nice Jewish Girl your-self?"

"I'm contemplating a Nice Catholic Boy."

"And just in time for Christmas . . ."

"Dan, this is my lighthearted attempt to introduce a se-rious topic that's been on my mind."

"Oh, well then." His tone became more serious. "Tell me about this guy."

"You won't believe this: he's a handyman. My sister called him up off an ad she saw on the back of a church bulletin my parents left around. He worked on a couple things around the house, and I had him come out to put together some plans to renovate the kitchen—which really needs work—and he's just, interesting. We enjoyed having him around so much, we started just inviting him to come over, aside from the work."

"We?"

"Well, I. We. Katie and I are kind of like a family, I guess."

"So a handyman from a church bulletin. What's he like?"

"He's . . . Man, that's a terrible question. How can you just explain what someone is like? Could you describe me to someone?"

"I could come up with a few things. But also, I don't feel the sudden need to bring you up to people. There must be something that catches your imagination about him. What's his name, for starters?"

"Paul. His name is Paul Burke. I think he's a few years younger than I am. Maybe twenty-eight or twenty-nine. He spent some time in seminary and realized it wasn't for him, started his own company doing handyman work, mostly on old houses. He has seventy acres of land he wants to turn into a sustainable agriculture farm."

"A farm?"

"See, that's . . . He's rooted. There's a solidity to him that's attractive. He works with his hands and knows how to do things. He has a beard, and wears jeans and suspenders, and plays Johnny Cash songs on his guitar. I feel like there's something real about him that's been missing in men I've known before. He's very educated. He just prefers to work with his hands."

There was a slight pause before Dan responded to this onrush of description, and when he did so, it was not in the most gratifying tone. "Do you picture yourself living that life?" he asked. "On a farm and everything?"

"Well." Somehow, picturing herself with Paul had not worked itself out to the point of picturing herself living on a farm. "I don't know. Maybe. His ideas about business are a little unrealistic in some ways. I think I could help him run things."

"If he's the sort of old-fashioned, hands-on guy you're describing, do you think that he'd want you to help run things? Maybe those unrealistic ideas are his ideals?"

"Dan, I—" Jen started off indignantly, but Dan cut her off.

"Look, I'm sorry. I don't know the guy. I'm just asking because what you're describing to me sounds a lot more like an idea than a real guy. Maybe what you need is a guy totally different from the sorts you've known before. But make sure it's the *guy* that you're actually attracted to, not just the novelty."

From this point, the call wound its way rapidly to a close. Jen soon found herself looking at the darkened screen of her phone with a feeling of general dissatisfaction.

Katie and Pat arrived back shortly thereafter and began a whirlwind application of holiday cheer to the otherwise restrained bungalow. Jen tried briefly to join in but soon found that the Christmas decorating annoyed her. As it was decorated, the house seemed to become gradually less hers, as if she were in her family's house rather than they in hers. Each piece of decoration began to look garish and cheap.

Sensing that, with her looming mood, nothing would please, she extricated herself from the Christmas preparation, changed, and went running instead, trusting in the exercise and the shock of frigid air to clear her emotions.

Three miles later, on her return, the house seemed blazing with cheerful light and warmth. As Jen pulled off her fleece jacket and tried to rub some feeling back into her face, Katie handed her a mug of cocoa with a candy cane in it.

"Your father and I are going to go to Mass tonight," Pat said, as Jen sipped her cocoa. "The vigil is always beautiful, and that way, we can have the whole day together for family time tomorrow. Do you want to come, Jen?"

"I'd be happy to," said Jen.

"Oh, I guess I'll come too," Katie added.

The Mass was at 10:00 P.M., but Pat had insisted that they arrive half an hour early in order to be sure of getting a seat.

Besides, she assured them, the choir would start Christmas carols at 9:30, and this was not to be missed.

Though the weather remained cold, there had been no more snow since the first, hesitant fall the previous week, and that had since melted away. During the days, this left the landscape a dreary brown, all of autumn's bright colors leached out by the winter wet and chill. Now, however, with the stars dancing madly in the clear black sky and freezing air of a December night, the lack of snow simply made for a darker night and removed the danger of mud and slush.

Jen led the way up the church steps with the firmness of tread that marks those who know how to look their best: silk scarf around her neck, fitted black wool coat lying smoothly over her slim navy blue dress, heels lending the right air of confident femininity. Katie followed less eagerly, hunched against the cold, despite the bulky down jacket she was wearing over her sweater and long red skirt, flats leaving her looking distinctly shorter than her sister.

The vestibule was full of milling and talking people, and Tom and Pat soon stopped to talk to another couple they recognized from a retreat they had taken. Over the noise, the choir could be faintly heard from inside the church, offering an enthusiastic, if very white, rendition of "Go Tell It on the Mountain". Jen, drawn more to the music than to the conversation, edged toward the glass doors that led into the sanctuary. She had just situated herself where she could hear better, yet still keep her family in sight, when she noticed a familiar figure also standing near the doors.

"Paul!"

He seemed to take a moment to recognize her, then smiled. "Jen, I hadn't expected to see you here. I thought you said you didn't go to Mass."

"My parents asked us to come. It seems like the right thing to do for Christmas."

"Yes," Paul looked away, as if slightly uncomfortable. "That makes sense."

Paul was wearing a heavy tweed coat, a white shirt with a bowtie, slightly rumpled khakis, and what appeared to be his usual battered brown work boots. This seemed peculiarly appropriate to him, and Jen found herself charmed by it, though it was not a fashion she would have approved on anyone else.

"You haven't met my parents yet," she said. "Come over, I'll introduce you."

Paul hesitated a moment, casting a quick glance at the main part of the church, then followed her.

"Mom, Dad," said Jen, breaking in on the conversation her parents had been conducting with the couple from the retreat. "I want you to meet Paul. I was telling you last night about how he was helping us redesign the kitchen."

Greetings were exchanged, and hands were shaken.

"Are you here with anyone?" Katie asked, and when Paul responded in the negative, she urged him to join them.

"We should probably go in soon," Paul said. "The pews are filling up fast."

Tom and Pat said their goodbyes to their friends, and the whole group made its way into the main body of the church and occupied a pew halfway up the aisle.

The choir, whose members were formed in ranks on the

steps in front of the altar, all of them wearing matching red sweaters, was beginning "Do You Hear What I Hear?"

Paul, who was seated between Jen and Katie, shifted slightly in the pew and remarked in a low tone, "They could try to sing *some* good Christmas music."

"I like that they're singing so many ones that I know," Jen offered.

Paul shrugged. "There's so much sacred music out there they could have picked, but they seem determined to do only popular carols."

"What would you want them to sing?"

" 'O Magnum Mysterium'," Paul replied promptly.

Whether appreciated or not, the choir's singing seemed to encourage silence. Jen found her attention captured by the large manger scene set up to the left of the altar. The church that her family had gone to when she was a child had possessed a similar one, and among each year's Christmas pictures was inevitably one of Jen in her Christmas dress, posing in front of the plaster figures. The most memorable of these featured a twelve-year-old Jen, looking as if she felt too old to pose in front of a mock stable, and a two-year-old Katie, who had, unaccountably, become terrified of the plaster cow and was sobbing and trying to hide behind Jen, despite all the coaxing and threats of her mother behind the camera.

The Mass itself held fewer strong memories or impressions for her. There was a certain calming solemnity to the words and the changes of sitting, standing, and kneeling. Jen found her mind wandering back over her conversation with Dan earlier in the day, but she did not feel drawn to put herself in this place every week, as he had described. If anything, the changes that had evidently been made over the years served to emphasize her distance from the people around her, who said "And with your spirit" in well-informed unison while she blurted out "And also with you."

When Communion came, Jen sat next to Katie, watching Paul and her parents move together through the long line toward the front of the church. It seemed somehow strange that Paul, whom her parents had not met until that night, should have this in common with them and yet not with her and Katie. She could not resolve in her mind how she felt about this element of universal, instant familiarity that believers shared and from which she was excluded.

After Mass, as they were waiting for the crush of people in the aisle to die down enough for them to get out of the pew, Katie asked Paul if he would like to come to the house briefly for hot chocolate in honor of the day. Paul seemed to hesitate, but Jen and even their mother joined in the urging, and he agreed to come. Soon they were gathered around the dining room table. Katie passed around steaming mugs of cocoa, and Jen produced a large tin of fudge that she had bought at Andrea's "Christmas for the Troops" fundraiser at the office.

Paul seemed to accept with equanimity being the center of attention, as Tom asked him about his business and his farm and Pat asked him about his time in seminary and his family. Jen, once again, found it strange to see her parents interacting so naturally with someone she had thought of as belonging to her and Katie's world.

"But you must have someone to have Christmas dinner with?" Pat objected.

Paul shrugged. "I haven't spent much time with my mother since she remarried when I was in high school. I always lived with my dad, and I never got along with my mother's new husband. Since Dad died, I've seen even less of her. I used to spend holidays with my buddy Joe's family, but he got married this last year, and he and Maria moved to Green Bay. Joe's family invited me anyway, but I felt odd about going if he wasn't going to be there."

"You can't have Christmas dinner alone, though!" Pat seemed shocked.

"It's usually a pretty quiet day for me anyway."

"No, no. We can't have that—a nice boy like you eating alone on Christmas. If you don't have somewhere else to go, come here for dinner. Katie and I are making a ham and pies and all sorts of things, and it's just the four of us. I'm sure the girls would love it. They like you."

Paul looked startled at this abrupt invitation and set of observations. "Umm."

"No um-ing about it. You come right on over for dinner. You don't mind, do you, Jen? I don't mean to be rude inviting people to your house, but it's a family dinner, and Paul is a friend of yours, after all."

The exchange had played out so quickly that Jen had sat watching it happen without thinking to participate.

"You're certainly welcome here, Paul," she managed. "We'd love to have you, if you don't mind. But don't feel pressured. Mom is just so . . . generous. Sometimes, she can be a bit overpowering."

Paul looked from Jen to Katie and then back to their mother. "Well . . . okay then. Thank you. I would be glad to come. Is there anything I can bring?"

That night, when Jen and Katie were lying next to each other in the dark of Jen's room, Jen asked her sister, "What do you think?"

"It'll be nice to have Paul over for Christmas dinner," Katie replied. "But . . . that was just so weird! What is it with Mom?"

Oddity aside, the meal proved to be a social success. Paul arrived at three with two bottles of wine as his contribution to the feast. Katie and Pat had been in the kitchen since ten that morning and laid out, when the time came, a ham, mashed potatoes, curried vegetables (according to Katie's recipe) and green-bean casserole (according to Pat's), cranberry sauce, fresh-baked rolls, and three kinds of pie. Jen had pointed out that this amounted to more than half a pie per person, but Katie had countered that pie leftovers make the perfect breakfast and predicted (accurately) that Jen would sample all three kinds.

Conversation ranged freely and, to the relief of both sisters, did not consist unduly of their mother's probing Paul for personal details or relating embarrassing stories about their youth. At last, Tom, Katie, and Paul retired to the living room, and Jen and Pat gathered the dishes into the kitchen and began to clean up.

"I'll be glad when Paul gets the dishwasher installed in here," Jen said, at a juncture when the silence had stretched to several minutes between mother and daughter.

"A dishwasher is a very nice thing to have," Pat agreed, "though Grandma never got one. She said that she had five dishwashers."

This oft-repeated story elicited its usual laugh.

Silence descended again, except for the clinking of items in the sink and the running of water, and Jen felt that intimacy that dishwashing sometimes brings between female family members.

"What do you think of Paul?" she asked, failing to imbue the question with the casualness she had intended.

Her mother contemplated her for a moment. "He's a very nice boy," she replied. "I like him."

"I've been thinking about him a lot the last few days," Jen confessed. "He's not like other men I've known, certainly not like the kind of man I would have imagined being interested in, but there's a lot I admire about him."

Her mother made a prompting sort of noise but did not reply. Jen plunged on. "But, even if he's not the sort of guy I'd pictured . . . Maybe I've been unrealistic, or maybe my ideas haven't been right. I've been thinking lately that Paul's a really good guy. Maybe I need to forget all the ideas I've had and settle for someone like him. Maybe having too many ideas ahead of time just results in passing up guys you could be happy with."

"I really like Paul," Pat replied after a moment, but her tone already indicating the "but" that was coming. "But I'm not sure anyone wants to be settled for. You'd better work it out in your mind whether Paul himself is what you want most, and if not, no kind of 'settling' will make up for it."

"No, you're taking it all wrong. I don't mean settling for something I don't like. I mean, dropping my preconceived ideas and just looking at the person."

"Well, if that's what you mean, make sure you say that. No one wants to hear 'I'm settling for you'. And there's just one other thing you should probably think about a bit too."

"What?"

"Is he interested in you? It does take two, they say. Has he shown any interest?"

Having started at Schneider and Sons late in the year, Jen had not yet accrued enough vacation time to take off the whole stretch from Christmas to New Year's. Even had this not been the case, she had always found that week to be an ideal time for getting things done, since the number of other people taking vacation kept distractions and meetings to a minimum. And while, thus far, the experience of all four family members sharing the small bungalow had been surprisingly peaceful, after three days of close quarters, Jen was looking forward to the eight hours of comparative solitude that each workday promised.

It was thus with a certain eagerness that Jen set her alarm Christmas night and set off early the next morning for the office. Only the first row of the parking lot was full when she arrived. The fountain was still running in the corporate lake, but ice had advanced to within a dozen feet of it on every side. A singularly determined duck could be seen waddling across the ice to the open water.

Inside, the halls were uncharacteristically silent. Jen was the only person present in her row of offices. Out in the bay of cubes across the hall, she could hear someone in the IT section playing Punjabi dance tunes at full volume, secure in the knowledge that there was no one to disturb. Jen paused for a moment in the doorway of her office, listening to the music and trying to imagine a Bollywood movie that featured its hero or heroine leading a dance number through the maze of cubes of a corporate headquarters nestled in the

American Midwest. Then she went inside and shut the door so that she could concentrate.

Immediately after New Year's, she was scheduled to spend three days in Washington, D.C., on LeadFirst training, so these days between Christmas and New Year's represented Jen's best chance to get line-review materials finalized before she began the long slog of convincing leadership that she had developed a sales and trade program that would both be attractive to the home-improvement box stores and profitable for the Schneider line.

When she got home that night, Pat and Katie were in the throes of disassembling the kitchen. Cardboard boxes from the move-in had been reassembled and stood in huddled clusters on the floor. The countertops were piled high with dishes and gadgets. Mother and daughter were discussing spiritedly, though surprisingly cordially, the merits of various items—which should be packed and which would be needed during the renovation.

"I need at least one cookie sheet," Katie objected, pulling one out of a box. "And the hand mixer."

"The kitchen will be all torn up," Pat said. "You won't want to be baking."

"We may have to live on takeout eaten off paper plates, but if the house is in chaos, we will need fresh-baked cookies," Katie countered.

"I still think you won't want to be cooking in here, and no one is going to want to have to clean up."

"Jen," Katie said. "Should we pack the coffee maker or leave it out?"

"Leave it out if you don't want anyone to get hurt," Jen

said, depositing her laptop bag on the dining room table and heading off to her room to change into casual clothes.

"See?" Katie said. "Sanity comes first. That goes for baking the same as coffee."

"Wait and see how you feel about it when this place is all lumber and sawdust," Pat warned.

Paul arrived early the next morning and was already moving tools and wood into the kitchen as Jen left for work. When she returned at six that night, the island stood complete—though the drawers and cabinet doors were as yet missing, and the wood was unfinished—and Paul and Tom were busily engaged in pulling apart the old wall cabinets. Jen stopped to watch for several minutes, but the two men were deeply immersed in their work and communicating in the sort of worker's shorthand that made little sense to those not familiar with the task at hand.

"Studs again?"

"Looks like."

"Driver?"

"Thanks."

Jen left them to it, wiping the sawdust off her shoes on the rug someone had thoughtfully placed in the kitchen doorway, and passed through the dining room into the living room. Katie was curled up in one of the armchairs, reading a book. Jen deposited her laptop bag on the couch and sat down next to it. Her sister, contrary to usual practice, did not move or look up from her book.

"What've you got there?" Jen asked.

Katie lifted the book so she should see the title: *The Unsettling of America.*

"What is it? A novel or something?"

"It's about farming and culture. By a guy called Wendell Berry," Katie explained, with the short sentences of one who is trying to continue reading while conversing.

"What got you interested in that?"

"Paul was talking about it. Got it at the library."

Jen waited a moment to see if any more comment would be forthcoming from Katie, then got up and started toward her room to change. "Do I need to go pick something up for dinner?" she asked from the doorway.

"Mom went out to get sandwich fixings." Katie paused but didn't look up from her book. "I told Paul to feel free to join us if he wants to keep working. He and Dad are having a blast."

Conversation at dinner centered on the kitchen. Paul and Tom discussed the ongoing removal of the old cabinets. After a time, Katie broke in on this to ask how they would go about finishing the cabinets and whether a different finish was required for the wood counters than for the cabinets and drawers. Pat advised that they work through the job one wall at a time, rather than removing all the old cabinets at once, then doing all the building at once.

"It will be a lot easier if all the storage is not out at once," she explained.

Katie opined, rather bluntly, that this was a stupid idea and would take longer—necessitating a much longer and more tactful explanation from Paul and Tom than would otherwise have been necessary, punctuated by Pat's repeating, "I don't know anything about building cabinets; I'm just telling you what people like."

Finally, Tom changed the subject entirely. "What about you, Jen? How are things going at the office? What are you working on?"

This was the sort of query Jen would normally have brushed off with an "Oh, you know. Just taking the chance to get some projects done when there's no one around to interrupt me", but this seemed an appropriate time not to skimp on detail, regardless of whether it proved of general interest.

"I'm trying to come up with a workable strategy to pitch during line reviews at the big-box retailers—that's Home Depot and Lowe's—in a couple months. Schneider and Sons has always wanted to get the consumer-tools line that I manage into the big retailers, but they've never been able to come up with a strategy that stays profitable, keeps our current retail partners—the specialty carpentry and woodworking retailers—happy, and satisfies the big-box stores."

"Why is it different selling the products to Home Depot and Lowe's than it is selling them to Woodcraft?" Paul asked. "They are the same products."

"They have different selling strategies," Jen explained. "The specialty stores have staff that can make a feature-based sale and customers who are willing to pay a premium price for a premium product, so they're willing to pay a relatively high wholesale price and sell our products at full MSRP. They seldom do discounts or promotions. Home Depot and Lowe's are all about volume, and while we can count on the customer to understand that our products represent higher quality than the other products on their shelves, they don't have staff who can explain the differences in detail and make a value sell. They also focus heavily on periodic discounts and promotions. Plus, for a product that's going to sit on the shelf a long time and have slow inventory turns, they want a higher profit margin than on their other products. So, they demand a lower wholesale price than our other customers are willing to pay, and then they're going to want trade dollars so that they can promote the products at prices lower than our other customers charge. All that is going to disrupt our existing channel, so while the increase in volume would be great, and our total margin dollars might go up, my go-to-market plan has to account for blowback and still be profitable."

"What are trade dollars?"

"If the retailer wants to do a promotion, like putting the product on sale or featuring it in an advertising circular, they ask the vendor to pay some of the cost. That money from the vendor is called 'trade'. If you go into a Lowe's or Home Depot, virtually everything that's on an end cap or sitting on a pallet out in the middle of the aisle is something that the vendor paid trade dollars to have featured more prominently."

"Wait," said Paul. "Do you mean that they ask you for bribes in order to sell your products?"

"No, it's not a bribe, it's—they have only a limited number of products that they can feature prominently, rather than just on the shelf. And they have expenses they have to meet, like leases on the building and pay for their staff and so on. The vendors whose products get featured prominently stand to benefit the most from the retail relationship, so they ask those vendors to provide extra funds to help meet those expenses. In return, the vendor gets higher sales from the prominent placement. It benefits both."

Paul seemed to find each explanation a further source of indignation. "And then, on top of that, they want to engage in predatory pricing and steal business from the stores that currently sell your products? Why would you even want to do business with them?"

"They're not trying to steal business, exactly. I mean, sure, they'd be happy to have people buy from them instead of specialty stores (and the consumers would probably be happy to pay less), but mainly it's just that the big-box stores have a different kind of customer than the specialty retailers, and a different kind of business model, so they have different needs."

"But surely there's only one fair price for a product. The product itself is the same. Why would you charge two re-tailers different amounts, or let them charge their customers different amounts, for the same product?"

This was an objection to a principle so basic that Jen was not at first sure how to answer it. "I don't know. Different consumers are just . . . different. Some are willing to pay more than others. By working through different retail chan-nels, we're able to reach more consumers at prices they can afford."

"But it's not honest," Paul objected. "That's not charg-ing the fair and honest price."

"The problem is," Katie observed, as if this got to the heart of the matter, "that there are these big companies that only care about profit. In a more human economy, the price would be based on the real value of the product, and every-one would charge the same."

Jen responded to these newfound convictions of Katie's with a derisive snort.

"Would anyone like dessert?" Pat asked. "I bought an apple pie at the store. I could even warm it up for a few minutes. How about hot apple pie?"

Friday passed much as Thursday had. By the time Jen got home from work, the old cabinets had been removed and the skeletons of new ones had risen on one wall. The renovation continued on Saturday—Paul insisting that he was used to working six days a week and Tom saying he didn't consider it work at all and was glad to help. Katie sat in the doorway, alternately watching and reading her book, occasionally reading aloud sections that she thought were particularly interesting. It had begun to snow, and the light from outside that filtered through the windows was dim and bluish, the sort of light that makes one glad to be inside and makes the lights inside seem brighter and the heat warmer. When people say they love winter days, they often mean not the winter day itself but the sense of warmth and security that one feels when sitting inside and reflecting on the contrast between one's surroundings and the weather outside. Jen felt this warmth and security strongly as she sat in the dining room with her newspaper and her mug of coffee, listening to the work and talk in the kitchen, and reflecting that she had seldom felt so strongly the draw of family.

In the afternoon, Pat received a call from someone at the apartment complex she and Tom would be moving into in the new year, alerting her that their apartment was now empty and could be viewed. Pat was clearly eager to go but was hesitant about driving in the increasing snowstorm. Jen, crossword completed, offered to take her, assuring her that the BMW did well in all driving conditions.

The apartment, all white walls and white carpeting, seemed bare and sterile to Jen's eyes, which had become accustomed to the wood and age of the bungalow. Her mother, however, saw only her plans. "I think the hutch will go here. And the sideboard over there. We'll leave the couch in storage and just put the recliners in the living room here with the coffee table. There's just room. It's small, but it will be cozy, and we'll find a house before long. I'm so glad to be near you girls," Pat concluded. "This last week has been . . . Oh, Jennifer, you can't imagine how much it means to your father and me to be with you girls and have everyone getting along so wonderfully. We're all so blessed."

Pat and Katie were united in their determination to hold a New Year's Eve party. Pat explained (as she did every year) that she had watched the ball drop in Times Square on television every year since she was sixteen and, to that end, procured a bottle of inexpensive sparkling wine, plastic champagne flutes, party hats emblazoned with the year, and noisemakers. Katie invited Paul, announced that the food would be Mexican, and forsook her own Little Kings slim cans to lay in a case of her father's favored Budweiser longnecks and a case of Guinness in honor of Paul. Jen urged Paul to bring his guitar, but he repeatedly demurred.

The New Year's party, more than any other point during her parents' stay, felt to Jen like a throwback to her youth; she felt more like a child living with her parents than an adult whose parents were visiting. Katie made delicious enchiladas and chile verde for dinner, Jen mixed cocktails, and Paul drank beer and chatted with both of them, but once the lead-up to midnight on the East Coast began, the parents and the television became the centers of gravity for the evening. Tom dozed in his chair with a bottle of Bud in his hand, while Pat provided running commentary on the televised proceedings from Times Square. The ball dropped in New York, they switched to local programming for the last hour, and Pat bustled around, distributing hats, noisemakers, and champagne glasses as the moment approached.

The local countdown did not have the sense of its own limitations that New York's did and began with fully ten minutes to spare. As the numbers changed and the local anchor provided patter, Jen found herself contemplating, through the soft focus of her Manhattan, the last year and the changes it had brought: Katie, China, Schneider and Sons, the new house, Paul, her parents. She looked around at all those assembled with a feeling of warmth for all of them and upward-spiraling hopes for what the new year might bring.

At last the countdown began in earnest. Thirty, twenty-nine, twenty-eight . . .

Pat pulled the cork out of the bottle of sparkling wine and filled everyone's glasses.

Thirteen, twelve, eleven, ten . . .

They were all on their feet.

Three, two, one.

"Happy New Year!"

Pat gave a tremendous blow on her noisemaker, then turned and planted a New Year's kiss on Tom. Jen took a sip of sparkling wine, then received and returned her mother's New Year's hug. Then Pat led off:

"Should auld acquaintance be forgot / And never brought to mind?"

Tom's deep though slightly quavering voice joined Pat's,

and Jen joined in too, though at a volume designed to keep her voice, of which she was not proud, from being distinguishable from the others. She waited to hear Paul's strong bass join. At this thought, she turned to look, and saw Paul and Katie in the doorway to the dining room, kissing.

She stopped singing. Ceased to hear the song. Felt herself to be staring. Looked away. Looked back in time to see Paul's hand reach up to stroke Katie's hair gently.

Then the two seemed suddenly to feel the attention on them, and they separated abruptly, looking away from each other, flushing, yet uncontrollably smiling.

It was with a wish to adjust her desires and hopes in peace after the events of the night that Jen retreated to her room, pleading tiredness, as soon as the family saw Paul off. For something so unsubstantial, a dream dies hard and often leaves a clawing pit in the stomach as its memorial. She was all too conscious of the fact that she would have to share her room and bed with her sister, but perhaps she could arrange to be asleep before the newly blissful Katie came in.

Katie, on the other hand, seemed to be in the stage of happiness that cannot easily be kept to oneself. She followed Jen into her room almost immediately and cast herself on the bed with a happy sigh.

"Just think of all the things that have changed in the last year," Katie said, lying on her back and looking up at the ceiling. "I finished my degree, moved out to California with you, moved back, met Paul. Think how much will happen over the next year!"

Jen climbed under the covers with her, turned off the light, and lay looking up into the darkness.

"Did you know Paul liked you before tonight?" Jen asked after a moment, her desire to understand the parameters of her disappointment overcoming her reluctance to hear Katie talk about it.

"No. I mean, I hoped. We talked about things. And he seemed to understand me so well," Katie said. If a sound could be said to glow, Katie's voice did so. She continued —by the sound of it, more for the sheer joy of reciting the events than with any consciousness that Jen was listening. "He said, 'Happy New Year!' and hugged me. And then he said, 'May I kiss you?' I couldn't talk, I just said, 'Mmm hmm.' And he kissed me, and it was such a light kiss, I was afraid he was just giving me a New Year's kiss and didn't mean anything more than that. But I thought that if he was going to kiss me, I would at least let him know how I felt. So I pulled him close and really kissed him. And he kissed me back. And I felt him stroking my hair and pulling me close. And then it was all over so fast. I wish we could have had hours more to talk about it. And kiss some more. But of course Mom and Dad are here, so I guess that would be weird. But he gave me a hug and another quick kiss as he was leaving. Oh, Jen, isn't it wonderful?"

"Yes," Jen made herself say, before any hesitation could become noticeable. "I am very happy for you."

IO

Pat and Tom rose early the next morning so that they could go to Mass before the broadcast of the Rose Parade began, a ritual to which Pat was as deeply devoted as watching the ball drop in Times Square the night before. Jen had intended to sleep in, but having wakened briefly, she found herself unable to get back to sleep with Katie in bed next to her.

The main rooms were silent and orderly. Pat had evidently cleaned up from the party after the sisters had gone to their room the night before, or else had embarked on an early-morning cleaning frenzy. Looking at the cabinet frames that now lined the walls of the kitchen, Jen found herself thinking back over the past week and the familial glow that had filled the house: Tom and Paul working in the kitchen, had seemed, she now realized, not unlike father and son. Pat and Katie seemed to have found a new common ground in preparing meals together. Setting firmly aside the hopes that had ended in disappointment last night, the week had been the most enjoyable family time she could recall.

Tomorrow her parents would move to their new apartment, and she herself would fly off for three days of LeadFirst training. The kitchen would probably be done by the time she got back. And if Paul and Katie proved to be a lasting couple, they would doubtless withdraw increasingly into their own world in the manner that couples invariably did.

A sense of loss struck her, and with it the impractical desire that somehow the experience of the last few days could be continued indefinitely.

This last morning with the four of them together seemed to call for some celebratory gesture. Her eye fell on an open cardboard box sitting in a corner in which the cookbooks that Katie used most sat in semi-storage. She pulled out *The Joy of Cooking* and started paging through it. Waffles were her father's realm, into which she dared not tread. Muffins? The pans were packed. There was a cookie sheet; what could she cook on that? She flipped pages until her eye fell on scones. "Bake 15–17 minutes." If she hurried, they could be done just as her parents got home. Perhaps they would watch the Rose Parade together.

It was still dark when Jen rose the next morning, getting ready as quietly as possible so as not to wake Katie. Her roller luggage was waiting for her by the front door. She had only to wrestle it down the icy walk and load it into the BMW's trunk. She could get breakfast at the airport.

Any news-watching American has heard of General Benjamin Palliser: famous for his leadership in the war in Afghanistan and even more so for his sudden ejection from that post after explaining all too candidly in a major interview his differences with the administration over the conduct of the war. F. Scott Fitzgerald claimed that there are no second acts in American lives, but when he said this, he did not anticipate the creation of Palliser Associates: "Providing combat-tested organizational awareness and leadership solutions to today's ever-changing business environment".

Rumor abounded at Schneider and Sons as to how exactly the company had become one of Palliser Associates' first clients. Some claimed that Gus Schneider IV and General Palliser frequented the same glider club in the Colorado Rockies. Others maintained that the connection stemmed from the general's widely rumored political ambitions. Whatever the origin, for three years now, the LeadFirst Management Boot Camp seminars had been a staple of the Schneider experience, providing just the right combination of useful content, mockable buzzwords, and memorable "team-building" physical activity (and the resulting colorful injuries) to be an endless source of anecdote and commonality among "all Schneider leaders of director level and above, as well as select managers in strategic lines of business".

Jen had experienced team-building and leadership exercises ranging from cooking classes to rock climbing, from group meditation to personality analysis, but next to her Silicon Valley experience, this blend of management consulting and military trappings was wholly novel. She found herself wondering if Palliser Associates drew any of its clients from the Coasts, or if this was a uniquely Middle-American business experience.

On arrival at Dulles Airport, Jen collected her baggage and found the middle-aged man who stood holding the LeadFirst sign—obviously military-looking in his crew cut, khakis and dark-blue LeadFirst fleece. Several other seminar attendees already stood waiting, though no other members of the Schneider and Sons contingent had arrived yet.

A paunchy attendee in polo shirt and blazer sidled up to Jen, wheeling his luggage behind him.

"Hi there. Joe Smith. Insure America," he said, inspiring in Jen curiosity as to whether he spoke exclusively in two-word sentences.

"My name's Jen Nilsson. I'm from Schneider and Sons."

"You gonna run? With the SEALs?" he asked.

"I haven't decided. It sounds like fun, but I've heard the history jog with the general is very good as well."

"I heard that too." He sucked in his gut slightly each time he was about to speak, perhaps out of self-consciousness, but giving the impression that he was slightly out of breath. "I want to try. I heard it's tough. Running with SEALs, though. Can you beat that?"

Jen allowed that this would be difficult to beat and looked around for someone else to talk to.

"My company sends everyone here," he continued. "Say it's a great experience."

At that moment, Jen saw another woman approaching the group and hastened to introduce herself to her.

"Sarah Walters," the woman said, replying to Jen's introduction. "Sales strategy director at Midwest PVC."

"PVC as in plastic pipe?"

Sarah nodded and launched into the kind of expertise talk that Jen knew well, though the variety she was familiar with addressed network speed and chip architecture, not drainage systems. "Yep. Polyvinyl chloride. Plastic pipe. Everything from your half-inch pipe for interior lines up to twelve-inch water mains. We don't actually make the dinky white stuff you buy at Home Depot. Our products are all industrial grade, sold to construction companies, public works, that kind of thing."

"I'd never really thought about plastic pipe, but I guess someone has to make it."

"Oh, we make it. Over six million feet of it last year alone. Turns out making it isn't the hard part, though. Everyone can make it, including the Chinese. You know how much PVC they can put on one of those mega freighters?"

"No. How much?"

Sarah laughed. "Well, okay, I don't actually know. But a lot, I can tell you that. And the surface shipping across the Pacific only adds pennies per foot to the price. The point is: the money isn't in manufacturing anymore. The money is in design and installation. And consulting. And selling that is my new job, which is why I'm on the national tour of training seminars. Before Christmas, it was negotiation training. Now it's this. Next week is pricing for consultative selling. No one's sure quite how to turn a brand manager into a sales director, so they're just throwing everything at me, and then they'll see if I sink or swim. But at least with this one, I hear they've bundled a run in with the official activities, so I don't have to get up at four to get my miles in before things get started."

"You run?" Jen asked. Of course she ran. What did she not do? And a director. The list of accomplishments and breezy confidence would be annoying if it weren't for the easy way she rolled them out.

"Yeah. I'm signed up for a half marathon in March, so I have to keep my training up." As she spoke, Sarah rested a hand on her stomach. It was a bit rounder than the rest of her. Perhaps she was doing the half marathon to lose weight.

"Is this your first half?" Jen asked.

"Oh no. I've done a dozen or so. The last few years, I've done a full in the spring, but this year I didn't want to put that much time in with the promotion. And now with the baby, I'm glad I didn't."

"Baby?"

"Yeah." Sarah drew the syllable out in a way that indicated mixed pride and self-consciousness. "I found out just a couple weeks after signing up. I'll be five months when I do the race. My time will be lousy, but the doctor says I should be okay if I don't push too hard."

Jen shook her head. Go to a leadership seminar, bump into superwoman. "So you're going to be running with the SEALs?"

"Yep. I assume we'll get at least three or four miles in, so I should be covered even if it's a bit of a light day. You look like you run. Are you going with the SEALs?"

She could hardly back out when this woman was going to be running it pregnant. "Yeah, I guess I am."

When the half dozen people on the driver's list were all assembled, the group piled into a shuttle bus and drove off. The seminar was evidently to be a study in contrasts. Each attendee was handed a "briefing paper" assigning him to a "squad" and listing activities for the next two days. As they were driven to LeadFirst headquarters in Arlington, Virginia, video screens in the shuttle bus played a talk delivered by General Palliser propounding "strategic awareness" and emphasizing that "in our global economy, as on the modern battlefield, information is the most powerful weapon." After the general's talk, they saw another video in which instructors in athletic garb with whistles around their necks propounded the importance of "working hard, playing hard" and team building.

With all this buildup, Jen had almost begun to expect the shuttle bus to stop in front of corrugated metal barracks, where she would spend her night in a bunk or a cot. Instead, it pulled up in front of a picturesque hotel whose gracious lobby featured a "Welcome LeadFirst!" sign. She took her bag up to her room and, consulting her briefing paper, saw that she had free time until the "Welcome Dinner with General Palliser and LeadFirst Team" in a couple of hours.

Skimming over the schedule for the rest of the seminar, she learned that in addition to the near legendary "06:00 Physical Training: Participants to choose between 5-mile run with the SEALs or historical sightseeing jog with General Palliser", there were a mix of physical activities and seminar topics ranging from the banal to the arcane:

Strategic Awareness and the Power of Information
Leadership and Knowledge Networks
Ropes Course
Building an Understanding of Routine: Lessons from
    de Vigney
Conquering the Infoscape
Team Building: Relay Race by Squads

A note at the bottom of the briefing paper advised her, "LeadFirst emphasizes a holistic approach to leadership, incorporating knowledge building and physical activity. We strongly encourage all participants to take part in physical training and contests. However, participants are encouraged to know their physical limits and avoid unaccustomed exertion, which may lead to injury. The attached waiver must be signed before participation in any physical activities."

At 5:50 the next morning, a milling crowd of LeadFirst attendees in various styles of athletic gear filled the hotel lobby, most of them grasping cups of coffee to fend off the early-morning hour and the temperature outside, which was hovering around freezing. Three facilitators stood at different points in the room, holding up signs saying "RUN", "JOG", and "WALK".

Jen made her way to the first group and found Sarah as the group was boarding the bus. The running group was heavily male, a mix of men who looked as though they regularly did triathlons and others who perhaps had not run regularly in years but couldn't pass up the chance to run with the SEALs. By securing a pair of seats together, Jen and Sarah avoided any risk of being talked at before the sun was up and sat in companionable silence as the bus took them across the Potomac and dropped the group off near the Jefferson Memorial.

The three retired SEALs were waiting for the group on the memorial's steps. One gave a brief talk about Jefferson and the memorial, then told them that the route would take them around the Capitol, down the Mall, and end at the Lincoln Memorial.

"It's just under five miles," he concluded. "At a comfortable pace, we should be able to make that in forty minutes, which will allow you to watch the sunrise from the Lincoln Memorial. Don't stop unless you drop. Let's go!"

Even at early-morning rates of multiplication, Jen quickly arrived at the conclusion that this meant eight-minute miles. With dedication, she could do that for five miles. She set off with the determination not to be the last in the group. It quickly became clear, however, that the real pace setter would be Sarah, whose fluid, long-legged gait quickly took her to the front of the group, where she stayed.

The three SEALs had nothing to prove. Two kept with the front of the group. The third brought up the rear, offering encouragement to the clump of gasping, unpracticed runners who were suffering for their decision to join the group based more on bravado than on ability.

But for those able to keep up with the front group, "don't be outrun by the pregnant lady" became the consuming challenge. The synthesized voice of Jen's iPhone running app informed her at intervals that they were exceeding the pace promised by the SEALs as they rounded the white-columned Capitol, ghostly in the predawn half-light, and set off down the tree-lined pathways of the Mall.

Sunrise was still some ten minutes away when they reached the Lincoln Memorial. Jen leaned against an icy block of marble wall as she tried to stretch the threatening cramps out of her calves. The cold morning air wheezed and rattled in her lungs, and when a facilitator handed her a bottle of water, it was tempting to splash some on her burning face, though she knew that if she did that, she'd be shivering from the cold in a few minutes.

Sarah was also stretching; then she jogged lightly up the stairs to the memorial above. Jen followed her at a more plodding pace.

"The bragging rights will be that I ran with the SEALs,

but you were the hard one to keep up with," Jen said, as they stood beneath Lincoln's knees.

The other woman shrugged. "Everyone already knows the SEALS are tough. I was trying to show myself I could lead the pack now, even if I won't in March."

"Well, you won."

"I guess so. Funny, isn't it, that winning some kind of status with people you'll probably never actually see again can seem important. But we do it all the time. That's how I keep going after a water stop in a race. I tell myself I don't want the people giving away cups to see me drop into a walk. Not that they have any idea who I am."

"Here, at least, you've got two more days of LeadFirst to glory in your reputation."

Turning away from Lincoln, Jen could see the sun breaking the horizon, the Washington Memorial a black spire silhouetted against it. The reflecting pool mirrored the fiery colors of the sky.

"Impressive view, isn't it?"

Sarah turned to face the dawn as well. "Wow. Yeah. Makes the early morning worthwhile. If I lived around here, I'd run this route every morning."

"And yet it's just us tourists."

The two of them stood looking at the view for a few moments longer. Then calls from below summoned them to a group picture with the other seminar attendees on the steps below.

The day's seminar ran its course, some sessions thought-provoking, others dull, like any of its kind. Dinner was at a seafood restaurant down by the piers, the whole upper floor reserved for the crowd of businesspeople, which became more boisterous as the open bar did its work on them.

At nine o'clock, LeadFirst closed out the tab, and those not ready to open their own took the short walk back to the hotel.

Groups of attendees gathered in the lobby to head out for a second round at one of the local hot spots. Others headed for the elevators to turn in for the night.

It seemed early to go to bed, and an evening spent with the minibar and HBO was too dismal to contemplate, but the groups going out seemed heavy on the middle-aged party-boy type. Jen had already been cornered and talked at by several of these at the LeadFirst-sponsored dinner. Experience said it would only get worse during the course of the night, unless she could find a group to join with a critical mass of other women.

As Jen hesitated, the lobby gradually cleared out. Perhaps the decision had been made by default. She was on the point of heading for the elevators when Sarah came in through the rotating doors, stopped, and looked around.

It was worth a try.

"Are you turning in or getting ready to head out?" Jen asked.

Sarah shrugged. "I won't get to sleep this early, but I don't know that I'm looking for a night on the town. I was thinking maybe I'd run into a group here, but I guess everyone headed out while I was calling home. What are you doing?"

"More or less the same." She looked around for inspiration. "Want to step into the hotel restaurant for a bit? I noticed earlier they've got a big dessert menu. Drinks are at hotel prices, but for one or two, it won't break the bank."

"I'm game."

At that hour, the hotel restaurant was nearly empty. A few recent arrivals were loading their company cards at the bar, but it was past the dinner hour and not yet to the point where late arrivals would take shelter there rather than hitting the pavements for the uncertain chance of finding a cheaper option still open. The lone server put them at a high top along the front plate-glass windows, where they could watch people walking by outside, and left them to peruse the thick, spiral-bound menus.

"If this double-chocolate cheesecake is as big as it looks, will you help me finish it?"

"Sure," Jen said. "I think I'll get the barrel-aged Manhattan."

"Hmmm. They have a whole tequila menu."

In the end, Sarah ordered an extra añejo that came at cognac-level prices and the cheesecake. "Don't tell on the pregnant lady, okay?" she added once the server was gone. "I haven't had a drink all night, and I seem to have gone over from the stage where I sleep twelve hours a day to the one where I get muscle twinges that keep me up all night. Do you have kids?"

Jen shook her head.

"I love babies, but believe me, being pregnant is the worst," Sarah said.

"How many kids do you have?"

"This is number three. And not one bit planned, before you ask the next question. Having a baby on the wrong side of forty was not my idea. But hey. The best-laid plans."

"Wow. How old are your others?"

"Twelve and nine. I figured I was done for good with diapers and all that stuff. Thought I was on the verge of being too old to have to worry about it. There's a milestone I'm looking forward to. And I'd just gotten this promotion. For the first time since kids, the husband and I caught a getaway to Cabo. Five days of beaches and drinks by the pool and . . . well, here I am. I'm sorry. The drinks haven't even come yet, and I'm in confessional mode. I'll shut up. Tell me about you."

Self-consciously, Jen summarized her past year: the layoffs at AppLogix, the madness of Aspire Brands, and the challenge of getting the consumer line into the big-box home centers for Schneider and Sons.

"Too bad they're not sending me to negotiation training like you. Maybe a negotiation expert would be able to explain how to make Home Depot keep their prices at a decent level, or else make Wood Craft and the other niche stores accept their place in the world."

Their drinks and the cheesecake had come during Jen's narration. The dessert was indeed massive, and they were slowly eating through it, one from each end, while sipping at their drinks.

"You know, I went into the training thinking that it would be like negotiation in movies," Sarah said. "I figured they'd teach us some badass techniques for maneuvering people into doing what we wanted, even if they didn't want to. But it's really not like that. One of the things they had us spend a lot of time doing in negotiation training was writing down matrices of what we want and what the other party wants, and then applying values to both. If you want the other party to do something for you, you need to figure out what you can do in return that's of equal value to them. Negotiation isn't about making people do things they don't want to do. It's about figuring out a proposal that gets both of you what you want."

The conversation wound on for another hour from there, but it was this point that stuck in Jen's memory for the rest of the seminar, turning and needling at the back of her mind. If negotiation meant determining what each party really wanted and offering it to them in a way that caused them to make decisions, what did each retailer want, and how could she give it to them?

Although LeadFirst had concluded after lunch on Friday, and the time change was with her as she returned home, it was nearly eight o'clock by the time Jen arrived at the house on Friday evening. She had texted Katie from the airport. No response had been forthcoming, but she had nonetheless allowed herself to hope that she would see the windows glowing with light as she pulled up to the bungalow and that the smell of Katie's cooking would waft out to meet her as she opened the door. The house, however, was dark.

She turned on the light, dragged her luggage over the threshold, and shut the door against the cold, then took a long moment to look around the kitchen. The newly finished cabinets gleamed, and the smells of wood and varnish were heavy in the air. The kitchen had that showroom quality that a room has so briefly after it has been finished and loses quickly upon use. She opened cupboards and drawers. Most of them were still empty. Paul had evidently finished the work that day, and Katie had not yet begun unpacking the kitchen wares.

After wandering admiringly around the kitchen for some minutes, she took up her bag once more and rolled it back to her room, where she began to unpack. As she was finishing, she heard the door open and close and, returning to the kitchen, found Katie taking off her coat.

"Sorry, I just got back," Katie said. "I haven't thought at all about dinner. Doesn't the kitchen look great, though? Paul just put the hardware on the cabinets this afternoon."

Jen nodded. "Have you eaten?"

"Not really. I had a late lunch with Paul, and then we were out at his farm. Sorry I didn't respond to your text. The reception is terrible out there."

"Well, I'm starving," Jen said, pulling her coat back on. "Let's go out to dinner. And you can tell me about what's been going on while I was gone."

What had been going on was, apparently, Paul. Katie told about the work on the kitchen, about what Paul had been reading, about what they had discussed, about his plans for his business and his farm. She checked her phone every few moments, and though she had said that reception at the farm was bad, this seemed not to impede Paul from sending her a half dozen texts over the course of dinner.

Were it not so already, the weekend that followed made it clear that Katie and Paul were at the ecstatic early stage in a relationship when it is impossible to spend enough time together. Katie left the house early on Saturday and did not return until after midnight. On Sunday, Paul stopped by in his truck, on his way back from church, judging by his clothes, and Katie immediately rushed out. Jen contemplated the empty house for several minutes. It was difficult not to feel a certain bitterness. Was the home they had built together over the last half year to be cast aside so quickly? But then, what had they built? Had they built anything, or was the comfort of their situation wholly the result of Katie's having no one else on whom to lavish her attention?

For a moment, the house began to seem very empty and bleak. Jen could leave it that way or find some way to fill it. She contemplated the silent kitchen, then called her parents and invited them over for brunch, throwing herself into chopping and frying until they arrived and the house felt comfortably populated again.

It was not until Jen was getting ready for bed that night that Katie returned, calling, "I'm home, Jen" and then flopping onto the couch with a contented sigh.

Jen padded out in her bare feet. "Have a good day?"

"Mmm hmm," Katie responded, snuggling back into the embrace of the couch.

"Are you hanging out with Paul again tomorrow?"

Katie's expression lost its glow. "No. He has to go install a furnace. Running ducts and stuff. Nothing I even know how to help with."

"Too bad. Will you be around for dinner?"

Katie nodded. "Paul says he'll work late and has to be up early again the next morning. I won't get to see him all day."

"Well, maybe we can catch up over dinner, then. Do you want to cook, or would you rather we go out?"

"Oh, I'll cook." Katie rolled onto her side and put an arm under her head.

"Good night, then."

Jen returned to her room, hearing the TV start up back in the living room. Perhaps tomorrow they could regain some normalcy.

11

"So," Brad asked as Jen sat down for their weekly one-on-one meeting on Monday afternoon. "Did you run with the SEALs or jog with the general?"

"I ran with the SEALs. For all it gets talked about, they honestly set a pretty standard pace. I'd feel bad bragging about it."

"It's grown into legend because of all the guys who have attempted it despite not having run a mile since they were in college. No need to brag, but I'd advise letting it drop every so often. So, aside from the SEALs, how was LeadFirst?"

Jen shifted slightly in her chair. "There was some good, generally applicable stuff, but to be honest, it's not closely related to what I'm doing right now."

Brad nodded. "It's a bit like going away to camp. More a life experience than job-related training."

"However," Jen said. "I was doing some thinking about my big-box problem, and I came up with an idea I want to run by you."

"Shoot." Brad leaned forward, his elbows on his desk.

"So, the big challenge, as I see it, is to move some volume through Depot and Lowe's without disrupting our existing retail channel too much."

"Correct."

"I started thinking about means of differentiation, and

here's what I came up with. Let's put together a couple of gift sets that include both the tool itself and all of its accessories, and place those with Depot and Lowe's for the holiday season only. We could allow them to offer a substantial discount, which would bring the price with accessories down to slightly less than we'd normally have as the MSRP for the tool, and we'd provide a good basket of trade dollars so they can advertise the heck out of it and drive traffic from Black Friday to Christmas. We can authorize the rest of the retail channel to discount during the same period, but we'll tell them that the gift sets are exclusive to the big-box retailers. After the holidays, we tell the big boxes that they can sell the line either in store or online (I'm betting they do online exclusively), but they have to abide by MSRP, or we'll cut them out of next year's holiday deal. End result: we get to move a bunch of big-box volume but do it with a differentiated product and keep it seasonal, so we don't disrupt the channel too much."

Brad leaned back in his chair, steepling his fingers. "This is good, Jen," he said after a moment. "This is really good. It'll take some work with the buyers to pull it off, but this actually stands a good chance of working if it's pitched right."

"I'm glad you like it," Jen said, with more relief than she allowed to show.

"I do. Now, there's still stuff to get past. First off, we need to get buy-in here. That'll take some work, because anyone who's been around the industry for a while has been bent over a barrel once or twice by Home Depot, and sometimes even by Lowe's. People will try to tell you it can't be done, but I think you just need to get it pitched right. Now, that may mean that you need to go out to Mooresville and Atlanta. The channel account team doesn't have experience with the big boxes, and the last thing you want is to hear after the fact that they screwed up your pitch."

"I've never negotiated with buyers before."

Brad shrugged. "I can't say it's fun. I did it a few times when I was with the business development team for Stanley. The formula for Home Depot works like this: You go in with a great pitch. The buyer makes you do exactly what he wants instead, and then, when he's through with you, he says, 'Thank you for doing business with Home Depot. I'll be happy to screw you again next year.' But you have a solid pitch. The beauty of it is that if they won't talk, you walk. You'll do fine."

Jen did not find this prediction wholly reassuring, but there was a strong allure to making the pitch herself, and she certainly had no desire to put all the work into preparing the line review and then have the account team give it all away when she wasn't even there.

"If you think I can do it, I'm happy to give it a try."

The next few weeks saw both sisters consumed by their different concerns. Katie continued to spend as much time as possible with Paul, which, given his work schedule, usually involved rushing off each evening at around the time Jen got home from work, and on weekends resulted in Katie's near complete absence.

For her part, Jen was busy producing a seemingly endless series of PowerPoint presentations as she and Brad worked to convince Schneider and Sons' leadership that pitching the holiday-gift-set idea to Home Depot and Lowe's represented the best way to begin a presence at those retailers. By the end of January, with internal support secured, she, Brad, and the account team flew to Mooresville and received a conditional approval: Lowe's would agree to the conditions of the holiday offer so long as Home Depot would abide by the same conditions.

In the first week of February, a week that in Johnson, Illinois, set record lows, Jen flew to Atlanta, where the high was in the mid-fifties and even the low was still above freezing. She and Brad were instructed to meet the buyer at Rooster's Barbeque, where he gazed at them balefully over a basket of chicken wings as Jen explained her program. When she had finished, he considered the matter for the space of four chicken wings. Then he announced, "I will take the cordless drill, the router, the circular saw, and the band saw, if you can offer eleven percent trade from Black Friday through Christmas."

Jen looked at Brad. Brad responded that they could.

"Well then," the buyer intoned. "Thank you for doing business with Home Depot. I look forward to talking with you next year."

He turned back to his wings, and Jen and Brad left. Before starting the rental car, Jen stopped to e-mail the buyer at Lowe's: "HD is in for drill, router, circular saw, and band saw. Are you in too?"

Before she boarded the plane back to Chicago, she had received a reply: "We're in."

It was almost eleven when Jen arrived home that night. Katie's car was parked outside, and the lights throughout the house were blazing, but Jen saw no sign of her sister in the kitchen or the living room.

"Katie?" she called. There was no response.

She pulled out of the pantry a bottle of wine she had been saving for some appropriate occasion, uncorked it, and carried two wine glasses into the living room. She poured a glass for herself, took out her phone, and texted: "Just got back. Trip was a big success. Got a glass of wine with your name on it. Are you going to be back soon?"

On hitting Send, she immediately heard the amplified *ding ding* of Katie's phone sounding from her room. Half wondering if Katie had, uncharacteristically, left her phone behind, Jen went to her sister's door.

"Katie?" she called again, opening the door.

Her sister was half sitting, half lying on the bed, looking at her phone. As Jen opened the door, Katie tossed the phone into a corner. "Oh, it was you texting," she said, flopping back down on the mattress and pulling the pillow over her head.

"What's wrong?" Jen asked, stepping over the mess of clothing and shoes on the floor to sit down on the bed next to her sister.

"I don't want to talk about it," said the pillow in a muffled voice.

"Is something wrong with you and Paul?"

The pillow was pushed aside, and Katie glared at her.

"Did you two break up?"

"No!" Katie objected, sitting upright.

"What's wrong then?"

"We were—we love each other so much . . . I thought—"

Katie kneaded and twisted the pillow. "I don't know if he doesn't love me as much, or—up till then, he seemed to want it as much as I did—ohhh!" This last rose to a wail. "I just don't *understand* Paul!"

"Katie, what happened?" Jen asked, in her most gentle tone.

"Nothing!" Katie shouted. "Nothing happened. Nothing, okay? Nothing, nothing, nothing!"

The pillow was hurled after the phone, and Katie collapsed back on the mattress with anguished sobs, which gradually diminished until Jen heard her say in a very small voice, "Is he too upset even to call?"

Jen gently rubbed her sister's back and asked questions in a soothing voice but could get no further explanation. After some time, Katie's breathing became regular, and her clenched hands relaxed. Jen quietly got up from the bed, retrieved the phone, and put it on the bedside table, within reach. Then she left the room, turning out the light and closing the door softly.

Back in the living room Jen stood looking at the empty glass she had brought out for her sister. The work victory was still there, still a path to recognition and perhaps promotion. But there was no one to share her triumph with. Her excitement was not Katie's excitement. Nor would it be.

If today's tempest in the new relationship had not overshadowed her sister's news, Katie would at least have been happy for her. But not with the concern of someone who truly shared a life. That had been an illusion of the last few months. Now it was Paul's triumphs and difficulties that most concerned Katie. And even if this relationship did not last, another would surely come in time. However close they might remain as sisters, Katie would not be the one to think of Jen's life as her life. Who would?

At last, Jen refilled her own glass and took it with her into her room.

Saturday was a restrained day. Katie slept late the next morning and, when she did rise, stayed mostly in her room. Jen cleaned and organized and even resorted to checking her work e-mail, but although, at most times, such things would provide the satisfaction she desired, what she wanted now was to bask in the familial glow that had been so plentiful over Christmas.

Noon came. Jen went to check on Katie and found her in bed, the covers pulled up to her shoulders, reading a book.

"Are you doing all right?" Jen asked.

Katie shrugged and only half lowered her book. "I'm sorry I went to pieces at you last night. I was really tired. And kind of upset."

"What happened? Do you want to talk about it?"

Katie raised the book again. "No. Not really. It's just . . . relationship stuff."

Jen waited to see if any more information would be forthcoming, but nothing was. "Can I get you anything?"

"Cocoa?" asked Katie from behind the book. "If you don't mind. You don't have to."

"Sure. I'll get you cocoa."

In the kitchen, Jen pulled down cocoa, sugar, and vanilla from the cupboard; measured, mixed, heated, and stirred; then brought the steaming cup to Katie, who sat up in bed with her back to the wall, pulled the blankets up over her knees, and sipped.

"Thanks. This is good."

Jen smiled, unexpectedly warmed by the offhand compliment. "Is there anything in particular you'd like for dinner?"

"Mmmm. It's so cold today. There's stew meat in the fridge and onions in the pantry. How about beef stew?"

"That'll make the kitchen smell good all day," Jen agreed. "Maybe I'll put the rest of that bottle of wine from last night in it. Didn't you make a stew with red wine once?"

"Yeah. There's a recipe in that Black Cat Bistro cookbook of yours."

"Okay."

Jen returned to the kitchen with a new sense of purpose for the day, found the book, and began chopping ingredients.

An hour later, with the pot simmering fragrantly on the stove and Jen contemplating the newspaper over an afternoon cup of coffee, there was a knock at the kitchen door. She opened it to find Paul standing on the step, holding a bouquet of flowers.

"Paul, hi. Come on in. It's cold! I don't want to stand with the door open."

"Thank you." Paul knocked the snow off his boots against the doorsill and stepped inside. Jen closed the door behind him. This flurry of activity past, Paul stood awkwardly, still clutching the flowers before him—not, Jen noted, roses, but a mix of gold, yellow, and red flowers with pieces of fern arrayed around them.

"Are you here to see Katie?"

"Yes. I . . . want to talk to her."

"She's been in her room all day," Jen said, circling around

the island to the stove, to give Paul an unencumbered path through to the living room and the bedroom beyond.

Paul seemed to hesitate. "Do you think I should just go back to her room?"

"She was watching her phone all last night, hoping you'd call or text. I assume she wants to talk to you."

Paul set the flowers down on the counter, took his coat off, and hung it on the hook by the door. Jen noted that he was wearing khakis and a blazer, as on Christmas, rather than his usual jeans. He took a slow breath, buttoned his blazer, then unbuttoned it again, started for the kitchen door, then turned back, picked up the flowers, and left the room again.

"The door on the right," Jen called after him, unable to repress a slight smile as she did so.

Time passed, and Jen suddenly began to feel awkward sitting in the kitchen, as if sitting with her newspaper and coffee, waiting, made her a spectator or a spy in relation to whatever was going on in Katie's room. She went to the stove, stirred the stew, washed the few things that were in the sink, and looked around for something else to occupy her. Stew for dinner. What else would Katie make if she were in charge of the kitchen for the evening? She examined the fridge and then the pantry. In the pantry, a plastic bag full of green apples caught her eye. Pie. Katie would definitely make pie. She pulled *The Joy of Cooking* off the shelf.

When Katie and Paul appeared, the dough was chilling in the refrigerator and Jen was occupied in peeling apples.

"What are you doing?" Katie asked, setting the bouquet of flowers on the kitchen counter and putting on her coat and hat.

"Apple pie," Jen responded.

"Isn't that on the list of things that make you fat?" Katie asked, grinning.

Jen shrugged. "I thought you'd like it. And now that you mention it, I haven't had any lunch today."

Katie finished buttoning her coat. "We're going for a walk. We'll be back in a little while."

"Okay."

Rolling out pie crust proved more challenging than Jen had expected—or at least, doing so without the dough either sticking to the counter or developing cracks that caused it to tear apart when she picked it up to put in the pan. At last, the pie was complete, if somewhat lopsided and patched. She put it in the oven and set about washing up.

It was as she was finishing with the cleanup that Jen noticed that the bouquet of flowers was still lying on the kitchen counter near the door. She searched through cupboards, found a vase, filled it with water, put the flowers in it, and placed it in the center of the island.

The pie was cooling on the counter by the time the kitchen door opened. Katie stepped in, then paused on the threshold to exchange a brief kiss, which became a longer kiss, with Paul. At last, she stepped back. "Good night, then. I'll see you tomorrow."

Katie pushed the door closed with her shoulder and stood leaning back against the door, hugging her arms to her and rubbing them for warmth.

"You guys were out there for more than an hour. You must be freezing," Jen observed. "Do you want some tea or something to warm you up?"

Katie nodded.

Jen started the electric kettle, and after a few minutes, Katie ducked into the other room to hang up her coat.

"So," said Jen, once both sisters were grasping mugs of hot tea. "Did you two make it up? Is everything okay?"

Katie stared down at her mug rather than meeting her sister's eyes and took so long before answering that Jen was beginning to think that she would not answer at all. "Things are okay," Katie said at last.

12

There were no more scenes like the one on Friday night. Katie seemed unusually restrained but not visibly unhappy. Paul came and picked her up the next day just after noon, but she was back by nine o'clock. During the following week, Katie either stayed home entirely or else went out for a couple of hours after dinner with Paul. Most nights, however, Jen could hear the low murmur in the next room of late-night phone conversations going long past midnight.

Katie also seemed to be on a reading tear. Gone, however, were Wendell Berry, Michael Pollan, and books on farming. Now Katie was working her way through a succession of religious titles.

"Why all the religion books?" Jen asked one evening, on coming home to find Katie making dinner with a book propped open on the counter. "Didn't you cover all that stuff in college with your religious studies major?"

"It's not the same kind of thing. We studied religion as a phenomenon. That's not the same thing as understanding the theology and morality and spirituality that people live by."

"Did you have some kind of a religious argument with Paul?" Jen asked, looking over Katie's shoulder at the book, but finding no explanation in the seemingly contradictory title *Theology of the Body*. "Did he want you to start going to church if you guys are going to stay together?"

"No!" Katie objected, closing her book loudly. "Paul would never do that. He takes his faith too seriously to try to force it. No, he—" Katie seemed to stop and gather her thoughts, then continued in a quieter tone. "I realized that, being in a relationship with Paul, I'll be living with the practical implications of his beliefs, so I figured that I needed to understand those beliefs better and decide what I think of them."

"Does it make that big a difference? I dated a vegetarian once; I didn't have to go read a bunch of books about vegetarianism. I just knew when we went out, we had to go to restaurants with good vegetarian options."

Katie sighed and opened the book again. "It's not the same. Paul's faith doesn't just affect what he's willing to do; it informs his ideas about what a relationship is and what it's for."

"I thought religious beliefs were all about God and heaven and what not to do. How can you have beliefs about what relationships are for?"

"You can't. Religious people are all crazy," Katie said, rolling her eyes. "No need to question your assumptions. It's just something a billion people believe that goes back two thousand years. I'll let you know when dinner is ready." She turned her back to Jen and ostentatiously returned to her reading.

The sarcasm stung. "Look, I'm sorry. I wasn't trying to be rude," Jen said.

"Well, it sounded pretty dismissive from here. Do you think people like Paul are stupid or something? I mean sure, disagree with him. Maybe I disagree with him. I don't even know yet. But don't act like there's nothing there to have beliefs about."

"I'm sorry." Jen turned to go, then stopped. Perhaps honesty was the best amends. "I was being dismissive because I don't know how to talk about this stuff without sounding stupid. It seems weird to talk about, and I don't know how, but I'd like to understand. Maybe you can tell me about it?" she asked as a final peace offering.

Katie smiled. Peace offering accepted. "Yeah, okay. I'll try." For a moment she chewed her lip, brow furrowed. Then she turned back to her meal preparations and began cutting vegetables again. "Okay, you're not such a jerk. It does feel weird to just start talking about God and faith and all that. Go grab a drink and sit down in the breakfast nook or something. Don't just stare at me like I'm some kind of freak. I'm gonna try, but this is hard."

Jen pulled a Diet Coke out of the fridge and obediently sat on one of the breakfast stools, turning herself away from Katie. After a moment's more vigorous chopping, and a gusty sigh, Katie began.

"One of the first things I noticed about Paul was how rooted he is. I mean, his handyman work, his farm, his ideas about sustainable living and a sustainable economy, all the stuff he's trying to do: it comes from a clear philosophy. And I admired that philosophy and wanted to be a part of it.

"But at first, I kind of thought of his Catholicism as being like a style he'd picked up to express that philosophy —you know, like the suspenders and bowties and Johnny Cash obsession. That's because I'd always thought of being spiritual as something that was, you know, out there. I mean,

261

sure, religious people try to be nice people (at least the good ones do) but they're not unique that way. We all try to be good people. So religion seemed like something extra, like a second family you call up sometimes long-distance. I mean, you hear people say, 'You can't do that, it's a sin', but that seemed more like just a way of trying to prove you were holy or controlling other people or whatever.

"Well, then there was that miserable night when I thought we were ready to . . . you know. And—actually, I don't want to talk about that. But the point is that Paul doesn't think about these things as rules. I'm starting to think that none of the smart religious people do. They see the physical world as shot through with meaning. Like the natural world is actually supernatural. And it all, like, ties together because God made the world a certain way, and so it's got meaning. There's a way that things are supposed to be. And most of that is messed up because of sin and stuff. But then they believe that when Jesus came, he kind of tied it all together, because he was both a person and supernatural at the same time. See? So, it's like he was the perfect person, and so being good is following that model and being like Jesus."

What had started as a painfully slow recitation had turned into a verbal torrent, until at the last Katie had become so occupied with articulating these newly forming ideas that she had turned away from her saucepan at the key moment when the butter was melting, and turned back to it with a yelp only as it began to smoke.

After some decidedly unholy exclamations and frantic efforts at recovery, she got her sauteing back on track. Her verbal rhapsody, however, had been interrupted, and so she concluded in summary form. "So, really, when I'd thought that Paul's lifestyle was compelling and his spirituality was like an expression of it, I had it totally backwards. For Christians like him, how they live is like a reflection of what they believe, not the other way around. And if I'm going to decide whether I want to be a part of that lifestyle, I need to understand what it comes from and whether it's true."

"I'm going over to Paul's house for the afternoon tomorrow," Katie announced on Saturday evening, emerging from her room after a several-hour-long phone call. "I'm going to make dinner for him there, so you'll be on your own for dinner. I'll be back around nine."

Jen shrugged. "I'll come up with something."

She contemplated the Netflix queue and the prospect of a long quiet afternoon, then went back to her room, shut the door, and called her mother.

"Jen, this is a surprise."

"Hey, Mom. I know it's kind of last minute, but I was wondering if you and Dad would like to come over for an early dinner tomorrow. Katie's going off with Paul for the afternoon and evening, and I don't have much going on. Seemed like it would be nice to do something with family."

"Well, sure. We'd be happy to. What time? Is there anything I can bring?"

"Oh, how about two o'clock and we'll eat at three or something? Don't worry about bringing anything. I'll come up with something."

"Sure, that sounds wonderful. How're you doing? We haven't talked in a while. Katie told me about your big Home Depot thing at work."

"Well, things have been a lot quieter at work since I got

the big-box accounts sold. Katie's been around a lot more the last week than she has been since she and Paul got together. I hope she's okay. She seems . . . different."

"I think she'll be fine. She's just . . ." Pat paused, and her tone suggested she was choosing her words carefully. "She and Paul are just working through some religious and moral issues."

"Has she talked with you about it?" Jen asked, surprised that her mother seemed at least as conversant on the topic as she.

"Well, yes. Katie and I have talked it over a few times."

"Wow. I didn't think—I mean—it's great that you two are getting along so much better."

"I was real glad she felt comfortable talking to me about it. She's grown up a lot while she's been living with you. Your father and I are very proud of her."

This routine held through the rest of February, with Tom and Pat coming over for dinner with Jen on Sundays while Katie spent the afternoon with Paul.

The first Saturday in March was unusually warm for Illinois. The sun was so inviting that Jen had gone out to the nursery and returned with several bags full of bulbs, which she spent the afternoon planting in the beds along the front walk. She had just finished one side when Katie, who had been inside reading all morning, suddenly issued from the house and drove off quickly in her red Focus. Almost an hour later, she returned, her eyes red as if she had been crying.

"Are you okay?" Jen asked.

"Yes!" said Katie, with a smile that was completely at

odds with the redness of her eyes. "Oh, Jen, I feel wonder-ful!"

"Umm . . . why?"

"I realized I was holding back only because I was scared to start. And I looked at the schedule and saw that confessions were going on right now, so I drove down to Saint Anne's and went to confession. It took twenty minutes, and I cried my eyes out, but I feel *so* good." The last two words were delivered with an emphasis that was almost a dance step.

"You feel good because you went to confession?" Jen asked skeptically. "I remember doing that as a kid. I hated it."

"So did I, then, but . . . I just feel new. And clean. And it's sunny out. And spring. And . . . I'm going to call Paul and see if he's free to have dinner! I feel like celebrating."

Jen shrugged. "Um, okay. I'll see you later."

Katie had already turned away and was pulling up Paul's number on her phone as she walked inside.

Jen continued working down the walk, planting bulbs. Just as she was finishing, Paul's truck pulled into the drive-way and Katie came rushing down the walk, dressed and made up. She leaned in the driver's side window to give Paul a long kiss, then ran around the truck to climb in the passenger door, and they were gone. Jen stretched, took off her gardening gloves, and went inside. It was time to pour herself a glass of wine and put her feet up.

The next morning, Paul arrived shortly before nine rather than after noon. Katie rushed out to the truck and was gone until nine o'clock that night. She brought back with her a little icon of the Virgin Mary, which she hung in the kitchen, next to the liquor bottles, on the stretch of wall between the countertop and the wall cabinets.

"Don't you want to have that somewhere nice in your room?" Jen asked.

"No. I want it in here where I can see it when I'm cooking," Katie replied.

"Isn't it kind of weird to have it near the alcohol?"

"No. Sheesh, I'm Catholic, not Baptist."

Jen's initial fear had been that Katie's sudden return to religious practice would result in her becoming even more quiet and reclusive than she had been the last few weeks. Instead, this seemed to mark something of a return of the old Katie. Monday morning, when Jen came into the kitchen to grab breakfast on her way to work, she found Katie already there, frying bacon and eggs.

"You're starting early," Jen observed.

"I thought you'd like a hot breakfast."

"It smells great."

"Coffee should be ready too," Katie said, gesturing toward the maker.

When Jen got home that night, Katie was again in the kitchen. The stereo was blasting dance music, and Katie swayed to the beat as she ladled out French onion soup into a pair of bowls.

Other changes were more peculiar. Katie had purchased a package of little votive candles and would occasionally light one in front of the icon in the kitchen. That Sunday, passing through the kitchen, Jen noticed that the candle in front of the picture had been left lit. She blew it out and thought no more of it until that night, when Katie came back, pulled a beer out of the fridge, popped it open, and then squawked, "What? You put out my candle?"

"Um, yes," replied Jen, from where she sat in the living room with her laptop. "You left it burning."

"It was *supposed* to be burning!" Katie objected, coming into the living room and planting herself in front of her older sister.

"What are you talking about? You weren't even here."

"Exactly. I lit it in front of the icon before I left so that if I was tempted while I was gone, I would remember that Mary was watching over me and stop."

"You lit a candle in front of a picture so that the Virgin Mary would make sure you didn't get in trouble with Paul while you were gone?"

Katie nodded firmly. "And you blew it out. Why can't you leave my stuff alone?"

"Katie, that's weird. No one does that."

"What do you mean 'weird'? I had a roommate in college who used to put a gold Buddha in the center of the room and smoke pot while listening to Pink Floyd. How is lighting a candle weird compared to that?"

"Lots of people do weird things with pot," Jen stated. "No one lights a candle in front of a picture so they don't go too far with their boyfriends."

"Well, I do," said Katie defiantly, taking a swig of Little Kings. "And next time, I'll thank you to leave my candle alone. It's not hurting you."

Late that night, after she had retired to her room, Jen called Dan.

"Please tell me," said Jen, after the usual greetings had been exchanged, "that when you started becoming religious you didn't start acting insane."

"Um . . ." said Dan. "Perhaps a definition of 'insane' would be in order?"

Jen described the incident with Katie and the candle.

"Well," said Dan with evident mirth, "I think I can promise you that I've never lit a candle in front of a picture of the Virgin Mary—whatever other 'insane' stuff, to use your evocative phrase, I may have done."

"I make a joke of it," Jen said, her tone turning serious. "But with Katie having a boyfriend and turning religious, it's really lonely. Sometimes I feel like everyone else is just crazy, but other times it's like being blindfolded while everyone else is sightseeing. Everyone is talking about things that I don't have any experience of."

"That doesn't entirely change," Dan said, his tone sympathetic now. "I've often heard people talk about religious experiences that are completely foreign to me. Even aside from faith, some people just feel and respond to symbols and words more than others."

"So, if you don't have all kinds of religious feelings, what made you go back to being a practicing Jew?"

"Ask an easy question, why don't you?" said Dan with a wry laugh. There was a pause, and Jen was on the point of withdrawing the question with apologies. "I guess the best way I could describe it is: I became convinced that there was something out there beyond just me that I had to acknowledge, something more than my everyday. And not just something abstract, but something that cared about me. And at the same time, I had this inescapable feeling that being a Jew was something that wasn't just a matter of chance. It was something in my blood and in everything I'd been brought up to. Like the way the language you're brought up speaking is the language you always think in even when you learn another language. I realized that when my parents and grandparents went to temple, they were talking to that . . . whatever it was that was out there. And that as a Jew, the only way I could acknowledge it was by going with them and learning to be a better Jew. I know that probably sounds pretty irrational, but it wasn't exactly something I reasoned my way into at first; that came later. At first it was just something I *knew*."

"No, that's . . . Thank you," said Jen, surprised and slightly uncomfortable with the honesty and completeness of Dan's answer.

Silence stretched on for several seconds, and at last Dan broke it with a lighter note. "So, the last time we talked, you were talking about settling down with a Nice Catholic Boy. How's that going?"

Jen found herself laughing wildly for a moment.

"What?" Dan asked.

"The Nice Catholic Boy, that's right . . . The Nice Catholic Boy is the guy who's dating Katie. He's the reason she's become all religious."

"Your sister stole the guy you were interested in?"

"Or he stole her. Take your pick. Somehow in all my plans, I missed the point that he might have ideas of his own. Says a bit about my own self-involvement."

"Well . . . are you okay?"

"Yeah." Jen felt a lump rising in her throat but swallowed it down. "My interest in Paul was just . . . just one of those crazy ideas one gets from time to time. I'm not upset about it. He and Katie are happy, and they seem to be good for each other. Watching them, I don't think Paul and I would even have got along. The only thing that's hard is that I see so much less of both of them now. The way it always is when a couple gets together. Though I'm seeing a lot of my parents now, and that's good."

"It must be nice to be back near family."

"It is. I hadn't thought it would mean much to me, but it really does. I miss all of you back in California, though. I know I was always pretty selfish about my social life—only showing up for things or calling people when I needed company. But I hadn't realized how much I relied on the circle of acquaintances I had out there. The new job is great. I really love it after Aspire and AppLogix. But it seems like everyone my age is married and talking about their children. The single people are all kids right out of college. And I don't know anyone else. I didn't think about it at first, because I was busy and I had Katie around for company. But with her spending all her time with Paul now . . . I miss all you guys."

"Well, for what it's worth, even without having uprooted and left everyone, I miss having you around."

"Thanks."

The call soon wound to an end. Once she had changed and gone to bed, lying under the covers in the dark, Jen couldn't help dwelling on the closing exchange.

It was Lent, and Katie threw herself into it with the enthusiasm of the neophyte. She fried her own fish on Fridays, because she had judged that the parish fish fry was too commercial. She went to the Stations of the Cross with Paul on Friday nights. She placed an Operation Rice Bowl carton on the kitchen counter and trimmed the food budget in order to stuff it with change. She stopped making desserts except on Sundays, the change that Jen found hardest to adjust to, despite the minor satisfaction of seeing her morning consultations with the scale confirm the accusations she had long leveled against Katie's baking.

As Easter neared, the preparations for it began to take over increasing amounts of Katie's time. Easter dinner was to be at their parents' apartment, and Jen, Katie, and Paul were to be in attendance. To the same extent that Katie's new religiosity had led to a certain asceticism of cuisine over the last few weeks, Katie was determined that Easter should be a notable feast. To this end, she seemed at particular pains to discover dishes that would require the maximum amount of preparation in the days before. Jen volunteered to bring wine and a salad and considered herself fortunate to be spared further worry, though, as she saw less of Katie, she began to wish that she had agreed to become involved in projects such as pickled eggs and homemade ravioli, if only in order to be included.

The Thursday and Friday before Easter arrived, and Katie seemed to spend virtually all of the evenings either away at church or going about somberly with a book by the pope about the life of Christ.

Work provided no effective source of diversion for Jen. Half the office seemed to have taken vacation. Brad wandered into Jen's office at three o'clock on Friday and advised,

"It's dead around here. Unless you've got something really important you're working on, just clear out and get a start on your weekend."

She drove home with a feeling of anticipation. An early weekend, the long week of preparation finally giving way to the celebration itself. Perhaps Katie would be in the mood for pizza and a movie or some other girls'-night activity after her long week. Or, if preparation was still in full swing, Jen could at least join in her mixing pie dough or stuffing ravioli or whatever task might provide some hours of camaraderie in the kitchen.

At home, however, she found the house empty. The kitchen counters were clean, and the dishwasher quietly murmuring to itself. A note from Katie stood folded by the liquor cabinet, near Katie's icon with its burning votive candle: "Headed off to church and then to spend time with Paul. Sorry to leave you to get dinner by yourself. Don't forget it's Friday!"

The last sentence seemed inexplicable, until it fell into place with her sister's newfound enthusiasms. Did Katie expect her to keep up her meatless-Friday kick when she was off hanging out with her boyfriend and couldn't even bother to be home?

What had seemed a yawning chasm of another evening alone suddenly filled itself. She was going to go find a great steak dinner, tender and rare, and have a bottle of expensive wine all to herself. That would get the weekend celebration started properly.

The Easter Vigil did not, in itself, hold a great allure for Jen, but it was a relief that she would at least be included in the main event of the day along with the rest of her family. Katie and Paul were going out to dinner together before the vigil, and Jen had invited Pat and Tom to have dinner with her, both for company and so that her mother would not have to cook amid the elaborate Easter preparations already underway. Thus, late afternoon found both sisters getting ready for the evening.

"Do you have a cardigan I can borrow that would go with this dress?" Katie asked, bursting into Jen's room without knocking as Jen was standing in her bra and slip, contemplating the relative merits of two dresses.

"There's a light pink one that might go. Second drawer down on the right," Jen said, her head disappearing into her own dress. Once dressed and adjusted, she turned back to Katie to see her rooting through her makeup drawer. "Wrong drawer."

"I found the cardigan. I just thought maybe you'd have some lipstick that matched it."

"Feel free," said Jen, shaking her head but smiling at the same time.

"Oh hey," said Katie into the makeup drawer. "Hmm. No. Not that." Sounds of more pawing around followed.

"Are you seriously wearing those scuffed old flats?" Jen asked, surveying Katie's outfit more critically.

"I don't want something really high," Katie said, contemplating the shade of coral lipstick she had just applied.

Jen disappeared into her closet for a moment. "How about these?" she said, reappearing. "Kitten heels. The shade matches your dress better. And they look new. I liked them but I don't have anything to wear them with."

"Oooh. I like those. Okay. Hey, can I use this eye cream?"

"No. That's for wrinkles, and it's really expensive."

"I might get wrinkles someday. I used the face wash of yours from the same brand, and it felt really good."

"You work yourself up some wrinkles and let me know. Now get out. I want to finish getting ready."

"Okay, okay. Thanks for the shoes. And the sweater."

Jen shooed her out and shut the door behind her, feeling as if she was back at home after a long absence.

Dinner with her parents was a quiet affair, and at their insistence, they left for the church with plenty of time to spare to be assured of getting a good spot. Mass was to begin at 10:00 P.M., but there was already a significant crowd gathering at 9:30, when they arrived. There was, it seemed, to be some sort of blessing of the Easter candle outside before the Mass started, and so the congregation was assembling on the patio in front of the main doors, enjoying the unusually warm April night air.

They had been standing there for only a few minutes when she heard an excited squeal of "Jen!" and turned to receive a sudden, fierce hug from Katie.

"Look! Look what—Paul—look!" Katie, who was almost bouncing up and down in her excitement, disengaged enough from the hug she was giving Jen to show her left hand, which sported a slim gold band holding a tiny solitaire. "Isn't it beautiful?" Katie asked.

Jen's first, if quickly suppressed, thought was how much smaller it was than the diamonds she was used to seeing on women at the office, but she assured Katie that it was beautiful and asked how it happened. Katie, however, had already turned to show the ring to her parents.

Paul ambled up, smiling proudly though looking some-what awkward.

"Katie was just telling us," Jen said. "Congratulations!" She gave Paul a quick hug. "And on Easter. Was she sur-prised?"

Paul nodded, his smile approaching a grin. "I thought, feast of eternal life, starting a new life together, you know . . . I asked your father for permission last week, but he said he wouldn't tell anyone."

"You asked Dad for permission to propose to Katie?" Jen asked, without thinking to prevent her disbelief from sounding in her voice. "What did he think of that?"

Paul shrugged and shifted from one foot to the other. "He seemed a little surprised. But I think he was pleased."

At that moment Katie seized Jen by the shoulder. "Jen! Come here. I want to tell you and Mom how it happened."

Discussion of the engagement, in one form or another, took up all of the Nilsson family's attention until Mass began.

The Mass was long, and for the first half of it, the church was lighted only by candles. A whole sequence of readings traced biblical history from the seven days of Creation to Jesus Christ. By turns, listening to these and looking over at Katie—who was so obviously trying hard to pay attention yet continually drawn to look at Paul or at her ring—Jen found herself thinking back over her own recent history.

Last April, she had been busily working toward the Pocket-DJ launch, with her only thought of Katie and her parents being that she would not have time to make it to Katie's graduation in May. Katie's unexpected arrival. Two new jobs. China. Moving back to Illinois. Christmas with Katie and her parents. Paul. And now Paul and Katie engaged. The hopes of a year ago now seemed remote. And yet the news that made it seemingly impossible for Katie, sitting next to her, to stop smiling even as she tried to look piously attentive to the Mass, was for Jen the final step in returning to the old way of things. Katie would move out, and once again Jen would be alone.

When Katie had first arrived, it had seemed a temporary disruption in the organized and satisfying life that Jen had created for herself. Now the prospect of Katie's leaving seemed like the breakup of a family. Katie would go on to form a real family, living in the broken-down old farmhouse Paul was fixing up, and probably having lots of babies. And Jen would be left with . . . what?

She looked over at Katie. Happy in love and deeply involved in the liturgy going on before them. Having all the things I lack. Things I've shied away from or just never found.

How was it that with Katie, a sister so much younger that they had barely known each other as children, she had at last created this deep attachment?

Twice in her life, she had picked someone to live with who seemed just the right partner for her life, a decision made over many dates and conversations and careful thought on her part. And each of those relationships had slid gradually into a fatal blend of frustration and indifference. Yet somehow a series of chance happenings—Katie's sudden phone call, Paul's handyman ad, and the faster-than-expected sale of her parents' house—had created a household that she would miss far more.

Had the necessity of getting along with someone familiar

but unchosen somehow been the key to forming a relationship when trying so hard to choose just the right person had failed?

The priest was raising the host. Katie, beside her, was watching raptly. Jen thought she could see the gleam of tears in her eyes.

"Behold the Lamb of God," he said. "Behold him who takes away the sins of the world. Blessed are those called to the supper of the Lamb."

The congregation responded with words that were unfamiliar and seemed out of place in the situation: "Lord, I am not worthy that you should enter under my roof, but only say the word and my soul shall be healed." Had they changed the words, leaving lapsed Catholics like her to feel even more out of place at Mass? Or had she forgotten even more than she realized?

As Jen sat watching Katie and Paul and her parents join the rest of the congregation in going up, row by row, to receive Communion, she found herself reflecting on the odd phrases.

The blessed did seem to be the ones going up to the supper of the Lamb. Having all these people come under her roof over the last year had brought her soul a certain healing and inspired in it a hunger for more.

Lord, she thought, in an unfamiliar, prayer-like mode. I'm really not sure I'm ready to have you under my roof. I'm not even sure what that would mean. Or if you exist. Or if I'd like you if you did. But I need someone under my roof if my soul is going to be healed. That much I've learned this year, whatever else is to come.

Mass concluded, and the family went their separate ways: Pat and Tom to their apartment; Katie and Paul, to whose happiness midnight still seemed early, to find somewhere to talk for another hour or two before parting for the night; and Jen back to her empty house.

Sitting on her bed, she thought over the string of memories and desires that had been crystalizing in her mind since that hesitant half prayer as she watched the rest of her family go up to Communion.

Jen pulled out her phone, scrolled through the contacts, and for several minutes sat contemplating the name long familiar but with a new possibility of significance. At last she pressed Call and waited, half hoping, half fearing, that there would be no answer.

"Jen? It must be late out there." There was an edge of concern in his voice. "Is everything okay?"

"Hey, Dan. Yeah, everything's fine. I know it's late. I just wanted to talk."

"Sure. Sure. It's not nearly as late here, so if you want to talk, I'm happy to."

The difficulty was how to begin, and now that Dan was on the phone, that difficulty seemed of a sudden to be extreme. A pause stretched out, and that, too, was painful. Jen launched into what came easiest, which was news.

"Big events here tonight. Katie and Paul got engaged."

"Oh. That was sudden. Haven't they been together only a few months? Are you feeling okay?"

"Okay?"

"I know you were originally interested in Paul yourself. It must have been hard to see all this happen so suddenly."

His tone seemed strange: concerned, certainly, but a hint of something else. It might have sounded like bitterness, had that not seemed such an uncharacteristic thing to hear from him.

"What? Oh, no, I'm fine. I don't think he was the guy for me. I'm happy for them. Though, like you say, it is awfully quick. And I'm going to miss having Katie here. I suppose at least it'll be a while. I don't think they'd move in while engaged, the way they are about those things."

She was babbling, and this was not why she had called. She struggled to make herself begin, but silence stretched on again. How was it that she could be so good at things that others found difficult, such as addressing a large business audience on a complicated topic, and yet this simple conversation turned her into a blushing high schooler?

"It was Easter Vigil here tonight," she offered, then suddenly wondered if this was a bad topic to bring up with a Jewish friend. She forced a laugh. "Which is a much bigger deal for everyone in the family except me." But as soon as she made this attempt to defuse the previous blunder, she realized that it, in turn, served only to emphasize that she was not religious and he was.

"Actually," she went on, in a more somber tone, "that was one of the things that left me thinking tonight. It's like I was doubly alone: Katie and Paul now an engaged couple and everyone so wrapped up in the service, while I was the outsider. Feeling on the outs from everything left me to really listen to the words they were saying and to think about them. And that got me looking back at the last year, and my life, and some of the decisions I've made. Or not made."

Her wont had never been intentionally to expose what might be seen as weakness, to ask for that which might justly be refused. It was a struggle to push past that long-trained reticence. But at least she was talking. And perhaps, now talking, she could make herself go through with the task she had set herself.

"What?" Dan asked, his tone one of searching curiosity, clearly aware that she was hesitating over something.

The words from earlier that night ran through her mind again: Enter under my roof. Say the word and my soul shall be healed.

She drew herself together. "There's something I want to talk to you about. I've been thinking back through my life. About what's important to me. And I realized that one of the things that's most important to me, and that I've taken for granted far too much, is having you around."

Memory is by turns harsh and merciful. For Jen it was the latter. The sentence fragments and run-ons of her first jumbled attempt to tell her friend all the things she knew now that she should have told him long before never came clearly to her memory. What she could always remember in later days was when he said, "I'm embarrassed to tell you how long I've wanted to hear you say this. And how many times I thought you never would. When we met, you were with someone else. And then I was. And then we were such established pals, and it seemed to me that you'd never think of me as anything else. Late last year, when you were back from China, it seemed like perhaps that was finally changing, but then you said you were moving away, and I gave up hope entirely."

It was not for any great eloquence that she recalled these words. Indeed, it was not exactly the words themselves that were so etched in her mind. It was the tone of his voice, caring as always, but with an edge of hope that only now made her realize how often those caring tones had masked an underlying disappointment. He cared for her, had done so as long she had cared for him, and without the blindness that had left her seeing him as merely a comfortable friend until now.

With that realization, the painful awkwardness of her declaration was gone. The blood was singing in her ears as her words continued to tangle up against each other on her tongue in the happy rush to express everything that should have been said long before.

And so, once they had found themselves to think the same way about the one thing that now clearly mattered, to both of them, it became necessary to discuss and rediscover many other things.

It was in the small hours of the morning, long after Katie had returned from her evening of bliss and gone to bed without Jen hearing her at all, that they at last recognized the necessity of ending the call.

"What are we going to do about this? We live two thousand miles apart," she said.

"They have these things called planes. I'll buy a ticket and come see you."

"I have a job. And I kind of like it."

"I know. So do I. But they have lawyers everywhere. And product managers, come to that. We've taken this long. We'll figure it out."

"I want to figure it out soon."

"We will. It is not good that Jen should be alone. I will make a suitable help meet for her."

"What?"

"It's an old story."

～

Acknowledgments

There are a great many people to whom a first-time novelist owes thanks. First and foremost, I owe more than I can express to my wife, Cat, for the many hours she spent with me discussing the plot and characters, for being the first eyes on each new chapter I wrote, and for her constant encouragement. And on top of all of that, I can't thank her enough for cheerfully excusing me from helping with household tasks night after night while I was in the first rush of composition. I'm also grateful to my younger sister, Rosamund Hodge, who set an example by preceding me into print by many years and who provided encouragement and advice as I sought to follow. I owe a debt to my first readers, who encouraged me as I worked, particularly Lois, Entropy, Melanie, Amber, Clare, and my mother, Mary Hodge. Thanks also to Sherwood Smith, who provided insightful comments on the initial draft. Finally, my heartfelt thanks to Suzanne Fortin, who provided a fresh eye and some needed encouragement at a point when this project might have gone no further, and to Laura Pittenger, who provided advice and encouragement at key moments.